A Ronnie Ventana Mystery

D1230134

WITHDRAWN

DEATH NOTES

DEATH NOTES

Gloria White

This first world edition published in Great Britain 2005 by
SEVERN HOUSE PUBLISHERS LTD of
9–15 High Street, Sutton, Surrey SM1 1DF.
This first world edition published in the USA 2005 by
SEVERN HOUSE PUBLISHERS INC of
595 Madison Avenue, New York, N.Y. 10022.

British Library Cataloguing in Publication Data

White, Gloria
    Death notes
    1. Ventana, Ronnie (Fictitious character) - Fiction
    2. Women private investigators - California - San Francisco - Fiction
    3. Detective and mystery stories
    I. Title
    813.5'4 [F]

    ISBN 0-7278-6198-0

Typeset by Palimpsest Book Production Ltd.,
Polmont, Stirlingshire, Scotland.
Printed and bound in Great Britain by
MPG Books Ltd., Bodmin, Cornwall.

Prologue

When I invited my friend and mentor, Blackie Coogan, to Match Margolis's comeback performance, Blackie said, 'Him? I thought he was dead.'

He wasn't – not yet.

1

It was dark and the stars were out. You couldn't see them from inside the Riff Club, but you could feel them, twinkling along with the jolting jazz rhythm that moved the crowd. When we had stepped inside, a warm wall of air hit us, steamy and smoky, smelling of sweat, perfume, and booze. Blackie headed for the bar but the music held me where I stood, mesmerized just inside the flimsy shack's door. Match Margolis, the greatest tenor sax player and jazz composer alive, had just started blowing his solo. Nobody in the room so much as breathed.

He was doing one of his old numbers, a song I'd memorized years ago when I was just a kid. He played it sweet and cool, just like I remembered it, with parts that were clear and so pure you could almost cry over them.

When he finished and looked up into the sudden silence, the roar and clapping that erupted drowned out whatever it was he started to say. He stood there, tall and rangy, a heroin-ravaged sixty-year-old man with more talent than a king, and drank it all in.

'Some of you probably heard this one before, too,' he said, when the noise finally died down. Then he turned his back to us and faced his band: trumpet, trombone, bass, drum, and piano.

'One, a-two, a-one and *two*!'

He snapped his fingers and the room exploded with music, then with cheers of recognition. The crowd was standing room only tonight, crammed into every corner and up against the back wall.

I stood with Blackie Coogan in the back, flagging waitresses for Anchor Steams, breathing in the tight, hot air and

2

feeling cramped and sweaty but not really noticing any of it because the music was all there was.

Then it ended. Match finished the set, hopped off the stage and headed for the bar with his band trailing after him like so many thirsty Bedouins.

I lost Blackie about midway through the crowd to a couple of co-eds who didn't look old enough to drink, much less stay out past ten, but that was okay. I was the one who wanted to talk to Match.

Weaving through the bodies seemed to take forever, but when I finally reached the bar, Match appeared to be alone. His band had vanished into the sea of glowing faces around us and the fans – cool, aloof jazz fans – were letting the man breathe. Not me. I was connected.

I told him my name and he squinted at me, blue eyes peering out of the boniest face I'd ever seen. Then he beamed.

'Damn! You're Cisco Ventana's girl, aren't you? Let me take a look at you.'

Everybody who ever met my father tells me I talk like him, have his brown Latin eyes and the same lopsided smile. I read it all in Match's look.

A squat blonde had somehow materialized beside him. 'Sharon, you ever meet Cisco Ventana? Cat burglar. Remember the guy? He was famous.'

The blonde pushed somebody else's back out of the way and stepped into our circle, then eyed me up and down. She was a thick, brassy little number in her forties, loaded down with cheap jewelry and more makeup than a circus clown. She was packed into a low-cut, sequined top over jeans that fit her like sausage casing. All this tottering on a pair of four-inch stiletto heels. If anybody ever deserved to be called a broad, it was her.

'Did you say something, sweetheart?'

'Cisco Ventana, remember him? Famous cat burglar?'

'Uuhmm?'

She wasn't paying attention. But then Blackie came up beside me and something flickered in her eyes.

'You remember the guy? He was cool,' Match persisted.

3

'Ya gotta remember him, Shar. This is his little girl here, his daughter.'

She smiled vacantly right through me and fluttered her lashes at Blackie.

'Why don't you introduce us then, honey?'

Match set his empty glass down while she draped her thick arm possessively around his skinny mid-section.

'This is my wife, Sharon. Ronnie Ventana. And . . .'

Blackie offered his hand to Match and ignored Sharon.

'Blackie Coogan.'

'The *boxer*?'

Match's bony face opened up with pleasure as he pumped Blackie's hand and slapped him on the back.

'Man, oh, man, Shar, you know who *this* guy is? Blackhand Coogan. He took the light-heavyweight title from The Hammer, what – twenty, thirty years ago?'

'Try forty,' Blackie said.

'Great fight, man. Yeah! I made two C's on that fight, man. That was a lot of bread back then.'

Sharon released his waist and glommed on to her husband's arm.

'I want something to drink, honey.'

Just then, Lucius the bartender set a fresh drink on the bar in front of Match.

'Here babe, take mine.'

He picked up a glass of what looked like ginger ale and absently handed it to her, then with a sly grin turned to me and asked, 'How about it? You follow in the old man's footsteps?'

'Not exactly. I'm a private investigator. But I do burglar-alarm consulting. I guess you could say that's close.'

Blackie made a noise midway between a snicker and grunt.

I handed Match my card. He glanced at it, then passed it to his wife. Sharon narrowed her eyes, read it, then tossed it into a puddle on the bar. She was eyeing me like I was trying to steal her man.

'What about those rumors?' I asked Match. 'Somebody said you're writing again.'

'Yeah, oh, yeah. Well, I never could write much,' he said, 'but I got some new tunes I'm gonna play tonight. Saved 'em for last. We'll see if they're any good.'

Sharon set her empty glass on the counter and stroked his narrow arm.

'Sure they're good, sweetheart. They're the best you've written, honey. *Ever*.'

The man could play like an angel and improvise with the best, but what really set Match Margolis above the rest were his compositions – songs straight from heaven that made you *believe*.

The piano player up on the stand sprinkled the room with notes and the whole place started to get quiet. As soon as she heard the cue, Sharon said, 'Come on now, sweetie. You're up.'

She made for the stand without so much as a goodbye, dragging Match behind her like he was an old man, which I guess he was, but he didn't act like one and she didn't need to treat him like one.

Blackie watched them go and shook his head in disgust.

'Too bad about him.'

'What do you mean? He seems to be doing all right.'

'All right? The guy might be an ex-junkie, but fuck . . . I don't know how he's gonna stay clean livin' with her. She looks like she could be a real pain in the ass.'

Sharon was helping Match up the two steps to the bandstand. Match didn't need any help. He walked upright and took the stairs in two strong, easy strides. Sharon looked ridiculous trying to keep up with him, much less assist him.

'Yeah, well,' I said, 'I guess that's love.'

The room went dark. The murmurs died as Match mounted the lighted stage and lifted a gloriously engraved saxophone from its stand. Behind us, somebody coughed. Then, with all the gravitas of a high priest, Match spoke.

'Here's something nobody's heard before.'

He raised his arm and suddenly dropped it. The horns broke the silence first. The drums and piano burst in a half beat later. Then finally Match put his saxophone to his lips and blew.

It was his new stuff – sweet and easy and low – entirely different from the numbers he'd done earlier in the night. A new style. A new sound. And better. He blew out the melody while the sidemen played around him, letting Match's awesome talent convince every soul in the room that this indeed was magic.

Every note lingered just the right beat, every song hit just the right chord, and every solo left us breathlessly aching for more. And Match gave us more. On and on he played, releasing everything he'd held back these last fifteen years. He filled us all with the sheer and simple beauty of sound as his music floated around us like a fine golden mist.

I stuck by the bar with Blackie until this last set was over. Match finished it up with a sweet, melancholy solo that brought tears to my eyes.

As the clapping and whistling and shouting died down, Match bent his ear to one of the guys in the band, listened for a minute, then threw his head back and laughed. It was a fitting finish to a grand performance.

I wasn't ready to leave and I guess neither was anybody else, so I ordered another beer with the rest of the masses while Blackie went trolling for the co-eds. We were all still packed in elbow to elbow, jostling and moving in the dark, charged up from the jazz and feeling good, secure in knowing we'd just witnessed the second coming of a great star.

That's why I didn't notice at first when somebody pushed up against my back. I figured it was just another drunk customer stumbling around. But the pressure didn't abate. I heard a grunt. Somebody grabbed my shoulder and hung on like I was a lifeline.

'All right, all right,' I said, fumbling to get the hand off my shoulder while I turned to see who it was. I pried his fingers out of my flesh and peeled him off me. When I turned I saw his face.

Match Margolis. His eyes caught me first: sunken blue eyes, glazed and opaque. They stared right through me. Something was terribly wrong.

He clutched at me again and this time I reached out to him. But I was too late. He slid right through my hands and slumped face down on the floor at my feet. That's when everybody finally seemed to notice what was going on.

The chatter stopped gradually. I heard something like a collective gasp. Some people were still smiling, the rest just looked confused. Sharon wasn't anywhere in sight.

I dropped to my knee beside Match, laid a tentative hand on his neck where I figured his jugular was and tried to find a pulse. Nothing. But what did I know?

I leaned down and tried to see if he was breathing. I put my lips close to his ear. 'Match! *Match?*'

Nothing.

'Call an ambulance,' I shouted.

Somebody shuffled behind the bar, probably Lucius the bartender. In the stark silence I heard a number being punched out on a touch-tone phone.

'What the fuck's wrong with him?'

I looked up. Blackie towered over me, then knelt down opposite, on Match's right side. He felt for a pulse like I had, being careful not to move him.

'He needs a doctor,' I said. 'I think it's a heart attack.'

Then I lifted my hand – the one that had been resting lightly on Match's back – and my fingers came away sticky. I held them up in the dim light and my heart sank.

'Shit,' I said. 'Blood.'

2

Naturally, it had to be Lieutenant Philly Post who showed up at the Riff Club after the paramedics talked to somebody over the radio and declared Match Margolis dead. Post didn't look happy to see me, but then he never did.

Post was supposed to be one of San Francisco PD's finest – tops in Homicide, unusually bright, a big man with a barrel chest, large, even white teeth, bushy eyebrows that hid his eyes most of the time – but he had the sourest disposition I'd ever run across. Once you've met him, he's the kind of guy you wouldn't hesitate to cross the street to avoid.

The uniformed cops all practically genuflected when Post walked through the club's double doors. He cut through the milling crowd and strode into the sacred space marked off with yellow police tape. From there, he stared at Match's body for a solid minute, scowling like he'd eaten something that didn't agree with him, then looked up and took in the room.

The uniforms had asked me to stick close by since I was the one nearest Match when he went down. And Blackie was special, too, since he'd come up to Match after I had. So Blackie stood beside me. We were just outside the yellow police tape while everybody else was sequestered at the far end of the hall.

'I should have known you'd be here, Ventana.'

Beside me, Blackie stiffened.

Post said, 'Well?'

'Well what?' I answered.

'What have you got to say for yourself?'

I glanced from Post to Match's body. Nobody had bothered to cover him and to me, at least, it looked like his skin was starting to turn gray. Post just kept staring at me without speaking and suddenly it sank in.

'You can't think I killed Match?'

'Why not? You were right here when he died.'

'So was everybody else. They . . .' I stopped. He was joking. He had to be. 'Look around,' I told him in case he wasn't. 'There's nothing here that says I had anything to do with this murder.'

'We'll see,' Post said, then turned his eyes to Blackie. Post didn't bother to speak, just shot him a dirty look.

Blackie smiled back at him with pure malevolence and said, 'Must be amateur night.'

Post muttered an oath under his breath, then squinted across the room at the corner full of subdued people. Everybody looked numb and deflated in rumpled clothes that seemed garish under the lights. They sat in little clusters of five or six at the cocktail tables or lined against the back wall, sipping free cups of coffee that Lucius had passed out while we all waited for somebody to tell us we could go home.

With the lights up, the Riff Club seemed suddenly cheap and dirty: sawdust on the floor, burn scars on all the stained table tops, and faded green walls, scuffed and marred with years of grime and graffiti. The band, so cool and self-possessed under the spotlight an hour ago, huddled near the stage with stony faces of disbelief. Except for the hawk-nosed Latino trumpet player. Poor kid. He was fighting tears.

Even Sharon Margolis seemed uncharacteristically passive, clinging to a young rookie cop's arm while she tottered dry-eyed between the tables, a dazed look on her face. The cop kept walking her around the room in circles, trying to calm her like you would a nervous poodle, but it didn't seem to be working. Every time they'd head for the side of the room where the body was, she'd start hyperventilating.

Post took it all in with a sigh of resignation.

'All right, Kendall,' he said to the uniformed cop at his elbow. 'Let's get set up.'

Kendall scurried around while Post mingled and murmured with the other official-looking types – a photographer, some guys with notebooks and tape measures, and some in uniform. The rest of us just stood around and watched, horrified and fascinated.

Blackie looked pained. In his book all cops are dirt, but Post was worse than most. I'd gotten them to shake hands once but that was about as far as they'd go.

'Why'd they send that fucker?' he mumbled.

'Thanks to me he's on permanent night call now, remember?'

'Fuck 'im,' Blackie said. 'They should have busted his butt, made him quit or retire without a pension or something.'

'He's not so bad, Blackie. Give the guy a chance.' I'd been trying to give Post a chance ever since we'd met.

9

'Come off it, doll. You heard what he said. He thinks you popped Match.'

'He was joking, Blackie.'

'Him? Joking? He wouldn't know a joke if it blew up in his face.'

Sharon Margolis watched stolidly from one end of the room while they finally carried the body out. She didn't cry. She didn't even blink. She just hung on to the little rookie's arm like he was her only link to the living.

'Damn shame,' somebody said from where the band members stood. It was the drummer. He was shaking his blond, coiffed head forlornly while beside him the young Latino guy snuffled into his fist.

The trombone player had picked up his instrument and was intent on polishing it with a soft beige cloth. Behind him a big black woman – the bassist – and the pianist clutched their coffee cups with white-knuckled hands and just stared at the floor.

I tried to imagine the roller coaster of emotions they all must be feeling: One minute they're on top of the world playing with one of the world's greatest jazz legends, making history, and the next, they've just seen their hero die.

Low murmurs eventually started up at some of the tables and one of the waitresses came around to offer refills on the coffee. Blackie wandered over to the far end of the bar – the only part of it not cordoned off – and tried to talk Lucius into pouring him a Scotch.

It seemed like a good time to talk to Sharon. The young cop released her arm and backed off when I approached, but he hovered nearby, alternately eyeing me with suspicion and studying her cleavage. It was obvious from Sharon's expression that she didn't recognize me. Understandable given all she'd been through.

'Mrs Margolis? We just met. Ronnie Ventana, remember?'

Her oily face glistened in the stark light, grotesquely pale under the mask of makeup. She narrowed her eyes at me and seemed puzzled, like somebody who just woke up on another planet and didn't speak the language.

I touched her arm. Her bare skin was icy, but she didn't seem to notice my touch or even the fact that she was cold.

'I'm sorry about what happened, Mrs Margolis. If there's anything I can do, let me know.'

'Sure, honey, sure,' she said absently.

Then she reached for the young cop and started off again, weaving aimlessly through the tables like a shell-shocked soldier.

To Philly's credit he let just about everybody go after the uniforms checked IDs and took down names and addresses and quick mini-statements. Me and Blackie he kept behind, along with the band, Sharon Margolis, Lucius, the waitresses, and a handful of others I didn't recognize. Then Post commandeered the manager's back room and started sending for us one at a time.

Sharon Margolis went in first. She looked sort of hysterical and nervous going in but when she came out about thirty minutes later it seemed that sitting with Philly had pepped her up. Her color was back and she seemed to have settled down a bit.

Whatever Post had done to soothe her, she zeroed in on Blackie as soon as she stepped back into the great hall. Most women went nuts over Blackie as a matter of course, but I didn't think a grieving widow'd fall for him two hours after her husband had died.

Whatever was on her mind, she made it a few feet from Blackie before her face crumpled and she started to sway. Everybody in the room – especially the cops – started for her, but Blackie didn't move a muscle. He just stood there and watched her go down. If the cops hadn't lunged for her from halfway across the room, she would have landed on the floor.

'What a gentleman!' Framed in the back room's door, Philly Post scowled at Blackie. His shirt was stained with sweat now, big double crescents under each arm and, now more than before, he seemed to be seething.

Before Blackie could curse at him, Post pointed a thick finger at me.

'You. Ventana.'

He gestured me to follow, then spun on his heel and disappeared inside.

'Tell him to fuck himself,' Blackie said, loud enough for everybody to hear.

Sharon Margolis's eyelids were just starting to flutter open as I tiptoed around her and entered the storeroom.

'Sit down,' Post said, and pointed to a pair of crates, one stacked on top of the other by a table in the corner. The other half of the makeshift office was packed three deep almost to the ceiling with cases and cases of liquor and beer. For some reason, the whole place smelled of seaweed and damp. I stood by the crates.

'Just because you're the law doesn't mean you can't be civil, Post.'

'Like your pal out there?'

Post hitched his hip on the table, hunched over to rest an elbow on his knee, then nodded at the little guy behind me.

'Shut the door, Kendall.'

Kendall shut the door, then pulled out a blue notebook and a pencil and waited.

'So,' Post began. He showed me his big, white teeth in what I guess was supposed to be a conciliatory smile. 'What's the story?'

'Am I a suspect?'

'Sit down, will you? Relax. Would I talk to the victim's wife first if you were?'

'I don't know.' I glanced over at Kendall. His pencil hadn't moved. 'When do we go on record?'

'We're on record.'

'Then how come he's not writing?' I took a step backwards in the direction of the door. 'I think I'd better call a lawyer.'

'Sit down, Ventana. You don't need a lawyer. If you level with me, I'll level with you. Isn't that how we work?'

Flash of the big, white teeth again. I wasn't quite sure how we worked, so I didn't respond. Instead, I watched a roach crawl up behind an auto parts calendar on the wall and thought about how much it was going to cost to hire a lawyer.

Post let out a loud sigh.

'Talk, Ventana. You're no more a suspect than anybody else out there.'

'They're all suspects.'

'Okay, okay. You're not a suspect at present. Can I just do my job here?'

'Write that down,' I said to Kendall.

Kendall glanced at Post, who scowled furiously, then nodded. I sat down and waited. Post leaned in toward me. He smelled of onions.

'Start at the beginning.'

'Match finished the set and I was at the bar. I didn't see anything.'

A flicker of annoyance crossed his face.

'Describe the people in the vicinity.'

I thought a minute. 'I can't.'

'What do you mean, you can't?'

'I was facing the bar. My back was to the room. I can tell you there was a heavyset bald guy with his date on my right. She was sort of sitting on his lap. And there were three Middle Eastern-looking types to my left. But none of them murdered Match because it all happened behind me. I didn't turn around right away. I don't know who was back there.'

I peeked over my shoulder to make sure Kendall was still writing. He was.

'You know the victim personally?'

'No – we just met tonight.'

'Tell me about that.'

Post's face had as much expression as a block of concrete, but something, maybe the timbre of his voice, conveyed suspicion. Kendall was still writing.

'I introduced myself to Match—'

'When?'

'Right after his third set. He said he remembered . . .' I stopped.

Post waited. Finally, he prompted me.

'Remembered what?'

'Okay. He knew my father.'

'Ah.'

'So then he played another set to wrap up the show. The next thing I know I'm ordering a beer and he drops dead on top of me. To tell you the truth I thought it was a heart attack.'

It was the first time I'd seen a corpse without throwing up and I was still trying to figure out why. I'd had a few beers. Maybe that had something to do with it. Or maybe it was because he was the freshest stiff I'd run into, or maybe it was because the only dead-looking thing about him had been his eyes. I just didn't know.

Post was scowling. Before he could start quizzing me again, there was a rap at the door. Kendall jumped. His eyes shot over to Post for permission. When he got the nod, he tucked his notebook under one arm and reached for the handle.

'We found it, Lieutenant.'

It was one of the official-looking guys Post had been murmuring with earlier. 'Under the bandstand. Perp must have kicked it there.'

'Let's see.'

The official-looking guy came in and offered Post a plastic bag with something in it. Post held it gingerly by a corner and lifted it to the light from the bare bulb over our heads. There was a knife inside the bag, a long ugly knife with a black corrugated handle – the kind that's impossible to get any prints from – and a narrow, smooth-edged five-inch blade. The metal glistened under the glare of the light.

I said, 'The bandstand? Do you mean he could have been stabbed over there and walked to the bar before dropping dead? Is that possible?'

The guy nodded and a gloom settled in the little office. That meant pretty much anybody out there could have killed Match. Three hundred suspects.

Post turned a dismal eye back to the knife in the bag in his hand. 'Prints?'

The guy shook his head. 'Doubtful. We'll work it some more at the lab.'

14

I stared at the clean knife blade and thought about the damage it had done. Then I thought of the tiny wet dot on Match's back.

'Seems like there should have been more blood,' I said. 'You know, like a trail.'

The official-looking guy said, 'He bled into the chest cavity. It was all internal.'

Post gave the guy a belated dirty look for talking to me, then handed the knife to Kendall. Kendall passed it to the guy at the door.

'Let me know what the lab says,' Post told him, then turned to me as Kendall shut the door and pulled out his notebook again.

'Give me some more, Ventana.'

'It's sort of like you had to be there, Post. I mean it was dark – nothing like it is out there right now – and crowded. Picture the whole room packed. And I wasn't paying attention, you know. I don't think anybody even noticed Match until he fell down.'

Post sighed dramatically in a big show of patience. I almost felt sorry for him.

'This guy was hot shit, Ventana. Star of the show. The stinking guest of honor. You can't tell me people weren't watching him, asking him for autographs and crap. How's a perp going to stab the victim in a situation like that without *somebody* seeing *something*?'

'Maybe somebody did see something.'

'Yeah?' He looked hopeful.

'But it wasn't me.'

Post dragged a hand across his face, then fixed his intense black eyes on me. The silence made the seconds seem twice as long.

To avoid squirming, I said, 'You don't like jazz?'

He scowled.

'Jazz fans are cool, Post. They don't hound the musicians. They offer them respect and applause, you know, like a reserved nod or a quiet compliment, and that's it.'

'What can you tell me about Margolis?'

15

'Not much. He is – or I should say, *was* – the best tenor sax alive.'

'What else?'

'He was a composer, too. But he dropped out of circulation a few years ago.'

'Why?'

'Ask his wife. All I can tell you is tonight was supposed to be his big comeback and everybody out there was celebrating that.'

Post reached down and flicked a small roach off the desk and onto the floor where it scuttled behind a cardboard box. 'He say anything before he died?'

'Like what?'

'Christ, Ventana, I don't know. Dying words, what do you think?'

'No.'

'Nothing?'

'It's not exactly something I'd forget.'

'Yeah, yeah, all right.'

He paused for a moment, as if choosing his words. 'The medics say his veins were shot. Tracks all over his arms.'

I'd heard rumors about a habit being what sidelined Match, but why sully his name now? I shrugged.

'I wouldn't know.'

Post gave me an appraising glance, asked me some other stuff, then asked if I'd ever worked for Match.

'I told you, I just met him.'

Post nodded, glanced down to where the roach had disappeared, then turned back to me. 'You got anything else you want to say? Anything else I should know?'

Kendall waited, hand poised over his pad. I'd gone over the whole short murder scene in my mind while waiting for the cops. 'There is *one* thing,' I said. 'Where was the little missus? I got the impression she never left his side, but when Match went down, I looked around for her. I thought maybe she'd know if he had a health problem, you know, or maybe she'd have some medication for him or something. But I didn't see her anywhere.'

'So?'

'Aren't most murders committed by people close to the victim? Spouses?'

Post was shaking his head before I'd even finished. 'You're wrong, Ventana. Mrs Margolis was in plain sight up on the bandstand. She was with Hank Nesbitt, the drummer. They were picking up . . .' He glanced over at Kendall. 'What was it, Kendall?'

'Sheet music, sir.'

'Yeah, that's it, sheet music off the racks. Everybody could see them. She's not going to stab him on stage.' He paused and nodded at Kendall who stopped writing.

'I want you to stay out of this, Ventana. Don't get any ideas about working it. It's too high profile, understand?'

'No problem.'

My rent was past due. I needed a case that paid.

'Good. Go home, Ventana. We're done. Take Coogan with you. I don't even want to talk to him.'

He straightened his back and stretched, thick arms raised high over his leonine head.

'He didn't see anything, did he?'

'Ask him yourself.'

'Forget it. Go home. Get outta here. We're done.'

3

'You all right, doll?'

We'd left the Riff Club and were making our way down the block to Blackie's old rusted Buick. Post had changed his mind and asked Blackie a few perfunctory questions that left Blackie swearing all the way out the door. But the night was warm, the stars were out, and the perfect September Indian summer weather seemed to soothe him.

'Sure,' I answered.

Blackie glanced sideways at me with those sexy I-don't-give-a-shit-about-the-world eyes that made most women drool, then reached into his shirt pocket for a cigarette.

'Sure you are,' he said.

I was probably the only woman Blackie'd ever met who hadn't made a pass at him, but I'd just signed the divorce papers the night he offered to buy me a drink in a bar four years ago and, basically, I wasn't functioning quite right. Later, I'd found out there was more mileage in being his friend than his lover. He taught me everything he knew about being a private investigator and bailed me out when I needed it. I'd seen his girlfriends come and go in droves.

'Blackie! Blackie!'

The two co-eds from the Riff Club popped out of a recessed doorway in the next building down. They skipped over to us and the tall, blonde one – the one built like a Barbie doll – smiled seductively at Blackie.

'You're not going home now, are you, Blackie?'

'Nah,' he said, grinning and fingering his cigarette. He was obviously pleased to see them. 'Too early.'

'Who's she?'

They both stared daggers at me with a boldness I hadn't seen since high school. The short blonde had a pout straight out of a *Glamour* magazine cover. Blackie winked at me.

'This is Ronnie Ventana,' he said.

'Is she your girlfriend?'

'I'm his *friend*,' I told them.

'Oh!' They both brightened. 'We're going to a party, Blackie. Wanna come?'

The short one added, 'She can come, too.'

'Can't make it tonight, girls. How about we do it some other time?'

He winked at them and they both practically fainted. The tall blonde pulled something out of her pocket.

'I want you to have my phone number, okay? I'm Charlene.'

'And here's mine. I'm Sandra.'

Blackie stuffed both slips of paper into his breast pocket. Each of the girls kissed him, then scampered off, giggling like schoolgirls. They dove into a red Jaguar convertible parked across the street and sped into the night. When I turned to Blackie, he was jotting their license plate number down on the back of one of the slips of paper.

'Cute, Blackie.'

He chuckled. 'They loved it.'

'I think *you* loved it. I hope you're not planning to call them, Blackie. There are laws about girls that young.'

'I always run a check on 'em first, doll. If they don't show up on the DMV I leave 'em off the list.'

Blackie's version of safe sex.

'That's disgusting.'

'What the fuck's disgusting about it? Weeds out anybody under sixteen.' We walked a couple of paces in silence, then Blackie said, 'So what'd the fucker ask you?'

'You mean Post?'

He struck a match, cupped his hand over it, then held the flame to the tip of his cigarette. The tobacco caught and smoke billowed out into the warm night air of the waterfront.

'He tell you to stay out of it?'

'He's just doing his job, Blackie. It's not personal.'

I opened the Buick's door and tossed my jacket and bag inside.

'He's an asshole, doll, and you know it. Listen to the old teach here.'

Blackie piled into the driver's side while I kicked the empty liquor bottles, discarded fast food cartons, and crushed empty cigarette wrappers under the car seat to make a space to set my feet. The clock on the dash said nine A.M. It was five hours fast, as usual.

Blackie jangled his keys into the ignition. 'Joey's playing after hours at the Dock,' he said. 'Want to check him out?'

'Sure, why not?'

19

It would beat going home and brooding about the soulless look in Match's dying eyes.

Blackie pressed on the gas and guided the car onto China Basin Street. The mostly empty warehouses and just-barely-getting-by factories along China Basin yielded to cheesy cafes and hardware stores in the next few blocks, then nicer cafes and shops farther on, and finally to office buildings, the ballpark, and dozens of skyscrapers packed together, blocking out the night sky.

Driving down this stretch was like a trip through time, a panorama of the short, ten-year history of downtown and South of Market – the 'Manhattanization' and 'dot-comization' of my beloved San Francisco. It was progress, but just the same it made me sad.

'Did the asshole have any leads?' Blackie said.

'Uh-uh. All he's got is that knife and it didn't look like anything special. You could buy one like that anywhere.'

'Prints?'

'They're going to check but the handle didn't look like it would hold a decent set, not even that precious square millimeter they need for the computer to work it. But who knows, maybe they'll find something.'

'How about yourself, doll? You got any ideas?'

'I like the wife but Post says she was in plain view up on the bandstand. Did you see her there when Match went down?'

'Yeah.'

He seemed reluctant to agree with anything Post said. A bump in the road jiggled the two-inch ash off the end of Blackie's cigarette. I imagined the carpet of trash on the floor exploding into flames but nothing happened. Blackie rolled his window down and tossed the butt out, then swerved around a corner.

'Shit,' he said. 'Match musta crawled through fifty people to get from where he was to where he dropped. Could've been anybody along the way. What about the list the cops made?'

'What about it?'

'That's a start.'

Blackie's eyes sparkled in the glare of oncoming headlights.

Back when Blackie was showing me the ropes we used to work a lot of cases just for kicks. It was sort of his hobby, trying to beat out the cops.

'Think you can get a copy?'

'From who? Aldo Stivick won't do it. He's in love with that judge's clerk now so I've lost my leverage with him. Post's all I've got and we both know he won't give me a thing. He warned me to keep out of it and this time I think I'll listen. There's no money in it, Blackie, and Hakim's nagging me about the rent. I've got to land something that pays.'

'I hear anything, I'll pass it on.'

Blackie pulled out another cigarette, careened through two stop signs, then braked for a red light.

'He say anything?'

His voice was oddly casual.

'Who?'

'Margolis. Word out on the floor was he slipped you a couple of hints before he croaked.'

'Post had the same idea. Who told you that?'

'About fifteen different people.'

The light changed and Blackie smashed his foot on the gas. We flew up the Bay Bridge on ramp and sped toward Oakland. A horn blared. Blackie swerved to miss a diesel truck, then accelerated as he glanced across at me.

'Better keep your eyes open, doll. Whoever took him out heard the same rumor I did.'

4

I was awake before the phone rang. I'd spent most of Sunday recovering from Saturday night – B-complex and Bloody

Marys – and fighting the urge to look into Match's murder. Now it was Monday and I should have been out running instead of moping in bed thinking about jazz and Match and how the kind of music he made didn't happen too often and wasn't ever going to happen again. Never.

There wasn't time to get any more philosophical than that because the phone rang and I had to catch the call before the answering machine snatched it.

'Hello? Miss Ventana?'

The voice was a woman's – throaty, rough-edged, vaguely familiar and a little breathless.

'Yes?'

'This is Sharon, honey. Sharon Margolis. Match's wife.'

Considering what she'd been through, I was surprised she remembered me.

'I lost your card but Lucius gave me your number,' she said. 'I need to talk to you.'

'What about?'

'Lucius said he knew you.' Her voice started to rise, not strident, but not calm, either. 'He's the bartender at the Riff, honey. He said—'

'I know who Lucius is.'

I'd burglar-proofed his mother's house in East Oakland last year and he hadn't let me pay for my own drinks at the Riff Club since.

'What can I do for you?'

'I don't want to talk about it over the phone, honey. Can you come over?'

Philly Post's hot little words of warning flashed across my brain.

'I don't know. It depends. Do you mind telling me what this is about?'

'You want me to come to your office? That's what you're trying to say, isn't it, honey?'

I looked around my one-room North Beach walkup (two rooms if you counted the bathroom): a single table, chair, sofa bed and kitchenette with a hot plate. If she wasn't put off by the bar downstairs, this would be the 'office' Sharon Margolis would see.

'Not exactly,' I said. 'Does this have anything to do with the murder?'

'Please, honey, let's not talk about it over the phone. I don't want to leave the house, but if you're going to insist, I can—'

'Your place is fine,' I said. 'I'll be over in an hour.'

5

I skipped my run, showered, brewed a quick pot on the Mr Coffee and found a box of Cheerios I'd forgotten I owned. The milk in the fridge had gone sour, though, so I threw the whole mess out and ate an Italian pastry from Cafe Roma in the car on the way out to her place.

I felt stagnant, but the sun was out and by the time I pulled up to the curb on Molimo Drive in Miraloma Park, I was actually halfway looking forward to talking to Match's widow.

The Margolis house sat at the end of a cul-de-sac, set apart from the others on the block by a yard and a newly painted fence. The back of the lot abutted the foot of Mount Davidson, the hill with the big white cross on it where Clint Eastwood knifed the psycho punk in the leg in *Dirty Harry*. There was more history to the place than that, I was sure, but I wasn't up on it.

From the outside the place was nice. Two stories of eggshell-blue stucco with a terrazzo tile roof, a carved oak door and big, solid trees all over the yard. She had a lot of green and a lot of space for being in the city.

The grass in front hadn't been mowed in a while, but the

growth along the edges of the path to the door was freshly trampled about a foot and a half on either side. The reporters had obviously come and gone.

When Sharon opened the door she didn't look like somebody who'd seen her husband die just two nights ago. Her thick, middle-aged body was packed into a loud, flower-patterned dress that strained at the seams. She'd dabbed her eyes with too much purple shadow and her cheeks with pink, draped a couple of colored ropes around her neck and dangled some big, clanging loops from her ears. None of it helped. In the bright light of day Sharon Margolis looked old and used.

'Good morning,' I said, and offered my condolences.

She said, 'Yeah, isn't it awful?' without much conviction, then waved me into the house, locked the door, and hurried me down the hall. The air inside smelled of burned toast and bad coffee.

Sharon wasn't bossy and bustling like the other night before Match was killed and she wasn't in a dazed fog, either, like she'd been afterward. She acted like a woman with a mission. And I got the distinct impression she wanted me to be part of it.

'Look at this,' she said, leading me through inexpensively furnished rooms into a dining room. I couldn't understand the barely contained excitement in her voice. 'Just look at all this.'

The big oak table was strewn with newspapers and telegrams.

'They loved him.'

She picked up yesterday's paper and slapped the above-the-fold front-page heading: JAZZ GREAT SLAIN.

'See those telegrams over there? Recording companies. They want to reissue all his albums. The phone's been ringing off the hook. Agents are calling me to do a book. Everybody wants to deal. *Now* he's important.'

She wasn't exactly tearing her hair out with grief.

'This is how it should have been,' Sharon said, and set her mouth with determination. 'I want it to stay like this.'

I couldn't fault her for that but I still didn't see where I fit in.

24

'Mrs Margolis, I—'

She tossed the newspaper back into the pile on the table and said, 'Not here, honey. Let's talk in the living room.'

I followed her through to the next room while I tried to figure her out. Sharon had steered Match around like a doddering old piece of property Saturday night and now, less than forty-eight hours after his brutal murder, she was beaming like she'd just hit the Lotto. My guess was that theirs was a marriage of convenience – hers.

Before either of us could sit, a phone rang down the hall.

'I'd better get that,' she twittered. 'It could be Hollywood!'

I wandered around the room, marveling at how absolutely ordinary the house was. Nothing screamed 'jazz genius' like I'd expected.

The place was sparsely furnished in gold and green brocade fabric over blocky furniture that filled up the small space. Cheap oil paintings hung on each of the four walls and the carpet on the floor looked like it'd missed its last ten scheduled shampoos. There was a roll-top desk over in one corner with a tiny brass key jutting out of it, a bar in another corner, and two large fake Tiffany lamps at either end of the couch. The only clue that somebody special belonged here was a framed metallic disc – a Blue Note Award from 1975 – over the mantel.

Sharon bustled back in.

'I unplugged the phone so we won't be bothered,' she announced, then pointed a painted fingernail at the green brocade chair and sat down in the matching one opposite. I guess it hadn't been Hollywood calling.

She sucked in her fleshy cheeks and narrowed her eyes behind a ton of mascara like she was trying to size me up.

'Tell me something, honey. I've never hired a private investigator before. Is everything I tell you confidential?'

I hate it when people call me 'honey,' but I hate it even more when they start talking confidentiality. It's always a bad sign. No job's ever perfect, though.

I said, 'If you want it to be.'

'Thank God!' She sighed and sort of fell back into her chair. 'What a load off. I was worried about that one.'

She leaned forward conspiratorially. The cloth of her dress swished as it brushed over her stockings.

'I heard some people talking Saturday night. They said Match whispered something to you right before he fell. Is that true, honey, or did they just make it up?'

'I wish he had, Mrs Margolis. Maybe we'd know who murdered him then.'

Her pencilled-in eyebrows furrowed.

'You're not just saying that, are you?'

'Mrs Margolis—'

'I have a right to know – I'm his *wife*, you know.'

As abrasive and obnoxious as she was, I felt sorry for her.

'Not a word, Mrs Margolis.'

She stared at me with hard black eyes. I could tell she wanted me to keep talking but I didn't have anything else to say. I stared right back at her.

'Would you tell me the truth even if the cops asked you not to?'

'I don't know,' I answered honestly. 'But they didn't.' I cleared my throat. 'If that's all you wanted to discuss, I'll . . .' I stood up.

'No, wait!'

Her chunky little body shot out of the chair. She moved faster than I thought she could move.

'I was just curious, honey, so I had to ask. But that's not what I want to talk to you about. There's something else. Sit down, honey. We haven't even got started yet.'

I made a point of glancing at my watch, then sat down again. I didn't have any place else to go but I wanted her to think I had appointments lined up from here to next week.

She didn't even seem to notice, though. All she did was sink back into her seat with an unconscious grunt and pin little pig-like eyes on me.

'Did your parents teach you about breaking into people's houses?' she asked.

26

I didn't even bother to hide my annoyance.

'What's your point, Mrs Margolis?'

'I want a burglar alarm for the house, honey. Lucius told me you're the best. That's why I called – I need one by tonight.'

'Tonight?'

I'd seen enough of the place to know it was an easy mark: high shrubs around the house, isolated from the rest of the block, and piece-of-cake locks on the doors and windows. By the same token, it'd be a quick and easy installation.

'What's the hurry?'

She flushed. 'I'm all alone now, honey. You saw those papers. All that publicity means kooks are going to start coming around.'

I could've been wrong, but somehow she didn't strike me as the defenseless type. And her rush to get a system seemed a little overblown given her explanation. I took a guess.

'Did somebody break in?'

She hesitated. 'Well . . . somebody tried. Last night.'

'What did the police say?'

'The police?'

The way she said it, I knew she hadn't called them.

'They ought to know,' I told her.

I could feel the specter of Philly Post breathing fire in my face.

'It might have something to do with Match's death,' I said. 'Maybe they'd step up their routine patrols in the neighborhood. Maybe post a man out front.'

She waved the idea away impatiently.

'I need publicity, honey, but not that kind. Some crackpot'll read that and it'll put notions in his head. Then I'll have ten people trying to break in instead of one. No thanks!'

'The police don't give out everything to the papers, you know.'

'Where've you been, honey? I asked them not to tell the reporters about Saturday night until I was ready and look where it got me. My doorbell started ringing at eight o'clock yesterday morning.'

27

'That was a murder, a homicide. There's no way they could suppress that. We're talking about a little break-in here. An *attempted* break-in. The smaller the crime, the easier it is to keep out of the papers.'

Her eyes focused on the disc over the mantel. She wasn't listening any more.

'Can you handle a gun, honey?'

'No, and you don't need—'

'I need somebody who can handle a gun, honey. Now are you going to help me or not?' She drew her squat body up, bristling.

I told her to check the Yellow Pages.

6

I tried to worm out of the burglar alarm deal, too, but she wouldn't hear of it, so we talked money. Most contractors will quote some exorbitant sum if they don't want to be bothered with a job. I usually just say I'll pass, but that didn't work with Sharon. So I asked for enough to cover six months' rent and ballparked a figure I thought my friends at Electronic Systems would charge for a quick installation if I designed it. I knew it wouldn't do me any good, but I asked her not to call me 'honey' any more as part of the deal.

Without a blink, she agreed and gave me five hundred dollars cash and promised to write a check for the balance when we finished. I got the impression she didn't really care what it cost.

Afterward, we went around outside and she showed me the windows, doors, and basement entrance in the back, while I took notes and sketched out the schematics on paper I borrowed from her.

'Where'd the burglar try to get in?' I asked her.

'Over there.'

She pointed to a window at the back of the house partly obscured by some tall bushes. We were standing midway between the house and a dense thicket of brush that marked the beginning of Mount Davidson.

The day was warming up to another typical Indian summer high and little beads of sweat were popping out on Sharon's forehead. She looked out of place and artificial outdoors, sort of like those pink plastic flamingos people put on their lawns. The natural light exposed all her painted wrinkles and covered bulges.

'I couldn't sleep last night,' she said. 'You know how it is, honey, so I went downstairs for a little nightcap. I never would have heard him otherwise.'

The burglar knew what he was doing. If I was going to hit the place, I would have picked that very window. Any of them at the back were fair game, but that one was the best. A tall pine blocked it from view on the right and from behind. Nobody could see anything from the left, and there weren't any exterior lights nearby, so a burglar could work as slowly and carefully as he needed to. No rush, no fuss.

'Did you see him?'

'I heard him. That's why he left, honey. I turned on every light in the house and shouted that I had a gun.'

'Why not just call 911?'

She looked at me like I was crazy.

'Oh, right. I forgot. The reporters.'

We went back indoors and it turned out that, had the burglar gotten inside, he would have ended up in Match's music room. When Sharon took me there I forgot all about checking out the jimmied window.

Standing just inside the door I felt like I was in a shrine. The air was dry and sweet with a vague aftershave scent I hadn't noticed in the rest of the house. My guess was that Match spent most of his time back here.

There were a couple of easy chairs, folding chairs, an over-stuffed couch against the far wall, and a workhorse upright piano in the corner. Music stands were scattered arbitrarily around the room and mounds and mounds of sheet music lay all over the place. An open cupboard against the wall was crammed full of records and music books, and in the center of the room, on a separate stand next to an open case on the floor, was Match's saxophone. It glittered like a diamond in the sun, its body engraved with a filigree of design that was a piece of work in itself.

The last time I'd seen it was at the Riff. Match had made it come alive then when he'd treated it like something sacred.

'I set it up like that for the reporters,' Sharon explained. 'They just ate it up.'

I'd read the stories. Like most of the stuff the local media printed, they were high in sentiment and low on facts. The bulk of the stories had been a simple chronicle of the songs he'd written and performed, most likely played out with tentative first notes on this very sax. With my fingertips, I traced the engraved initials on the stem.

'Do you play?'

She made a face and shook her head. Her earrings jangled some more.

'Not a note.'

I forced myself to leave the sax and go to the window. That's when I noticed the small plug of metal embedded waist-high in the molding left of the window frame. I turned to Sharon.

'You *fired* at him?'

'Sure, honey. He was a prowler.'

I was surprised the neighbors hadn't called it in. Maybe they'd heard it but just wrote it off as a car backfiring.

I raised the window to study the frame. Deep gouge marks scarred the underside where the burglar had started to jimmy the window. Maybe he'd been professional about choosing the right window, but he was strictly amateur about getting it open.

30

I thought again about Match and about the rumors that he'd been an addict.

'What did Match do those fifteen years he didn't play?' I asked as I continued to poke around.

What I really wanted to know was how somebody like her had snagged Match.

'We just got married two years ago, honey. I didn't know him before that.'

And she probably never thought to ask.

'How did you meet?'

'Rehab.' She said it matter-of-factly. 'We were both in rehab and we hit it off. It was his fifth time there and he started to backslide again but I pulled him through. You heard of tough love? Yeah. Well, that's me. I made him stick with it. Told him I wasn't a junkie anymore and I wouldn't live with a junkie. So he said he needed me to keep him off the stuff and would I marry him. He was in rehab the whole first year we were married. I figured I needed to stick around for him to make it.'

Somehow I couldn't picture Sharon being altruistic.

'Besides,' she continued, 'I figured if he made a comeback, I'd be on easy street. But let me tell you, honey, I've paid my dues. These last months he's been pulling together the band and the new songs, it's been tough. That took up most of his time. That, and that whining little Cuban.'

'Who?'

'Dickie.'

She said the name like she was saying the word 'slug.'

'You know who he is, honey, he's Match's trumpet.'

The hawk-nosed, snuffling Latino. The one who'd been crying at the Riff.

'They were friends?'

She snorted. 'Friends! He's a little leech, just like all of them. Match could've done better. All kinds of people offered to work with him, but who does he choose? Some little Cuban who shows up on his doorstep one day with a trumpet. Match could've had his pick of anybody and he picks a bunch of unknowns. I told him to fire the Cuban. He refused. I told him to fire them all! But he had no business sense. If it weren't for me he wouldn't have been putting the band together in the first place. He'd still be . . .' She drew up short and shook her head. Bottle-blonde curls bounced. 'It doesn't matter now.'

'Did Match ever talk about why he stopped playing?'

She looked at me like it was a trick question. 'No, why?'

'Why did he decide to start up again?'

'That little Cuban,' she said. 'He showed up at our door a few months ago, out of the blue, and wormed his way in. Next thing I know, Match comes home with his sax and sets up in this room. It was okay with me, kept him out of my hair, but I don't know why he liked that little Cuban so much.'

I shut the window and locked it, then thought of Philly Post.

'You really ought to report this,' I said again. 'Even if you don't think it's tied to Saturday night, the police ought to know.'

Her eyes blinked purple at me, beady under the mauve.

'You finished in here, honey?'

'Just about.'

I'd seen enough but I wanted to stay a little longer to bask in Match's presence, his history, his music.

'Well, I can't wait, honey. I need a drink. I'll be in the living room.'

And without another word she trotted out of the room.

7

I found Sharon sipping neat whiskey at the bar in the corner of the living room. She drained her glass, refilled it, then held up the bottle.

'Care for some medicine, honey?'

I shook my head and tapped the sheets where I'd roughed out my specifications.

'I'd like to get started on this. I'll call to see how soon my contractor can come out.'

'Wait a minute, honey. Sit down. There's one other thing.'

I sat down on the awful green couch and watched while Sharon slugged down another half glass behind the bar, then topped it off and came around to stand over me.

The drink had done her good. The tight little lines around her mouth had eased and she looked, if not relaxed, at least less used-up than when she'd opened the door an hour ago. She took a deep breath that stretched the limits of her flowered bodice.

'This still confidential?'

I sighed. 'Yes.'

'If I tell you and you don't agree to do it, will it still be confidential?'

'Mrs Margolis, what exactly do you want?'

'I'm just being careful, honey. Don't get mad. I don't want this leaking out to those reporters, that's all. You can understand that, can't you?'

I told her I could, so she sat down, cleared her throat, then paused dramatically.

'Like I said, Match wasn't any good with money,' she began solemnly. 'He just couldn't keep a budget. Now, I don't want any of this to get out, honey, but he owes some people money. At least I think he does.'

'And you want me to find out for sure?'

She sat back. There was a satisfied look on her face. 'You're smart, honey. I like that.'

She rose, got a piece of paper off the desk in the corner, came back and handed it to me.

'Here. There's four of them.'

I took the list and read it. No addresses, no phone numbers, just four names printed in block letters. Siegfried Malone. Buddha Teagues. Nick DuPont. Eugene Tobinio. None of the names meant a thing to me.

'Who are these guys?'

33

'Friends of Match's.'

'Musicians? Business partners? Patrons?'

'Friends.'

She said it a little too casually.

'Were they at the Riff Club Saturday night? Are they suspects?'
Her beady little eyes went wide.

'Oh, no, honey. It's nothing like that. They *liked* Match. I
told you he didn't have any enemies. If you ask any single
one of them they'll say Match walked on water. Go ahead.
Don't take my word for it, ask them yourself.'

I decided I would.

'Tell me about the loans.'

'What do you mean?'

'Do you know if Match signed anything? A promissory
note, an IOU? How much do you think he owes them? Is the
debt separate or combined?'

'Match didn't like paperwork. I wouldn't even know about
this myself except he let it slip one night. He said he'd pay
them back if he ever cut another album. I asked him what for
and you know what he said? He said, "For believing in me."'

I studied the list while Sharon clanged and shimmered in
front of me like some kind of giant decorated amoeba. She
reached out and laid a fake purple fingernail next to Siegfried
Malone's name.

'This one he made a deal with, but I don't know for what.
All I want you to do, honey, is talk to them. If they tell you
how much, then tell them I'm closing these deals, see, and as
soon as I get some cash, I'll settle up.'

I looked at Sharon, her dirty-blonde hair curled and unkempt
around her fleshy, tinted cheeks. She was sort of seeping out of
her clothes, bulging seams and distended zippers. Her short little
fingers twisted like bloated worms in her lap. I felt sorry for her.

'Match wasn't big on the fine points,' she said, 'like who
he owed money to or who owns what. Proprietary – that's
what he called it. He said he just wasn't proprietary.'

I thought about what she was asking. It sounded simple
enough. Post couldn't say I was horning in and it'd only take

me a couple of hours to do it, max. But why didn't she just talk to them herself? I could have asked, but for private investigators there's a fine line between asking enough and asking too much. With clients like her, I preferred to err on the side of ignorance. Ignorance of the law won't get you off the hook, but ignorance of a client's motives might. As far as I was concerned, it was her dime and her show.

8

I spent the next hour working out the plans for the burglar alarm and setting up the place for installation while Sharon polished off half a bottle of Scotch and haggled over the phone with recording companies. Hearing her 'honey' and wheedle and whine at them made me wonder how I ever could have felt sorry for her.

My pal, Toby, down at Electronic Systems, was glad for the business but griped about the short notice.

'I gotta pull four guys off a job in the Sunset to do this, Ron. That's gonna cost. And this shit you're asking me to bring – hell, it ain't cheap.'

I ended up short, with just two months' rent instead of six, but that was okay. Toby'd be doing the bulk of the installation anyway.

They showed up forty-five minutes later, an army of six, carrying everything I'd asked for and more. I found out Toby'd promised them double time if they worked through their lunch hours in between their other jobs. And that's all it took. We were done by one fifteen.

'Is it finished?' Sharon glanced at the retreating back of Toby and his workers.

'All done.' I led her back up the walk and inside to show her the numbered digital keypad we'd installed just inside the front door.

'This is where you turn the system off when you come home,' I told her. 'You punch the code in. Here, like this. You've got four seconds after you unlock the door to get inside and shut off the system before the alarm kicks in. Think four seconds is enough time? We can make it longer if you'd like.'

'No, no, honey. That's fine.'

'It's a great system.' I was proud of it. 'It's a central alarm. That means it's wired over your phone line into the security office over on O'Shaughnessy. If anything happens, they'll know it as soon as you do. A guard can be here in a matter of minutes. Guaranteed. If anybody cuts the phone line, the alarm goes off. If your power goes out, there's a backup that'll kick in. Nothing's completely foolproof, but this one's close.'

'What about the police, honey? Will they come?'

'Do you want them to? We can set it up to notify the local station simultaneously if you'd like.'

'No, honey. Don't bother. Leave it the way it is.'

She smiled. I tried to remember if she'd smiled any time before, but couldn't.

'What a load off,' she said, then invited me into the living room so she could write me and Toby the final check.

'How's the police investigation going?' I asked as we trudged down the hall. I'd been wanting to ask her since I'd arrived.

'Lieutenant Post called this morning, honey, with more questions. But I'll be honest with you, nothing's changed since Saturday night.'

Not surprising given he had about three hundred suspects to slog through. Not too comforting, either. She sat down at the roll-top and flipped open her checkbook.

'What about your assistant? Does he want a separate check?'

'One's fine.'

Sharon filled in the amount, stood, then held on to the check. She was sweating: tiny beads of moisture covered her upper lip and forehead.

'The funeral home called a minute ago, honey. I need to pick up the remains.'

'The police released the body already?'

I knew from other cases that Post always kept his homicide victims' bodies at least five days.

Sharon just shrugged.

'Did Philly Post okay the release?'

'Please don't make this harder than it is, honey. I had to make the choice to cremate and that was tough enough.'

'Did they do an autopsy?'

'Sure, honey. How hard can it be? He died from being stabbed.'

She had a point. Still clutching the check, her face started to crumple. She dabbed at her eyes with a manicured finger.

'I don't think I can do this,' she said between sniffles.

My guess was that was my cue to offer to stick around.

'It must be tough,' I said, then stuck my hand out for the check. 'I wish you luck.'

In the end, she asked me to drive her over to the funeral home and I relented and said yes. They gave her an urn which we took out to the cemetery and locked up in a beehive vault that had a temporary label with his name on it. No priest, no rabbi, just me and Sharon and the caretaker.

'That's how he wanted it, honey. No ceremony.'

I could understand that. I don't want anybody to make a fuss over me, either. But Sharon didn't even leave him flowers.

9

Blackie was at his usual table at the Quarter Moon Saloon – in the back, away from the light, bent over a racing form. Five empties were scattered on the table and the ashtray should have been dumped three packs ago – especially since smoking in bars is against the law. When Harry the bartender greeted me by name, Blackie looked up and grinned.

I brought my beer and a fresh one for him over to his table.

He said, 'There's money on it now, doll. A reward. Want to nail the fucker?'

'Who?'

He chugged some beer, belched softly, then set the half-empty bottle down on the table next to the racing form.

'Match's killer. Ten grand. The musician's union put it up. What do you think? Want to go for it?'

'Post said—'

'Fuck Post. He's got shit for brains. What's he gonna do?'

'He'll arrest me, Blackie. He's already put me in jail once.'

'Thought you were short. What was all that shit about not making the rent?'

I pulled out Sharon Margolis's check and waved it under his nose. 'Burglar alarm for the little missus,' I said.

'Yeah?' He sounded more disappointed than impressed.

'And there's something else, too. Have you ever heard of Siegfried Malone?'

'Siggy Malone? Sure. Malone Junk. Owns that junkyard down off Toland. Runs a chop shop out of it.'

Gangster number one.

Blackie scowled.

'You workin' for him?'

'No. Match Margolis did some kind of business with him. Owes him and some other people money.'

'No shit.' Blackie looked pensive. 'Could be a motive.'

'Sharon swears it was friendly.'

I asked him about the other names on the list, but none were familiar.

'You workin' for the widow, are you?'

'Sort of. It's all supposed to be confidential.'

'Ain't it always?' His grin widened. 'Sounds to me like you're buckin' Post.'

'Not really. The main thing was she wanted me to set up

a system for her. Seems all his stuff is suddenly collectable now. Everybody's coming out of the woodwork offering her deals.'

'Too bad about that, huh? Old Match gets famous all over again and he can't even be around to enjoy it.'

Blackie glanced around the room, then said, 'When you talkin' to Malone?'

'Tonight if I can find him.'

Blackie inhaled again, then blew smoke towards the ceiling. 'Want me along?'

'I'll be fine,' I said. 'Unless you're bored.'

'Not even close. Got to meet a young lady at seven thirty.'

'I hope it's not . . .'

Blackie grinned. 'The tall one checked out.'

10

Halfway from the Quarter Moon to my car, I heard someone call out my name. When I turned around to look, a solid forty-something, sandy-haired guy was puffing after me, his hand raised in a salute. I didn't recognize him, but he was smiling like we'd been separated at birth.

When he caught up, slightly out of breath, he said, 'Got a minute?'

'That depends.'

He liked that. He had a slight overbite, but everything else about him looked nice: a sturdy build, muscular, a healthy complexion, and earnest green eyes.

'I'm Glen Faddis. *Faddis at Eleven.*'

'A reporter.'

My budding interest took a dive. He laughed.

'Could you sound any *less* enthusiastic?'

I didn't smile. But I didn't walk away, either. I guess I was curious.

'Look, Ms Ventana – can I call you Ronnie?'

'No.'

'Okay. Ms Ventana, I know you're not a big fan of the press. You ought to be, though. The press loved your parents. I haven't read a negative word about them. Ever.'

'Good for you. What is it you want, Mr Faddis?'

'It's about Match Margolis.'

'What a surprise.'

'I'm just trying to do my job.'

He seemed genuine, not a thick-skinned oaf like other reporters I'd spoken to.

'How long have you been a reporter, Mr Faddis?'

'Three years. I used to practice law. Criminal defense.'

'Then Hollywood called?'

'I do good work, Ms Ventana. Investigative work. Like you.'

Out of nowhere, a group of Chinese kids swarmed around us as they passed by, their chatter a mix of English and Cantonese, laughing and smoking cigarettes like it was their first time. They all looked way under age but they were probably grad students somewhere out for a night of letting off steam. Once they passed, other people seemed to follow. It was like somebody had opened up the gates.

I turned back to Faddis.

'What do you want?'

He glanced around at the steady stream of people squeezing past us on the narrow sidewalk.

'Can I buy you a drink?'

'No, thanks. If you want to talk, you can do it here.'

With a practiced, graceful motion, he whipped out a little notebook and a Mont Blanc pen.

'There's a rumor going around, Ms Ventana. A rumor that says Match Margolis whispered his killer's name in your ear before he died.'

'Were you there Saturday night?'

He shook his head.

'You're not a fan of jazz?'

'I was working on something else. Undercover. What did Match say to you? What were his dying words?'

'Where'd you hear this?'

'It's common knowledge.'

'Do you want an answer?'

'Yes.'

He fixed eager eyes on me, fingers tense as he poised pen over tablet.

'Then tell me who told you.'

'A source. I can't reveal a source.'

'Nice talking to you, Mr Faddis.'

I turned and started down the street toward my car.

'Wait!' He jogged to catch up with me. 'Okay. You win. It was an anonymous call.'

I studied his face.

'I don't believe you.'

He blushed deep red and turned instantly sheepish.

'Can't blame a guy for trying. Look, you'll tell me if I tell you?'

I'd already said as much.

'You're wasting time, Mr Faddis.'

'Okay, okay. It was Yvette Fields.'

'Who?'

'Match Margolis's daughter.'

'I didn't know he had one.'

'She's illegitimate. Lives in the Richmond. Her mother died of an overdose.'

'Was she there Saturday night?'

He nodded, then paused, waiting.

'So? What did Match say?'

'The rumor you heard? It's just that: a rumor. There's no truth to it at all. Match didn't say a word.'

He stared at me, mouth fixed in a straight line, fighting his own annoyance at being duped. Finally, he broke out in a good-natured grin and chuckled.

'Okay. You won that round.'

'If you're looking for a story, Mr Faddis, why don't you find out why Match's illegitimate daughter is spreading that rumor. And when you find the answer, let me know. Goodnight.'

I started back down the street for the third time and he chased me again.

'Hey,' he said when he caught up with me. 'Here's my card.' He slipped it into my hand. 'Have you got one?'

'I'm in the book.'

11

I'd been on my way to Malone Junk, but if Yvette Fields was telling anybody who'd listen that I knew who killed Match, she suddenly shot to the top of my list.

She was easy enough to find. Just like me, she was in the phone book. Twice. The first address was in a residential section of the Avenues in the Richmond. The other was in the Tenderloin, the San Francisco neighborhood that played host to most of the city's resident released sex offenders, winos, and a lot of just plain poor people, not to mention a growing and thriving, hardworking Vietnamese community of families.

In the business phone listing, after Yvette's name, were the initials CMT – certified massage therapist. But, given her address, I didn't think massage was all she offered.

The store front was the picture of good taste: a poster of a recumbent, big-busted brunette in a bikini lolling on a bunch of brightly colored pillows. With a smile. And a blue neon sign that flashed: MASSAGE NOW!

I opened the door and stepped into a linoleum-tiled room

the size of a bathroom stall. An exotic-looking woman sat at a card table with a cash box, a ballpoint pen, and one of those slider gizmos you need to process credit card sales. The harsh light from the bare bulb overhead didn't diminish her beauty. Her features were vaguely Asian, but she was full-bodied and was dressed like a hooker. She had Match's cheekbones and his full lips.

I smiled at her, but she didn't smile back. Instead, she rose halfway out of her folding chair, fear in her eyes. For a minute, I thought she might bolt through the door behind her, but she held her ground.

'What do you want?'

'Hi, Yvette. Nice place.'

'Why are you here?'

'I want to know why you're telling people I know who killed your father.'

'Because it's true.'

She didn't even sound like she believed it herself.

'You know it isn't. Who put you up to it?'

She tossed her head defiantly but that wasn't very convincing, either. She was too young to be doing what she was doing. Somehow, she looked like a cornered rabbit – a very pretty cornered rabbit.

'I don't have to talk to you,' she said.

'You're right. You can talk to the police instead. You can explain to them why you're spreading false information about a homicide.'

'Why are you threatening me? I don't know anything.'

The door behind her sprang open and we both jumped. A young captain of industry stepped out – blue suit, tie and brief-case. Techno music blared from inside, then stopped suddenly as the door shut behind him. Soundproof. Our eyes met, then he ducked his head and made for the door. I'd seen guys look less guilty coming out of a bank they'd just robbed. I stepped aside to let him pass and got a whiff of soap and sweat and cigar. He was probably on his way home to the wife and kids across the Bay in Orinda.

'I bet the cops would be really interested in a place like this.'

'They're not,' she said, suddenly on solid ground. 'I've got it covered.'

'Maybe Vice. I'm talking Homicide. They're different.'

'They're men, aren't they?'

I stepped in closer and mustered my meanest glare.

'Let me explain to you why I'm not going to go away: you put a premium on my head the minute you started that rumor. Now you're going to tell me who put you up to it or I'm going to park myself outside with a video camera and film every customer who walks through your door. And if that doesn't clear things out, I'll hand them letters telling them your staff's got a dozen different kinds of STDs.'

She looked horrified. 'That's illegal.'

'So's what you're doing.'

'It was one of his pals.'

'Which one?'

'I didn't see who it was. I was just standing near them and I heard somebody say my dad had whispered a name before he died.'

'I need more than that.'

'Nick DuPont. Sig Malone. Buddha Teagues. They're all friends of my dad's. Clark might have been with them, too – my half-brother. That's all I know.'

'And you didn't recognize the voice?'

She slammed her petite hand down on the cardboard tabletop in a sitting down version of stamping her foot. The ballpoint pen bounced.

'I told you I didn't! Now will you please leave me alone? I'm still grieving.'

Another guy popped out from the back, eyed me with suspicion, and scuttled past to the door. He didn't smell as clean as the other guy had. And he didn't look as clean, either.

'Right,' I said. 'Call me if anything jogs your memory.'

I tossed my card on the table, then followed the john outside and inhaled a deep breath of clean air.

12

By the time I got out to Malone Junk, it was past dusk. I parked on the street and slipped through a narrow gate in a tall wooden fence that surrounded half the block. There was just enough light left for me to make out the faded hobo drawn above the name MALONE JUNK.

The neighborhood wasn't the best. A million years ago it used to be industrial and dotted with tenements. Now it was stark and colorless with boarded-up windows, rundown metal-sided warehouses and the sad, ominous feeling of most ghettos.

A handful of bums were hanging out on the corner – not the usual innocuous homeless, but sinister men, wary and vigilant. Trash was everywhere and I felt at a disadvantage right off because my clothes were clean.

The dirty little shack just inside the fence had a big, lighted window under a sloppily hand-painted BEWARE OF DOG sign. A lot of people like the idea of a dog for protection but get turned off by the prospect of dog food, vet bills and dog shit, so they just post a sign and pretend. I was hoping Malone was one of them.

All the same, I looked around for Rover. If he existed, he must have been resting his jaws. Music – soft, easy jazz – filtered out from the open door. It turned out to be the only pleasant thing about the place.

Since the door was propped open with a blackened metal remnant from a car engine, I just walked right in. The two goons behind the counter – a man and a boy of about twelve – had to be precursors to the back-hill folks in that movie *Deliverance*. All they were missing was the banjo.

The sweat and grease-stained tee shirt the man wore had seen better days. So had his face. He had the kind of repugnantly friendly look I hate to see when I'm working alone and it's dark outside. He blinked and massaged his bulging stomach while he eyed me up and down from behind the counter.

The kid didn't look any more promising. He was sitting at a desk behind the counter pounding his open palms against his cheeks and making nasty, snot-sucking noises while he rolled his eyes and generally looked like he needed an emergency exorcism. The man acted like the kid was normal so I took my cue from him and tried not to stare.

'Whatcha need, hon?' the man said.

'Are you Siggy Malone?'

He picked at a scab on his chin.

'Could be.'

The kid went suddenly quiet so I looked past the big guy to see what he was up to. As soon as the kid knew I was watching he started making retching sounds and pretended to vomit. I looked back at the older guy and heard the kid laugh.

'Are you Mr Malone?'

'Depends. Who are you?'

'My name's Ronnie Ventana. I'm a private investigator. I need to speak to you regarding your business partner.'

'My business partner's dead, lady. What's there to say about him?'

The kid was still making disgusting sounds and from what I could glimpse over Malone's shoulder, he was making faces. Maybe he really was mentally disturbed.

'I understand your business partner owed you some money.'

'Maybe.'

He hitched an elbow on the counter and leaned on it. I could smell his rotting breath and count the little black holes in his front teeth when he smiled.

'Who sent you over here, hon?'

'I'm representing Mrs Margolis—'

He stiffened and pushed himself off the counter.

'That bastard.'

I assumed they'd met.

'She asked me to assure you there won't be any problem making good on her husband's debt. You will be paid back. She's concerned and she doesn't want any hard feelings between the two of you.'

'She should've thought of that when she walked out on me. Stupid whore.'

'You and Mrs Margolis . . .?'

I tried to hide the horror in my voice. Sharon Margolis was no princess but I couldn't picture anything female wanting to get nearer than ten yards from Sig Malone.

'You got it.' Malone jerked a thumb over his shoulder. 'Squirt back there's her kid. Soon as the judge said "guilty" she went after Match like a bitch in heat. I know it wasn't him. The whole year I was in Quentin she worked on poor old Match. Just 'cause he was living upstairs and running the yard for me she figured I give him the whole business instead of just half. Left me and the kid and look what she got. Nothin'.'

'When did your wife lea—?'

'Wife?' His laugh sounded more like a snarl. 'I wouldn't marry a cow like her. Hell! She begged me to take her back a week after she married poor old Match. Did she tell you that? Nah, I didn't think so. I wouldn't have her. Hell, Match did me a favor.'

Match stole Malone's lover. Match owed Malone money. Some people might figure Sig Malone had a motive.

'I understand you were at the Riff Club Saturday night.'

Malone only *looked* stupid.

'The day I croak a man for twenty grand is the day I cut off my balls.'

I wanted to say that I hoped he already had but I didn't think he'd take it well. The kid went quiet again and this time he rose from behind the desk and came toward the counter. He slipped under it, to my left, and walked around behind me. I acted like he wasn't there and wondered if I was making a mistake.

'Did you tell anyone Match named his killer?'

'Whah?'

He looked like I'd lost him entirely.

'Did you tell your friends or did any of your friends tell you that Match named his killer just before he died?'

'I heard somethin' like that, but I didn't pay any mind.'

'Think,' I urged him. 'It's important.'

'Look, lady PI whatever your name is. About the business. After the music bellied-up for Match, he worked here. He made a few deals, pumped up the profits, stood by me while I was doing my stretch. What am I going to do? Match says he wants to borrow against his share and so I give it to him. Twenty grand. But I'm not dumb, you see. Before I give it to him, I made him sign a note that says I get his piece of the business if he doesn't pay me back.'

There was a clank behind me and I spun around. The monster kid had a slim jim – one of those long metal slats that unlock locked car doors – in his dirty hand and he was brandishing it like a sword, poking holes in the air with his back to me. Two strong overhand thrusts, then one quick underhand jab – probably the same kind of single, swift motion Match's killer had used.

'Ditch it, boy,' Malone snarled. The kid dropped it and scuttled out the door like some kind of subterranean prairie varmint. I turned back to Malone.

'But, Mr. Malone an agreement like that—'

'You trying to say I killed Match?'

The look on his scabby face dared me to say yes.

'Not in a million years.'

He stuck a grimy finger in my face.

'You investigating this thing, you snoop into *her* business, lady. Not mine.'

'Sure,' I agreed. 'I'll do that.'

'That fat bitch has got more schemes than Houdini. She couldn't pull crap with me. Poor bastard Match wouldn't keep her in line. Couldn't. He was a nice guy but he was a fool. She walked on him, poor son of a bitch.'

He grunted and picked at the scab on his chin until it bled. Then he held his finger out, looked at the blood on it, and licked it.

'Match was all right,' he muttered almost to himself. Then

he fixed his nasty eyes on me. 'Tell her I don't want her money. I'd rather have the business and I've got it fair and legal and square. Tell her that. And tell her I hope she rots in hell.'

13

The night was young and Buddha Teagues was a cinch to locate. Sharon mentioned that he owned a bar in the Avenues and I stumbled across one on Clement called 'Teagues.' How hard was that?

It turned out the place was an Asian gay bar and I stuck out like a sore thumb.

When I asked the bartender if Buddha was around, he acted like English wasn't even close to being his second language. I tried City College advanced Japanese, a couple of words my father had taught me in Spanish, then quickly found his mother tongue: cash.

I slipped him a Jackson on top of paying for my beer and he opened right up.

'Buddha? Ya.'

He bobbed his head up and down and motioned for me to follow. I crossed my fingers, left my beer behind, and prayed Buddha had at least an ounce more polish than Sig Malone.

The bartender stopped outside a moldy wooden door between the men's room and the pay phone, away from the coy noises the fellas were making up front.

'Buddha here,' he said, pointing, then ran back to the bar as I knocked.

'Come in!'

At least Buddha Teagues' voice was more refined than Malone's. And when I opened the door, I had to smile.

Buddha was a fastidiously dressed fat man who looked like, well, like a buddha. His small bullet-shaped head was bald, with short tufts of white hair above his ears and eyes that beamed beneficence. He wore an impeccably tailored, tent-sized plaid suit, a couple of diamond pinkie rings on each hand, and he was listening to jazz from an old-fashioned tape deck in the corner. Match's songs. If he was a gangster, he looked pretty benign.

The office smelled musty, probably because it didn't have any windows, and the walls were covered with old black and white photos and yellowed newspaper clippings. Teagues was in all of them: Teagues with a jockey, Teagues with a race-horse, Teagues in Las Vegas, Teagues with a man in a tuxedo. Everybody smiling, patting each other on the back.

He raised his bulk out of the chair behind the desk, made little hamster-like *chuk-chukking* noises deep in his throat while he did so, and offered me his hand. My fingers vanished into it like I'd stuck them into a big, soft muffin. The *chuk-chuks* morphed into words.

'Sit down, sit down, my dear. Welcome.'

I took the only empty chair in the cramped room, an over-stuffed gold lamé job with a high back and claw feet.

Buddha's chair – a vast leather office job that looked like a bunch of pillows cobbled together into a chair – squeaked when he settled back into it. He clasped his thick hands over a vintage leather desk blotter and fixed me with a wide, mildly curious smile.

'We don't get many girls in here anymore. What can I do for you, Miss . . .?'

'Ventana. Ronnie Ventana. I'm a private investigator.'

'Ah.'

He raised his eyebrows in amusement. The smile deepened and he *chuk-chukked* himself into speaking some more.

'Very interesting, that profession. Or so I would imagine. I hope you're not bearing bad tidings.'

The way he said it, I could tell he didn't think anybody'd ever bring him bad news.

'They're good, as a matter of fact.'

'Marvelous! That's marvelous.'

He acted like a kid about to receive a present.

'It's about some money you've got coming.'

'Really? That's wonderful. From whom?'

'Match Margolis.'

The name hit him like a blow. The beatific smile vanished as every line in his face sagged. His eyes teared up. For a minute I thought he was going to cry, but all he did was pull out a spotless white handkerchief and trumpet into it.

'Forgive me,' he said, after composing himself. 'I suppose it's the will?'

'The will?'

'Match asked me once to be his executor. I told him it would be an honor. Of course, I had no idea I'd be paid for it.'

I watched him fold the handkerchief up neatly and pocket it.

'That *is* the money you're referring to, isn't it?'

'Actually, no. I haven't seen the will.'

'You . . . oh, my . . . what? I naturally assumed . . . Pardon me.' He cleared his throat. 'Do go on, then.'

The spirit in his hearty voice was subdued, just like the tune Match was playing on the tape in the background.

'Mrs Margolis asked—'

He bristled.

'Sharon Margolis sent you?'

'Yes, she . . . Her concern is that Match, er, Mr Margolis, owed you some money.'

'Money? I just lost one of the finest friends I ever had, a true gentleman. Not to mention that the man was a creative genius. A *musical* genius! Yes, that's what he was! His music was one of a kind. And she's worried about money! Listen.'

He whipped a remote control device off his desktop and cranked up the volume on the tape. Match's sax filled the room with a warm, sensual melody I recognized from my own collection. One of a kind. Buddha Teagues was right.

'Money!'

He jabbed a button with his fat fingers and the music stopped abruptly. His chin quivered with indignation.

51

'Why, that's absurd. It's *absurd* and obscene.' *Chuk-chuk-chuk.* 'But that's not what this is about, is it? She thinks *I* killed him, doesn't she?'

'I don't know what she thinks, Mr Teagues. And to tell you the truth, I don't care. I'm not investigating Match's murder; the police are doing that. All I'm doing is getting the word out about his debts. That's all.'

Buddha started in again with more *chukking* noises. It was like I hadn't said a word.

'If anyone had a motive, it was Sharon Margolis, not me. I loved Match. I'll tell you something in confidence – I spoke to Match on Saturday.'

He nodded for emphasis.

'If you're looking into this, Miss Ventana, I think you should know Match was extremely nervous. I asked him twice why he was so anxious. He blamed it on the new compositions. Of course, I didn't believe that for a minute. Match's talent has been undisputed since the first day he picked up a saxophone. He is – *was* a professional. No, I think he suspected something. I think he *knew* someone planned to do him harm. And,' he announced triumphantly, 'Match told me Sharon took out a life insurance policy on him this past year – a *very* large one.'

He sat there, jowls quivering, *chuk-chukking*, and staring at me like he expected me to run out the door and throw Sharon into leg irons.

'Mr Teagues, I'm not looking for Match's killer. I—'

'Talk to his son! Have you spoken to him?'

'Sounds like I should.'

'Of course you should. He's in Alameda. Clark didn't want Match to resurrect his career. They were tugging at Match from either side. His wretched wife, pushing him, egging him on, and the boy telling him not to listen to her. Neither of them did him any good. But Clark had good intentions. Ask him about Sharon.'

'What kind of good intentions?'

'Sorry?'

'The son. Why didn't he think Match should play?'

Buddha waved one of his big, puffy hands like he was swatting away a fly.

'The music milieu – it could expose his father to unnecessary temptations. Match's road to sobriety was a hard one.'

'I thought Sharon helped.'

Buddha's jaw dropped.

'That's the most ridiculous thing I've ever heard. She told you that?'

I nodded.

'The only reason she wanted Match sober was because she believed he would start writing again. She wanted a meal ticket. Match always saw the best in everyone, even Sharon.'

'Well, her plan seemed to have worked.'

'She didn't inspire him. He was clean for the last year and a half. He didn't go back to music until just a few months ago. It had nothing to do with Sharon. Not at all. I credit Dickie Almaviva. After he came into the picture, things picked up. Sharon always tries to take credit for everything.'

Buddha looked annoyed so I changed the subject.

'Did you hear anybody mention Match's dying words Saturday night?'

'Why, yes. As a matter of fact, Yvette – that's Match's daughter – told me he'd managed to whisper his killer's name into . . .'

He stopped and studied my face more closely, then recognition dawned in his eyes.

'It was *you*, wasn't it? You were the one.'

'I was there, yes, Mr Teagues. But Match didn't say anything. He was already dead when he fell.'

Buddha shook his formidable bald head.

'What a sad, sad state of affairs. That Sharon, she's a wretched piece of work, isn't she? Yvette isn't much better.'

He was quickly losing interest in the conversation, so I went for a second new tack.

'About the money . . .'

He waved his thick hand in dismissal.

'Match didn't owe me a thing.'

53

'Mr Teagues—'

'He's the one who insisted I keep track. There was the bar tab, and sometimes we'd make bets. You know, I take on wagers sometimes for the races. Match wasn't always so lucky, but we were friends. I never asked him to pay.'

'Never?'

'He was my friend. How could I ask him to pay when he's barely made a dime in fifteen years?'

Buddha Teagues obviously didn't know about Match's partnership with Sig Malone.

'Match made me keep track, but in all honesty, I never expected to see it again. I told him not to worry about it. I certainly don't expect it back now.'

'How much did he owe you?'

Buddha hesitated, shifting in his chair, lips pursed. Finally, he said, 'Roughly? Around ten thousand.'

'You're quite a friend.'

'It's nothing, really. Just paper.'

I wasn't sure whether to believe him or not so I just let him talk.

'Match and I went back a long time, you know. Since before Georgette died. He just fell apart when she passed away. Couldn't write another note after that. He played for a while, but his heart just wasn't in it. You'd understand if you'd seen them together. Georgette was a remarkable woman. Remarkable! Musical, too. They were made for each other.'

Her name wasn't on any of the records I owned. 'Did she play with him?'

'Oh, no. But she was always in the background though, supporting, advising. Never missed a rehearsal. Carried his scores for him.' He sighed. 'Poor Match. We tried to pull him through when she died, but you know how it is. He just let go. And that's when he found solace in drugs.'

His eyes stared out at nothing, the memories more vivid than anything inside the walls surrounding us.

'I've been giving some thought to this, Miss Ventana,' he finally said after breaking his reverie. 'If I could bring Match back, I would. I can't do anything about his . . . his passing, but I feel a need to act. I've decided to offer a reward – ten thousand dollars – to the person who tracks down the brute who took Match from us.'

Added to the ten from the musician's union, that made twenty thousand dollars.

'That's a lot of money,' I said, then felt stupid for saying it.

'It's not worth one man's life.'

I agreed, then out of the blue he suggested I talk to Nick DuPont and Eugene Tobinio.

'It will be excellent for you to speak with them. They'll tell you Match wasn't himself on Saturday. By all means, you *must* speak to them.'

Before I left, I gave Teagues my card and asked him to call me if he thought of anything else. I was halfway across town before I remembered I wasn't investigating Match's murder.

14

But somebody seemed to think I was. The same pair of headlights tailed me all the way down California. I made a couple of circuits around the block before I got to Gough, then made a U-turn and left him behind as I sped home. I was so sure I'd lost him that I bought a cold six pack and stopped by a place that sells takeout pizza by the slice. Then, once I'd parked and come around the corner to my building, I nearly tripped over Philly Post.

'Jesus, Post!' It was hard to ignore him, big and scowling, blocking my path.

'Ventana.' It sounded like an indictment. I decided to ignore his tone. Maybe if I sounded chirpy, it'd rub off on him.

'How's the investigation going?'

'You tell me.'

I raised the stuff I was holding – beer and pizza, my dinner – in case he'd overlooked it, and said, 'Your timing's bad, Post.'

'What I've got to say'll just take a minute.'

'Good.'

'What are you doing talking to Match's known associates?'

'*Known associates*? You make him sound like a Mafia don.'

'Didn't I tell you not to work this case, Ventana?'

'I'm not working it.'

'So what were you doing with Malone and Teagues?'

'What was I doing? I was *not* working the case. Just like you told me. And if you'd put your resources to finding Match's killer instead of tailing me, you'd probably save yourself a couple of weeks. Now, if you'll excuse me, my pizza's getting cold.'

I hurried past him, shoved open the door to my building and started upstairs. He scrambled in after me.

'Go away, Post,' I said, but he only hurried more.

Five minutes later, he was sitting across from me, eating half my slice of pizza. I was happy to give him half the slice, even offered him some beer, but I wasn't thrilled about his manners.

'I don't have to talk to you, Post.'

'Why'd you let me in?'

'A moment of weakness. Have you got any credible leads on Match's killer?'

Post snorted.

'What makes you think I'd give you confidential information about an ongoing police investigation?'

'You have before.'

He scowled.

'And it worked well for us, didn't it? I mean, we've got some kind of synergy, Post. Think about it. You just don't recognize it.'

He crumpled the paper towel I'd given him to use instead of a plate for his pizza and tossed it onto the coffee table between us.

'Spill, Ventana. What have Teagues and Malone got to say?'

'Why don't you interview them yourself?'

'We have.'

'And?'

'Just tell me what they told you.'

'Are we comparing notes?'

He hesitated, then nodded. His thick mane of hair swayed as his head moved.

'You're assuming I'm investigating Match's murder. I'm not. I do have one question for you, though. Why did the ME release Match's body already?'

Post straightened in his seat. His bushy eyebrows furrowed. 'What?'

'I thought five days was your own personal hard and fast rule. Who changed your mind?'

'What are you saying?'

'I'm saying I was with Sharon Margolis today when she put Match's ashes in their final resting place.'

Post sprang to his feet and yanked out his cell phone in one deft motion. He was punching buttons on it as he rushed out the door. By the time he was halfway down the stairs, he was bellowing at some poor soul on the other end who'd drawn the short straw of luck for the night when he picked up the phone and got Post.

Myself? I was just happy he was gone.

15

It'd been a full day but I wasn't tired. Jazz kept floating through my head, so I looked around and put on one of Match's CDs. Two minutes was all I could stand, though, before I shut it off. The music made me sad.

I was writing up a report that was way past due on an

insurance thing I'd worked last week when the phone rang.

'Ronnie! What are you doing?'

'Mitch?'

'Yeah. What are you doing?'

'Working.'

'Great. Listen, Ron, look out your window, okay?'

'Why?'

'Just look, will you? Walk over to your window and look out.'

I knew Mitch. He wasn't going to go away until I did. So I dragged the phone over to the curtainless window. I looked. Neon gleamed down the street off Columbus Avenue. The stars were out overhead.

'Down,' Mitch said through the receiver. 'Look down. Across the street.'

I did. There, double-parked, forcing every single car coming down the narrow, one-way street to slowly eke its way past, sat a shiny but vintage blue bathtub Porsche. There was a man inside it, a real knockout of a guy. I looked closer. He was waving at me with one hand, clutching a silver cell phone in the other. Mitchell.

The voice on the line chuckled.

'What do you think?' he asked.

'About what?'

'The car, Ron. It's me down here, can't you see me? I'm in the Porsche.'

'You bought another car?'

'Yeah.'

'What's that make, eighteen?'

He laughed and kept waving. The passers-by – tourists and drunks – were starting to stare.

I said, 'That's great, Mitch.'

'Yeah.' He sounded satisfied. 'Why don't you come down? We'll go for a ride.'

'I'm working.'

'We can ride around.'

'Sounds great, Mitch, but I'd rather not.'

'Come on, Ron. There's something else I wanted to run by you.'

Mitchell never saw me without 'having to talk' or 'run something by.' He seemed to forget we weren't married anymore, and one of the reasons we weren't was because we'd 'talked' ourselves out of being married.

I looked at my watch. It was ten o'clock. Mitch's crisis was probably about which kind of foreign car he should buy next. 'Some other time, Mitch.'

'All right. I'll come up. But if I get a ticket, man, it's on your head.'

He hung up before I could say no. I managed two quick gulps of beer before there was a tap at the door. I opened it a crack. 'Can't this wait, Mitch?'

He grinned. 'Come on, Ronnie. Let me in.'

'Mitchell, I'm really tired. I didn't run today and . . .'

His startling green eyes caught mine. I knew the look. He was as determined as he was handsome, and he wasn't going to go away. I sighed, let the door swing open and went back to my chair and my beer.

Mitch followed, taking in the laptop computer on the coffee table and the half-empty bottle of beer next to it.

'Beer?' I said.

'No, uh-uh. You go ahead.'

He was giving me permission again. At least in my mind, he was. I started to bristle, but caught myself. People only gave permission if you asked them, and I wasn't asking. I picked up the half-empty bottle and sat.

'Don't you want to know what's going on?' he said.

I drank some beer, then said, 'What's going on?'

'It's about work.'

I groaned. 'Not this again. Mitch, how many times do I have to tell you? I've got a job. I don't need another one, okay? Just because you don't think this kind of work is steady enough, doesn't mean it isn't. Quit talking your ex-fraternity brothers into offering me jobs. I'm tired of it. And I bet they're tired of it, too.'

He plopped onto the sofa and waved away my words. 'It's not that, Ronnie. It's *my* job.'

For the first time, I noticed he wasn't wearing his usual custom Italian-cut business suit. No power tie, either. Just an Izod shirt, Levi's and Topsiders. 'Didn't you work today?'

He grabbed a pillow off the couch and hugged it to his chest, then slouched down in his seat and let his head loll against the back of the couch. 'Nu-huh,' he said. 'I called in. I'm thinking of giving notice.'

'Why? Mitchell, you love your job. What happened?'

'Nothing.' He tossed the pillow back on the couch and sat up. 'I want to do something different, Ron.'

'Yeah?' I couldn't blame him. I'd rather spend a lifetime in San Quentin than a week as an accountant. But Mitch loved numbers. He thought ledgers were exciting.

'I want to buy a boat and sail to Tahiti.'

'Mitch, you don't have to quit your job to take a vacation.'

'I want to live there. Surf in the sun, eat coconuts all day, Ronnie. Just for a year. Time out. Reassess.' He said it like he meant it but I still couldn't believe him. Mitch wasn't fickle. He hated to let go. He took a whole year once just to decide whether to sell his Citroën or his Saab, then ended up keeping both.

'I don't think it's a good idea, Mitch. You'll curl up into a little ball and die without structure in your life. You going to sell your cars? Your house?'

'That's what I wanted to talk to you about.'

For one horrified moment, I thought he was going to invite me along, but what he said instead was just as bad.

'I was thinking you could stay at my house, look after—'

'No.'

'Why not?' He ran his eyes around the room. He didn't say a word but he didn't need to. I had one room. He had a big redwood house in Marin with a deck, a view, a private sauna, and enough furniture to fill a hotel.

'I like it here, Mitch.'

'Ron, I'm offering you a whole house to yourself. You wouldn't have to worry about working, about landing a case to pay the rent.'

'I don't worry about those things, Mitch. *You* worry about them for me. I'm not moving to Marin.'

He smiled.

'No,' I said.

'Come on, Ronnie. I know you don't really feel that way. What's so bad about Marin? Just think about it, that's all.'

I didn't get rid of him until after eleven. By then I was convinced he was having some kind of mid-life crisis. Thirty-four was a little young for that kind of thing, but in the age of technology, maybe Mitch had turned precocious.

Whatever it was, my worrying wasn't going to help him, so I finished my report, slapped a bunch of stamps on the envelope, and turned off the lights. I didn't go to sleep, though. I couldn't.

In the slice of neon from the sign outside my window I punched a button on the tape deck and lay down to let the heartbreaking wail of Match Margolis's sax wash over me. His song reached deep into the very core of my soul and stayed right there, filling the emptiness I was feeling tonight.

Right now, just for the moment, I wanted to feel sad.

16

Something clicked. Or had I dreamed it? I opened my eyes. The clock on the table by the couch said three A.M. I held my breath, closed my eyes and listened.

There. There it was again.

I was too groggy to tell what it was or where it had come from, but I was awake enough to have my instinct kick in. My instinct said not to move.

I circled the room with my eyes. All the hulks and shadows were in the right places. That, at least, was reassuring. I didn't exactly relax but I did start breathing again – short, shallow breaths that barely touched my lungs.

Then I heard it again: a grating, scratching metallic noise at the door, less than twenty feet from where I lay. I sat bolt upright. I knew the sound. Somebody – some fool – was working the lock.

I had a hammer out from under the kitchen sink within seconds. The fact that only about a dozen people in the country had the skills to pick my lock, and that I knew all of them, gave me confidence that nobody was going to come through the door any time soon.

Barefoot, in the oversized 49ers sweatshirt I sleep in, I tiptoed toward the tiny beacon of light coming from the peep-hole in the door, trying to step in all the right places so the floorboards wouldn't creak. I was doing great until the last step, the one that brought me up to the door. The hardwood under my foot cracked as loud as a pistol shot. I froze, then heard rustling on the other side of the door.

Was he running away or just moving around out there? I put my eye up to the peephole and blinked into the lighted hallway. Nothing. Nobody. *Shit.* I couldn't have imagined it all.

Just as I started to pull away, a dark specter skittered down the hall out of my range of vision. Footsteps thundered down the stairs. *Damn*!

I flung open the door and charged into the hall, barefoot, hammer in hand.

'Hey!' somebody shouted from the foot of the stairs. Then, 'Oomph!' and, 'What the . . .?'

Then a door slammed shut.

From the top of the landing I saw a bent figure struggling to stand; he was midway down the stairs.

'Blackie?'

I dropped the hammer and rushed down the steps to help him.

'Blackie, are you all right?'

By the time I reached him, he was on his feet, gripping the bannister, and weaving against the wall, reeking of aged whiskey and tobacco.

'Who the fuck was that?' he said. He *sounded* fine.

'Are you okay? Does anything hurt?'

He patted his torso, checking, then winked broadly at me and grinned.

'One fucking piece.'

He eyed me up and down, taking in my bare legs and the sleep shirt.

'You throw him out of your bed, doll?'

'Hardly. He was trying to pick my lock.'

'Yeah?'

I glanced past Blackie down to the front door.

'Did you get a good look at him?'

'A good look at him? Fuck. I got a look at something.'

Blackie started up the stairs, one staggering step at a time. I followed him.

'You're sure you're not hurt?'

'Yah, yah.'

'Did you see his face?'

'Fuckin' asshole . . .'

Blackie paused at the landing and picked up the hammer.

'You get a whack at him?'

'I didn't get near him. *Blackie*, what did he look like?'

'Nixon,' Blackie said, and tumbled into the apartment. I switched on the light in time to watch him collapse into the chair.

'Nixon?'

'Yah. He was wearing a fucking Richard Milhous Nixon mask, doll.'

17

A black leather jacket, jeans, blue Nikes and a rubber Richard M. Nixon mask. Not much to go on.

'What about his height, Blackie? His build?'

'Middleweight. Five-six, eight. Maybe ten. Average build, maybe bigger. Hell, Ventana, I'm drunk. I'm not supposed to remember shit.'

'I know, I know, Blackie. You want coffee?'

He rubbed the gray stubble on his chin.

'How about a beer?'

After he'd swigged down half a cold Anchor Steam, I said, 'You're sure you didn't twist or sprain anything?'

'Yah, yah. I been through worse, doll. Say.' He slipped a smoke from his pocket and fixed me with his handsome blue eyes. 'You step in some shit, or what? What the fuck's going on here?'

I'd gotten a beer for myself and sat at the table I use for a desk, my legs pulled up underneath me. I told Blackie about my visits with Yvette Fields, Malone and Teagues and how nobody was owning up to what I was starting to think of as my 'death warrant' rumor.

'Want me ta talk to 'em?'

Blackie flexed his right hand into a massive fist.

'I still need to see DuPont and Tobinio,' I said.

'Just say the word, doll. I'm your muscle.'

I told him about Teagues' observation that Match had seemed nervous. Blackie listened, massaging the stubble on his chin again while I talked and sipped my beer. The cold, malty taste was honest and comforting.

'Didn't seem like it to me,' he said, when I'd finished. 'How 'bout you?'

'Come on, Blackie. We spent all of three minutes with the man. Teagues has known him for decades.'

'Yah?'

'I think he could be on to something. I'm going to ask these other two guys when I talk to them tomorrow.'

Blackie had a satisfied smirk on his face. I knew he was thinking of Philly Post.

'Don't say it, Blackie.'

He rasped out a chuckle, blowing smoke as he exhaled.

'Fuck.'

Blackie's cigarette hissed when he dropped it into his empty beer bottle. 'You don't want to jack with Malone, doll. I should have told you before. He'll fucking put you away.'

'For what? I'm just a messenger. As disgusting a guy as he is, he strikes me as smart enough to know you don't shoot the messenger.'

'Whatdya expect?' Blackie said. 'You're it. The fuck who did Match thinks you're on to him.'

'But if I knew, if Match told me who killed him, I would have told Post. He'd be in jail already.'

'Fucks don't think like that, doll. The asshole probably figures you'll put the squeeze on him yourself.'

'Blackmail?'

'Tell it to the judge,' Blackie said, suddenly looking around the room like he'd misplaced something.

'You got another beer?'

'All out.'

'Fuck. Time to roll.'

Blackie stood up and started for the door.

'Keep your eyes open, doll.'

'Blackie?'

He stopped midway and turned to look at me, bleary-eyed but smiling and content.

'It's three in the morning, Blackie. What were you doing downstairs, anyway?'

'Fuck! I almost forgot.'

He pulled something out of his back pocket.

'Tickets, doll.'

'For what?'

'The musicians' local is putting on a show, a memorial for Match. Duddy Canuto, Spode Holcum, lotta old-timers. What do you say, Ventana?'

'I say I wouldn't miss it for the world. Goodnight, Blackie.'

18

I woke up to a splendid, cloudless morning, the kind that means it's going to be a hot day, the kind we'd been getting more and more of on account of global warming. Even though I'd only managed a couple of hours of sleep, I felt rested and refreshed.

I took a long, cathartic run through Golden Gate Park, then headed home for a shower. After last night, I couldn't shake the heavy paranoid feeling that I had to watch my back, but the run, at least, would help keep me centered for the rest of the day.

When I got back to my apartment, I could hear the phone ringing before I unlocked the door. When I grabbed the receiver and heard the voice on the other end, I was instantly sorry I had.

'Ronnie? This is Sharon. Sharon Margolis. You've got to come over, honey. I mean, right now.'

She sounded breathless, petulant and angry.

'What's wrong?'

'I've been robbed, honey. Somebody broke in last night.'

19

'What are you doing here, Ventana?'
Philly Post was not glad to see me but then I wasn't
thrilled at the sight of him, either. I hadn't expected him to
answer Sharon's door, which showed no signs of a break-in,
but there I was and there he was, bushy eyebrows, white teeth
flashing at me through his ever-present scowl.

'I could ask you the same thing,' I said. 'Are you working
Burglary now?'

'Didn't I warn you to keep out of this?'

'I wired the place. I need to know what happened, how the
system failed.'

A skinny black man in an expensive suit came up the hall
behind Post. Post exchanged glances with him.

'You hear that, Johnson? She wants to know how the system
failed. It failed, all right, didn't it?'

'Did it ever!'

Johnson chuckled gleefully as he walked past me and out
the front door.

'Care to let me in on the joke?'

Post jerked his head toward the living room and lowered
his voice.

'I'll let her do that.'

'What's missing?'

'Just a few collector's items.'

'How'd he get in?'

Post smirked. 'Ask your client, Ventana. The whole thing's
routine.'

'Is that why you're here?'

'I'm here because Johnson and I are working the homicide and the uniform who responded was sharp enough to remember the tie-in.'

'*Does* it tie in?'

He scowled.

'Whoever hit Margolis was a pro. This break-in's strictly amateur. I think even you'll see that right away.'

I ignored the barb.

'But the system—'

'Yeah,' he snickered. 'Tell me about your system. She's in there.'

He raised his bushy eyebrows long enough to reveal his eyes rolling in the direction of the living room. Then he sauntered down the hall toward the back of the house. I followed him as far as the living-room door and peered inside. Sharon Margolis was huddled on the couch next to a box of tissues, quivering and sniveling like a sloppy three-year-old.

When I tapped lightly on the door frame, she looked up. Her face was a mess – big crocodile tears running down both chubby cheeks, splotchy skin, red eyes. There was a jagged rip on the sleeve and a narrow brown coffee stain down the front of her faded green peignoir.

I felt sorry for her. She'd been good when Match died. She hadn't cried then, at least not in public and not in front of me. Seeing her now, I wondered if she'd finally reached a breaking point, a point where she couldn't hold her sorrow in any more. Then she spoke.

'What took you so long, honey?'

When she hoisted herself out of her seat, her painted red toenails squished out from under the dingy white pompons of her open-toed scuffs.

'Come on in.'

Having designed the system that had just failed her, I didn't expect her to be so civil, much less tame.

'What happened?'

'They took his sax,' she moaned. 'And his book, too.'

She raised the back of her hand to her forehead in a gesture worthy of an opera star and started to cry all over again.

'Sit down,' I said, and gently guided her back into the chair. Her muddy green peignoir contrasted horribly with the green brocade upholstery. I noticed a thin film of dust on the table by the chair that I hadn't noticed yesterday.

'And the sheet music,' she sobbed. 'His new songs . . . the original scores . . . all the copies.'

She wept inconsolably without grace, snorting and snuffling into tissues, while I sat across from her and just felt lousy.

'The system,' I said, after a moment. 'Where did they get in?'

She hiccuped twice, blew her nose, and eyed the worn carpet on the floor.

'The cops think it was just one person.'

'Oh?'

Why couldn't Post have told me that?

'Where did he get in?'

She squirmed, blew her nose some more and shifted her gaze from the carpet to the grungy pompons on her feet.

'Uh . . . ah . . . uh . . . the back door.'

'That's impossible! He couldn't have. The whole security office would have been here the minute he touched that door. I went over all the wiring myself. No, security would have been crawling all over the place. There is no way. Unless . . .'

I looked at her more closely. She still wouldn't meet my eyes.

'Unless . . . Mrs Margolis.' I raised my voice. 'Sharon, was the system *on*?'

She wrung her hands and stared at her pompons like her life depended on it.

'Did you remember to turn it on?'

Eyes pinned to the floor, she answered in a tiny voice. 'No.'

'Oh, no. *No*! Sharon, no. I *showed* you how – I *explained* it all to you.'

'You've got to understand, honey.' Her words spilled out. 'I've been dealing with a lot lately. I had an interview last night and it didn't go so hot. The pictures, well, they wanted pictures of Match instead of me, honey. I was so put out by the whole thing I just went upstairs and took some pills and went to sleep. I didn't even think to turn it on. I forgot all about it.'

I felt bad but I didn't feel half as bad as I had when she was sitting there, slobbering away, letting me think it was all my fault. I counted to ten, let go of my anger, and sighed.

'Show me where he came in.'

She led me to the back, pointed at the jimmied back door, then showed me into Match's music room. The sax was gone.

The impact of seeing the empty rack standing upright in the center of the room hit me with such force that I nearly missed Philly Post poking around in the corner.

'Mrs Margolis,' he said, and came over to join us at the door. 'I see you're feeling better. Do you think you can answer some questions now?'

Sharon batted her wet eyes at him and struggled to look seductive, but the effect was more horror than romance.

'Not now, Lieutenant. I just *couldn't*. I wouldn't be back here right now but Ronnie insisted.'

I bit my tongue and let my eyes drift back to the instrument rack. It stood erect, a lonely, empty symbol of what was once Match Margolis's world – his hope and his life.

Sheet music was strewn all over the floor like oversized confetti. Records and tapes had been tossed around, too. Except for the standing rack, the place looked like a cyclone had passed through.

'You slept through this?' I asked.

'I had three Seconals, honey. I needed my rest.'

She looked at me like she expected me to tell her that it was okay. When I didn't, she shrank backward toward the door. In her green peignoir, with her thick arms making fretful, waving motions through the air, she reminded me of an octopus.

'I need a drink,' she announced at the threshold, then left me alone with Philly Post.

We stood in silence amid the paper avalanche until her pomponed footsteps receded down the hall. Then Philly trained his hooded eyes on me.

'She told me,' I said.

'You working this case for her, Ventana?'

For a split second I considered telling him what I knew. Then I saw the corners of his mouth twitch and I resented the fun he was having over my burglar alarm.

'No.'

It wasn't a lie – any investigating I'd do, I'd do for me.

I couldn't be sure if he bought it or not but he didn't push. We talked burglar alarms for a while, then I looked out the window and decided to push my luck.

'Any big leads?'

He said nothing, so I turned around to face him. He was scowling.

'I got nothing,' he said. 'Three hundred interviews and nothing. A third of them have rap sheets and the rest are all PhDs or society types.'

'Any of them ever been arrested for knifing somebody?'

Post scowled. 'I didn't join the force yesterday, Ventana. I know how to do my job.'

'Well?'

'No.'

'What about the knife? Weren't there any prints?'

'Nothing we could use.'

'Didn't you say something about a professional hit theory?'

'For crying out loud, Ventana. Drop the goddamn blood-hound shit. That's the only thing I've got so far. And it's just a theory.'

He kicked at a bunch of sheet music. It splayed into the rest of the mess across the floor.

'She tell you she tried to keep Johnson out? Some neighbor called it in when she ran out the front door screaming she'd been robbed. Rocky somebody. Then Johnson shows up and she won't let him inside. Says it was all a mistake. He wouldn't leave, so she made him swear to keep it out of the papers before she'd open the door.'

'She's paranoid about the press. She wants to control what they say about Match.'

Post snorted. 'She should have thought of that before she charged out the door. You know what? Even though the old junkie's dead, I feel sorry for him. She's more wrung out over losing this crap than she was about losing him.'

Post had a point. Sharon wasn't painting herself in a very sympathetic light. Post tugged at his tie to loosen it, then squinted at me. He tried not to scowl, but I guess he couldn't figure out the right set of facial muscles to relax. They were probably stuck in place from being flexed all those years.

'You got any ideas?' he asked me. He actually sounded humble. 'Anything come up for you since Saturday?'

I wanted to throw the dog a bone but there was nothing I could tell him that he wouldn't throw a switch over.

'Have you tracked down who started the dying words rumor yet?' I asked.

'Looks like it was the son,' he said. 'It was something he overheard from the bartender.'

'Lucius?'

'The son misunderstood and spread it around.'

Great. I'd become a target for murder all because of a deadly version of 'telephone', the kids' game.

'Hell.'

Post rubbed his face with both hands, then glanced in the direction Sharon had gone.

'This broad's a flake.'

He trudged toward the door, leonine head bent, shoulders stooped like an old man's.

'Either that,' I said to his receding back, 'or she's smarter than both of us.'

20

As much as I hated to, I stuck around after Philly Post left. Somebody had to make sure Sharon was all right and it looked like I was elected.

'Isn't there somebody you can call?' I asked. 'Family, maybe?'

'I don't have any family.'

Her voice was stronger now and her expression was turning petulant again. The liquor had dried her tears. The only sign she'd been crying were the reddened eyes and the black smudges of mascara above her cheeks.

'You need somebody. How about somebody from the band? Would any of them come over and stay with you for a while?'

'I don't get along with the band, honey. They're nothing but a bunch of hungry mooches, anyway.'

'Who can I phone?'

'Nobody.'

Her choice. I wasn't going to ask again. I sat down across from her and waited until she looked up and met my gaze.

'Tell me about the sax,' I said. 'Post thinks a collector stole it. Can you think why anybody would take it?'

She swizzled her drink and stared out the window at the blue sky outside. The place was so depressing, I'd forgotten the sun was out.

'I told that lieutenant all this already,' she complained.

'Now tell me.'

'The museum. I was going to sign everything over to the museum. They were going to give me a hundred thousand dollars for it.'

'Did anybody know that? Who did you tell?'

'Why, everybody, honey. I told the whole world – the band, the reporters last night, record companies, agencies, every university that called, Match's old pals – everybody. That's how you get them to bid so high, honey, playing them off each other. Why? What are you thinking? Are you figuring one of them swiped it?'

'I'm just looking for a motive. Have you heard from anybody, anybody asking for a ransom or anything?'

She shook her head mournfully.

'Do you think the cops will find it, honey? I really need it back this week. I don't want to have to tell the museum people I lost it.'

I doubted the SFPD was going to make it a priority, but with one hundred grand riding on it, I didn't think she wanted to hear the truth.

'It's possible,' I said.

After all, anything's possible.

I filled her in on my visits to Malone and Teagues, but she didn't even pretend to show an interest. Not even when I told her they'd forgiven the loans.

'Look, Sharon, what aren't you telling me?'

'Why . . . I . . . What do you mean, honey?'

'You hired me to talk to these guys and now you act like they're yesterday's news. What's going on?'

She squirmed, then bit her lip and said, 'Is this confidential, honey?'

'None of it, starting from day one, is going to be confidential if you don't start talking right now.'

'It's like this, honey.' She got up, freshened her drink, then sat down again. 'The man who tried to break in Sunday night, before you put in the alarm,' she began, 'the man who broke in last night, I thought he was trying to kill me.'

'Why would anybody want to kill you?'

She stared at the ice cubes in her glass.

'I don't know, honey. Somebody killed Match.'

I jerked the list of names she'd given me yesterday out of my back pocket.

'You're thinking it was one of these guys, right?'

'I wasn't sure,' she sniffed.

'Why not just tell the police?'

'I can't, don't you see?'

She set her glass down on the table between us and let her hands drop into her ample lap. Her sigh was theatrical.

'You just don't understand, do you, honey?'

'No, I guess I don't.'

All I could think of was me, knifed in some back alley while Sharon wheeled and dealed over the phone for the movie rights. Or, if I survived, Philly Post screaming his brains out at me for withholding information.

'It's Match's reputation I'm protecting, honey. You see, his friends are no good. If it gets out that he was wrapped up with that kind, it could be that nobody'd want to touch him. I just want to close the deals first, see?'

'If anybody wanted to kill you, you were wide open last night.'

'I know, honey. Now I don't know what to think. Why would anybody want his sax?'

She looked so plaintive, so dejected and confused, I was starting to believe she really didn't know what was going on.

'I need the truth from you now, Sharon. It's important. Your life could depend on it.'

'Sure, honey. I understand.'

Her eyes were more feral than ever but there was an earnestness in her tone I hadn't heard before.

'Post said Match's killer was a pro.'

'Everybody Match knew was some kind of pro.'

'Did Post say why he thinks it was a professional hit?'

'The coroner told him it was, honey. Either that, or dumb luck. But Lieutenant Post said no amateur would be smart enough to murder somebody in a room full of people without anybody noticing. So it has to be a pro.'

I asked her if Match had seemed nervous Saturday and she thought for a moment.

'Why, now that you mention it, honey, he was kind of a wreck.

Ever since he started back with his music again, he's always been real particular about his sax and the scores. He made me promise I'd go up there to the stage and collect them after every set and put them in a folder. And the sax, he'd leave it on the stand on stage, but he made sure somebody was there to watch it.'

'Who?'

'One of the band. I hadn't ever seen him like that, honey. It was probably stage fright, you know. He hadn't played in years.'

'I don't suppose you asked him about it?'

'Why would I? What could *I* do?'

At least she was realistic. I asked her about the twenty thousand dollars Match had borrowed from Malone.

'I don't know anything about it, honey. Did Siggy say what Match wanted it for?'

'No. Do you have any idea?'

'Huh-uh.'

'Can you check your financial statements? That'll tell us where the money went.'

The paper trail would say a lot.

'It didn't go anywhere, honey. I would have known about it.'

'But you did. You knew Match had loans. That's why you asked me to talk to these guys.'

'I didn't think any of them were *recent* loans. I thought Match meant from years and years ago, honey. If it was recent, I would have known all about it 'cause I handled all the money.'

'Maybe Match had an account he didn't tell you about?'

'No.'

I gave up and point-blank asked her if she still wanted me to talk to DuPont and Tobinio.

'No, honey. Forget it. I don't care anymore.'

So I asked her for a check to cover an hour of my time and the ten miles I'd spent driving around town. She wrote it out, then announced she needed to rest. That was all I needed to hear. I was out the door like a bullet.

21

Halfway down the walk to the Toyota, I noticed a gray-haired man poking around under the hood of a blue vintage Mustang at the curb a couple of doors down. Tools were laid out precisely across a soiled towel draped over the car's front fender. Post said a neighbor had called the robbery in. Rocky somebody. I pocketed my keys and crossed the lawn.

Up close, in spite of his grungy coveralls, the man looked more like a Spanish literature professor than a home mechanic. He had eyeglasses, a receding hairline, and a serious, intelligent expression on his narrow copper face. He smiled warmly when he saw me approach and his thin mustache curved up at the ends.

'Julio Piedras.' He gave his right hand one final swipe with a pink rag, then offered it to me. 'My friends call me Rocky.'

Bingo.

'So the little widow, how's she taking it?'

'All right.' It seemed inappropriate to say the little widow had been wheeling and dealing like a street vendor.

'My wife's going to take something over to her later, something to eat.'

His eyes rested on Sharon's front door.

'Did that burglar scare her?'

'The burglar?'

'I saw him. Not the one last night but the one before.'

And Post had told me he had nothing.

'Rosario – that's my wife – she woke up. The lights and yelling woke her up, so she woke me up, and made me look out the window. All the lights were on over there and Sharon was cursing like she'd seen a ghost. I saw somebody run down the street. He got into a black car.'

'Black? What was the make?'

'I don't know. Black, dark blue.' He studied the line of grease under his fingernails. 'You know how it is at night. The engine sounded like a four-cylinder job.'

Great. That narrowed it down to just half the cars in San Francisco.

'Could have been dark green, too, now that I think about it.'

'How about the burglar? What did he look like?'

'Average.' He said it like it meant something. 'I'd say he looked average.'

'Caucasian? Black? Tall or short?'

'I don't know. That light –' He pointed to the cracked street lamp midway down the block – 'somebody should fix it, you know? Especially now. She's not scared, is she? Rosario won't let me go over there alone because Sharon was a dancer before and Rosario, well, you know, Rosario doesn't think much of dancers.'

I tried to picture Sharon's stout little form moving gracefully across a stage and didn't have much luck. 'Where did she dance?'

'Condor Club,' he said.

Topless dancing was born at the Condor.

'Most people, they hear Match was a musician and they think we get a lot of noise, but no. He was quiet. Real considerate.'

Rocky glanced past my shoulder to Sharon's house.

'Are you a cop, lady?'

'Private investigator.'

I could tell he had some doubts so I slipped him my card. His lips moved while he read it.

'If you remember anything else, or see anybody snooping around who doesn't belong, give me a call, will you?'

His chest puffed up with pride like I'd just asked him to guard the crown jewels.

'Of course, Miss Ventana. And Rosario, she'll watch, too.'

I left him hurrying up his sidewalk, clutching my card and calling his wife's name.

22

Sharon had said I didn't need to see Nick DuPont or Eugene Tobinio anymore, but under the circumstances that just added to their cachet.

DuPont's office was in a Sansome Street building in the heart of San Francisco's Financial District. I checked my rearview a dozen times on the way over, suddenly nervous and paranoid about being followed. I never saw the same car twice, but somehow couldn't shake the feeling that somebody was following me.

I looped around a few times over the one-way streets, drove through a couple of underground garages, then finally gave up and parked on the street a couple of blocks down, even though there was a parking garage in his building.

Thirty floors up, the plaque on the door said CREATIVE CORPORATE FINANCIAL MANAGEMENT. It sounded like an invitation for an SEC review, but nobody'd asked me when they named the business. The carpets were a rich mauve, and thick. Chrome and glass gleamed all over the place, and expensive-looking pieces of abstract art – not the kind some decorator just throws up for show – hung on the walls. The message was clear: Nick DuPont's office spelled big bucks.

While I waited for Nick DuPont to decide whether he'd see me or not, I wondered what connected him to Match. I couldn't picture Match, raggedly skinny, in jeans, strung out and sitting here amid all these polished surfaces like I was, waiting for an appointment. Then I wondered what tied Malone to DuPont. Maybe he liked to slum.

I was still trying to figure out why a corporate financial management consultant would lend a broken-down ex-junkie sax player money when his secretary told me DuPont was ready to see me. If I got nothing else out of this interview, I'd be happy to hear the answer to that one.

The secretary led me down a marble-paneled passage to a pair of huge, carved double doors. They looked like they belonged in a church. She threw the doors open and gestured with the grace of a geisha for me to go in. As soon as I was inside, the doors hissed shut behind me in what sounded like an airtight seal. I flashed back to an ancient history class I'd taken and I suddenly felt like I knew how the Christians felt when they were thrown into the arena with the lions. Then I heard the music – a sweet, cool jazz piped in from somewhere – and I relaxed.

It took me a few seconds to find Nick DuPont in the big, mahogany-paneled room. He was a teensy elf of a guy who, except for his wavy gray hair, looked like some kid let loose to play in Daddy's office. High-tech gadgets and flashing machines I didn't even recognize hummed quietly on his desk between beeps and whirring while he stabbed at a couple of keys on an exquisitely thin laptop.

He punched a final button that blackened the screen, then swiveled in his chair and looked up at me with that air of confidence little rich men seem to acquire with their seven-figure fortunes.

'Miss Ventana?'

His voice was deep, like somebody's twice his size.

'Maxine said you're employed by Mrs Margolis.'

'That's right.'

'It's a shame what happened to Match, isn't it? Did you know him? Personally, I mean.'

'I knew his music.'

'Well, then, you knew Match. A splendid composer. A piece of art incarnate. Every man has foibles, Miss Ventana, and Match wasn't unique. He had faults, but none of them – not a single one of them –' he punched the air with a dwarf-like finger for emphasis – 'overshadowed his talent. He was an artist, a great one.'

DuPont talked like he was giving a eulogy, quiet and all choked up.

I agreed that yeah, Match was a great guy, then watched him dab at his eyes and toss the crumpled tissue into a copper waste can that probably cost more than one month's rent for me. Then he cleared his throat and glanced at his Rolex.

'What can I do for you?'

'I'm here to talk about Match's debt.'

'Debt?'

He raised his clipped eyebrows like he'd never heard the word before.

'Right. I understand Match owed you some money.'

'I'm afraid you've been misinformed. Match owed me nothing.'

'That's not what he told his wife.'

It was tough trying to sound like I knew what I was talking about.

'What a shame.'

DuPont smiled at me with unbelievably white teeth and, even though his words showed concern, his expression was anything but warm.

'Tell her not to give it another thought.'

It was an order. His tone made the hair on the back of my neck stand on end. All of a sudden, he didn't seem so small or so harmless anymore. Or so clean, either. In spite of his expensive suit, his nice manners and his fancy office, he seemed just as creepy as Siggy Malone, clawing around his nasty little junk yard.

'If that's all . . .' He turned slightly and reached for his computer.

'There is one other thing,' I said.

His eyebrows slid up in a silent, surprised question.

'I talked to Buddha Teagues last night. He mentioned that Match seemed worried Saturday.'

No reaction.

'Did you get that impression, too?' DuPont picked up my card, the one I'd given his secretary, and read it.

'You're Cisco Ventana's daughter, aren't you?'

Now what?

'I met Cisco once, about thirty years ago in a poker game. Did you know that?'

'No.' My father hadn't made it a habit to talk about his poker partners to his three-year-old daughter. Now, looking into this little man's enigmatic face, I wish he had. And I hoped their meeting had been coincidental and brief.

'He was good, sharp. An honorable man.'

'Yes,' I said.

DuPont tapped the card against his temple and frowned. I could almost see the barriers dissolve. Then he seemed to make up his mind.

'Match seemed skittish Saturday, yes. But Buddha, I think, imagines too much. He considers himself perceptive, but reads more into things than what's really there. I don't think what Buddha saw was anything out of the ordinary given the circumstances. Match hadn't performed in fifteen years.

'If Match was nervous about anything it should have been about the caliber of musicians he'd picked. He could have been playing with Holcum and Canuto, established musicians who could complement his talent. I compose and play jazz trumpet myself and I don't understand why he chose the people he did.'

'Did you ask him?'

'I did.'

'And?'

DuPont shook his head. 'Match told me he had his reasons but he wouldn't elaborate.'

'What do you think he meant?'

'He meant, "butt out." He wouldn't discuss it.'

DuPont picked up what looked like a gold-plated pen from his desktop and fingered it.

'Have you heard Match's band? Were you there Saturday?'

I nodded.

'The bass, Rochelle Posner, is the only one to watch. The rest . . .' He sliced the air with the blade of his hand. 'Send them back to school. Train Harper plays better drums than Nesbitt. And Cheese – Match dragged him back for old time's sake. It doesn't take a rocket scientist to see that. But let me tell you, there's a reason why Cheese has been playing B-grade honky-tonk dives these last fifteen years.'

DuPont passed judgment on the whole band before he finally stopped for air.

'Any idea who'd want to kill Match?' I asked him.

He accepted the interruption graciously with a sad smile.

'The man had no enemies.'

'How about his sax? Any idea why somebody'd steal it?'

I'd asked to gauge his reaction and he seemed suitably surprised.

'His sax! Christ! Georgette gave him that sax. I kept it all those years he stopped playing. He'd hocked it and the pawn-broker knew me, called me up. I ran down there and took it home. I held it for twelve years, until he decided he wanted to play again. Who took it?'

'The police are still investigating.'

'My God, first Match, now the sax. How?'

I told him only that it had been taken from Sharon's house last night but he didn't press me for details.

'Are you investigating Match's murder?' he asked.

'I'm doing what I can,' I hedged. 'Someone started a rumor that Match whispered his killer's name to me before he died. It's kept me kind of jumpy.'

'Understandably,' he said. 'Now that you bring it up, Clark mentioned something to that effect Saturday night but I didn't really take it in. It was you he was talking about, then?'

I nodded. 'Is Clark Match's son?'

'Yes. He's devastated about Match's death. Just devastated.'

'They had a good relationship?'

'Excellent. Couldn't have been better.'

'How about his daughter? Yvette?'

'Ah. She's a disappointment, isn't she? But Match wasn't allowed into her life until the damage had been done. He loved her, though. Treated her far better than I would have in his shoes. Match was a good man. And patient.'

'In what way?'

'She never followed through on her promises. She'd promise to go to rehab and wouldn't, she'd promise to stop prostituting herself and failed. He never gave up on her. Even now, with her business, he said he was glad she'd gone into selling other women instead of herself. He saw it as a step in the right direction. He always felt she should go to college and he offered to send her every time they spoke. He made concessions for her because he felt her shortcomings were his fault for not rearing her as his own child. Even though Yvette's mother refused to let him see her until she was fifteen. Poor Match.'

He looked aggrieved, then his face hardened. His voice quivered with emotion when he spoke again.

'There's something I'd like you to remember, Miss Ventana. It's important, and since you're Cisco Ventana's daughter, I feel I can say this to you. I'd like to get my hands on the scum who killed Match. I'd give anything to have a crack at him first. Anything.' He held my eyes just long enough to make sure I got the message. 'Please remember that. It'd mean a lot to me.'

23

'Miss Ventana?'

DuPont's secretary swiveled at her desk and called out after me on my way to the elevator.

'Somebody dropped this off for you while you were in with Mr DuPont.'

She waved a letter-sized envelope at me.

'For me?'

I hadn't told anyone where I was going.

'Messenger?'

'No.'

Executive secretaries are supposed to be discreet. This one was going to make me work for it.

'Who?'

'It was a woman, Ms Ventana.'

'All right. What did she look like?'

The secretary shifted some stacks of paper around on her desk and smiled coolly.

'She had brown hair in a Dutch-boy cut. And glasses.'

No mention of a Richard Nixon mask, thank God.

'What makes you think she wasn't a messenger?'

'She was wearing a green suit and heels, Ms Ventana.'

I tore open the envelope in the elevator. The message was neatly hand-printed in black ink on cheap unlined paper.

Talk about Match? Parking Level 2, Section F.

I glanced at the bank of buttons next to the elevator door, considered punching Parking Level 2, but got out at the lobby instead and headed for the Toyota. Whoever was waiting for me downstairs would be expecting me on foot.

My third pass through Section F was my last one. The butterflies had faded from my stomach. The entire floor seemed deserted of people, and I was about to write the whole thing off as a prank when I beamed in on some movement behind a deep-blue Volkswagen with a dented fender. It was over by the center column. I pulled up in front of it, rolled my window down, took a deep breath and kept the engine running.

'Hey!' I shouted. 'I see you. Come on out.'

'Shut your engine off!'

The woman's voice echoed off the empty parked cars above the soft rumble of the Toyota. My starter was good, my engine in tune. I cut the motor.

'What do you want?' I asked.

'Get out of the car,' the voice said.

'Forget it.' I waited for an answer, then cranked the ignition when nobody spoke.

'Wait!'

A blur of green popped out from behind the VW. The Toyota's engine sputtered to a steady hum as a lithe feminine figure came toward me.

Her suit was impeccably cut and without a single wrinkle. It fit her slender figure like a glove. The cooler-than-cool trendy glasses looked more like a prop than a necessity. She was beauty-pageant gorgeous, tall and auburn-haired, without a blemish or a molecule of misplaced fat. I struggled to keep the annoyance out of my voice.

'What are you doing here, Abby?'

'I wrote the note,' she said.

'You idiot.' I reached for the gearshift and shoved it into first.

'Wait! You wouldn't have come if I'd signed it.'

'You're right about that.'

'I need to talk to you, Ronnie. *Please*. Just for a minute.'

'No reporter's ever satisfied with just one minute. Especially not you. Besides, have you ever heard of a phone? A lot of people use them to make appointments, you know.'

'It's about Match, Ronnie.'

'If you're trying to surprise me, Abby, it's not working.'

'Just hear me out. *Please*.'

I shut off the engine. Abby's notebook and pencil were in her hands, poised and ready by the time she reached the side of the Toyota. I stayed inside so she had to stoop down like a car hop taking an order.

'Are you working for Sharon Margolis?'

'I don't need my client roster published in your newspaper, Abby. Who I work for is nobody's business.'

'What if I attribute it to an anonymous source?'

'Look, Abby, just because we went to high school together doesn't mean I'm going to throw out my ethics so you can write a story. Since when did your paper start doing interviews? I thought you guys just made the stuff up.'

86

'That's not a nice thing to say, Ronnie. Are you working on Match Margolis's murder?'

'You're not listening, Abby.'

'What did Match say to you before he died?'

Shit. 'Abby, don't put that in the paper.'

Her eyes lit up. 'What did he say? Did he tell you who killed him? Did he say why? Why haven't the police acted on it?'

'Don't print that, Abby.'

'He told you something, didn't he? And you're working with the police to catch the killer, aren't you? Is Nicholas DuPont your main suspect? Is that why you were up there talking to him?'

'I could have been talking to anybody.'

'But you weren't.'

So much for discreet secretaries.

'Abby . . .'

'Why did Match pick you? Were you involved with him? How did you meet? If you were involved with him, why did Sharon Margolis hire you?'

'*Abby!*'

Her perfectly lipsticked but wide mouth slapped shut.

'Abby, I swear to you, if you print any of this crap in that cheap little rag you work for, I'll personally shove that notebook down your throat – sideways. Do you understand?'

Maybe I'd never quite forgiven Abby Stark for printing my name in the school paper under those who got an F in American History when she knew I'd pulled a C. Or maybe it was the time she'd written that feature about me without interviewing me or even *asking* to interview me when I was a parole officer.

She looked at me with huge, liquid eyes and a pretty-baby pout.

'I'm just trying to—'

'To what? Set the record straight? Get the story right? Forget it. You wouldn't know how to begin. Leave me alone, Abby. This is not a game. Somebody's been murdered. There's a killer at large. Keep away from me and don't you dare print a word about any of this. And if you ever pull another stunt like the little intrigue you used to get me down here, I'll have you arrested.'

'Ronnie, don't—'

'Goodbye, Abby.'

I turned the key in the ignition and my engine roared to life like a symphony. I left Abby Stark – girl reporter wannabe who never fact-checked a word in her life, much less an entire story – sputtering in my exhaust.

24

I regretted losing my temper with Abby Stark, but not as much as I regretting having run across her in the first place.

My threats wouldn't daunt her. She'd been sued a few times, assaulted more than once, and still she kept fabricating 'news.' Nothing would keep her from printing whatever she damn well pleased. And one thing I could be certain of was that Abby would paint me as the central force in the investigation.

Philly Post would love it. So would Match's killer. Either way, the clock was ticking. It was time to start asking serious questions and I knew exactly where to go.

25

Pear-face Barnes was a nerdy-looking guy with a soft, dumpy shape, slicked-back hair, and a complexion like dough. I guess you could call him a friend of the family's – he'd been my parents' fence way back when. He was one of those guys who, despite having done time, just wasn't capable of making that transition to working stiff.

Prison convinced Pear that fencing was bad, so when he got out, he opened a bookmaking operation in the back room of a Market Street tailor shop. From there, he kept his finger on the pulse of the city's underworld.

Pear knew more about snitches than stitches, though. He'd rip the labels from off-the-rack suits and pass them off as his own whenever the cops came around.

If any fool came in and actually ordered a suit or alteration, he'd have Mabel, his wife, take the measurements, then do such a lousy job putting the thing together that he never got a repeat customer.

Meanwhile, the numbers and dollars flew like confetti in the back room. If anybody could tell me whether Match Margolis had a real connection to bad guys, it was Pear. And even though he'd given up fencing, there was an off chance he might have heard something about the stolen sax. Or even Match's murder.

I parked in the Union Square garage and walked down to Market, stepping gingerly over Pear's lookout – a doorstop wino wired with a mike – and went inside. A brass bell clanged as I opened the door, then clanged again when I shut it behind me.

The place was dismal: gray plaster walls, a barren counter, and faded cloth bolts stacked on half-empty shelves. A pair of scissors and scattered straight pins had rusted into the surface of the counter like fossils from the Stone Age. The only window was so grimy, all you could see through it were shadows and shapes. Pear once told me he didn't want to look too prosperous, but he'd definitely overdone it.

A rush of sounds hit me as the door at the end of the counter opened. It was just like the noise you hear in the background when some poor jerk calls you up on the phone and tries to sell you something.

'Ronnie! How are you, gal?'

Pear's shirttail puffed up around his waist, drooping over his belt, and his Brylcreemed hair glistened almost blue under the overhead fluorescent light. One cheek bulged with chewing tobacco so his grin was lopsided.

'Where the hell you been hiding yourself?'

The busy sounds from the back room – phones ringing, machines pattering, and the low muttering of voices – were clipped silent when he closed the door behind him. Soundproof.

I ran a finger along the top row of cloth bolts and held it up to the dim light.

'Time to dust your props, Pear.'

He chuckled.

'What's it matter? These days, I'm taking action off the cops. Tuesdays, I even got a coupla sergeants come in.'

He leaned against the counter, weight on his elbows and grinned.

'You need a suit, gal?'

'If I did, I wouldn't come here.'

'Must be here for the ponies, then, huh, babe? Got a favorite?'

'I need information, Pear. Some background. Maybe you can help.'

'Anything, gal. Anything you want. Listen, listen up! I gotta tell you about Mabel and me first. You're not gonna believe this one.'

He was grinning from ear to ear.

'Me and Mabel, we're expectin'.'

'A baby?'

'Yeah. Ain't that something? Who woulda thought? A year in and I'm gonna be a Pop.'

His voice was full of wonder. Mabel was twenty-five, half his age, but the marriage thing had tamed Pear. He seemed younger and older at the same time.

'The doc says December. I'm taking action on it – you want in?'

'You're taking bets on your baby?'

His face clouded.

'You don't think it's bad luck, do you? I'll call it off if it's bad luck.'

'Of course not. These bets, they're if it's going to be a boy or a girl?'

'Sure, we got that. But we're taking action on the whole works. This is a big deal. We got the date, day of the week, time, eye color, weight, hair color, you name it. It's just a little something between friends, you know? What's your choice, gal?'

I reached into my back pocket.

'How about ten on a boy? What are the odds?'

'They're running three-to-one today. Boy?'

He jotted something on a slip of paper and stuffed it back into his own pocket.

'You're on! Wait'll you see Mabel – she's as big as a pumpkin! Eatin' nothing but vegetables and liver. I'm telling you, that baby's going to be smart and healthy. I guarantee it.'

Pear smoothed his hair, then wiped the Brylcreem off on his trouser leg.

Still grinning, he said, 'So what's this about some background?'

'I've got four names.'

'Who's number one?'

'Have you ever heard of Nick DuPont?'

He whistled. 'You go high class when you go, babe. That dude's loaded.'

'How'd he make it?'

'He's the West Coast snow connection. Supplies the suppliers. They get it from him and the street gets it from them.'

'He's got quite a front, Pear – the Financial District office, the paintings, the assistant.'

'Yeah, ain't that something?'

He rocked his round shape back on his heels and smiled with the left half of his mouth.

'He's about three-quarters legit now. Another coupla years he'll be outta snow entirely. So what'd he do to interest you?'

'How's DuPont connected to Match Margolis?'

'The hype jazzman who bought it a couple of nights ago? Didn't know he was. I can find out, you want me to. Tell you what, babe.' He leaned over and spat sideways into something that went *ping*. 'You come back here in a day and I'll tell you why and how.'

Sooner would have been better but Pear was thorough and accurate. I knew better than to rush him.

'What about Buddha Teagues?'

'You mean my competition? He's all right. His opera-tion's decent, no cheats. You could say, next to me, he's one of the best. But I couldn't say how he's connected to the hype.'

Pear said the same about Sig Malone and added that Malone was ruthless about running his chop shop.

'No morals, no scruples, that guy. He's dangerous. Not mellow.'

'What about Eugene Tobinio?'

'Tobinio? You don't even want to know about him, babe. You want my advice? Don't touch him.'

I thanked him, asked about the missing saxophone, without success, and went back out to Market Street. Once, just once, I'd like somebody to give me some advice I could follow.

26

I was headed home when the cell phone rang. Twice. The first call was Mitch. He wanted to know if I'd go look at sailboats with him. I told him no. Then he asked me to think again about housesitting for him while he was gone. I told him no again, wished him luck, and hung up.

The second call was Glen Faddis.

'Can you meet me at the Cafe Roma across from the Hall of Justice?'

'What's this about?'

'I'll tell you when you get here.'

I couldn't miss him. He was at one of the tables in front by the open door, two steaming cappuccinos and a big manila envelope in front of him. He lifted himself out of his chair when I walked in, then pulled a chair out for me. I guess he'd just passed Etiquette 101.

'Thanks for coming,' he said, looking happy to see me. His sandy hair was tousled and he wore jeans, Teva sandals, and an expensive-looking brown suede jacket over a white tee shirt.

'I assume this is about Match,' I said.

He gestured at the coffee. 'I took a guess and ordered you a cappuccino.'

'Thanks. About Match?'

'I've been researching.'

'And?'

'I'd like to help.'

'Go ahead.'

I knew he was about to propose some kind of trade, but I didn't feel like making it easy for him.

'I want an exclusive.'

'On what?'

'You solving the case. I know you're good at this – you've solved a few crimes lately, including some high-profile ones. I think you're going to figure this one out before the police and I want the story. From the inside.'

'And if I don't agree?'

'I'll have to do it from the outside.'

I pushed my untouched cappuccino away and stood. 'That's probably your best bet,' I said, and turned to go.

'Wait!'

93

He popped out of his chair. A couple of people at the table next to us looked up. Faddis reached over and laid a hand on my arm.

'Wait a minute. I want to help. Please, sit down.'

I sat.

'I'm not going to deal,' I said.

'That's okay. I'm in anyway.'

'Why?'

He shrugged and grinned. 'Maybe you'll change your mind.'

I laughed then, and he laughed, too.

'What have you got?' I said.

He slid the large manila envelope across the table. 'Match's autopsy.'

I opened the envelope and skimmed over the report. Death was caused by a slice across the aorta. He bled to death internally, into the chest cavity. It happened quickly but not instantly. He had time to walk a short distance which meant he could have been knifed anywhere between the bandstand and the bar where he fell. The skin between his ribs had acted like a squeegee when the knife was retracted so it came out clean. His liver was shot, his arteries clogged, and there were tracks covering every accessible vein all over his ravaged body. Other than that, he was surprisingly healthy. If he hadn't been murdered, he probably would have lived another five to ten years.

I shoved the sheets back into the envelope and gave it back to him.

'So?' I was glad I'd seen it but it didn't tell me anything I could use.

'So if you can trace Match's path from the band to the bar, then you've got a list of suspects.'

'It's not like there were assigned seats,' I said. 'Besides, by then everybody was standing. It sounds like police work to me. Why don't you give it to Post?'

Faddis frowned at me. 'He's already got a copy.'

I smiled, then rose. 'Thanks, anyway. Nice talking to you.'

27

Ihated to admit it, but the whole thing about the rumor that
Match told me his killer's name had finally gotten to me.
Every time I walked anywhere, I kept looking over my
shoulder. Every time I drove some place, I spent more time
looking in the rearview than at where I was going.

Then I realized I had to play it a different way. Even if I
tracked down the person who started the rumor, I still wouldn't
necessarily be any closer to the killer. The important part was
not who *started* the rumor but who *acted* on it.

And the best way to get some action was to keep digging.

So after I left Glen Faddis, I drove back to North Beach
and stopped in at Eugene Tobinio's favorite restaurant. It was
a venerated Italian place that had been in the neighborhood
for ages, just down the street from my apartment. It was the
kind of place Tony Soprano and pretty much any Italian would
love – rich food, lots of garlic and smiles, and Caruso and
Callas piped into the sound system around the clock.

Pear had phoned and told me Tobinio had lunch or dinner
there every day if he was in town. When I asked around, they
told me he was out of town, so I left my number and a twenty
with the kitchen boy, who also swept up at the Quarter Moon
after hours, and asked him to phone me when Tobinio showed
up.

Then I sampled their wares – a rich panini with a salad and
beer – and hit the Bay Bridge to Alameda.

Shade trees, with an occasional palm, dotted the wide residential streets when I swung out of Oakland into Alameda. I
liked the complexion of the town – it was a United Nations

kind of place with blacks and whites, Asians and Latinos, young and old, all sharing the same neighborhood.

As I turned down Sequoia, past big and little Victorians, I spotted more than a few gray heads working the gardens and heard a couple of babies wailing through open windows.

Nobody tailed me over there and that alone made it seem like a nice place to be. For suburbia, it wasn't bad. But like almost every place else outside San Francisco, it had seasons, and right now it was hotter here than in the city.

I took a left on Elm and midway down the block found Clark Margolis's piece of Alameda: a two-story low-slung bungalow. Nice but modest. I left the Toyota at the curb and rang the bell. A second later, the door rattled open.

Clark's resemblance to his father was startling. The same strong jaw, heavy brow, and naturally bronzed skin. He was about twenty-five or so, not much older than his half-sister, and looked like Match did on his early album covers, but neater and more handsome – like Match probably would have looked if he'd cared about things like haircuts and clean shirts instead of music and dope.

Clark blocked the open doorway with his tall, rangy frame and looked me in the eye with a challenge in his. Not friendly.

'Yes?' he said.

I smiled. 'You look just like him. Clark?'

He nodded but didn't smile back.

'My name's Ronnie Ventana. I'm a private investigator. Do you have a few minutes?'

'You're the one who was next to my dad.'

I nodded. 'Can I come in?'

'Please. Yes.'

He stepped back to let me pass into a cluttered room set up like an office with a desk and chair, a couch, a piano, and a clarinet in a glass case over the desk.

Above the brick fireplace were a bunch of dusty trophies and three eight-by-ten photographs in simple black frames. One, a faded black-and-white taken in some smoky nightclub, was of a young Match, sax in hand, beside a laughing, dark-eyed woman at a piano. The inscription, in bold, back-slanted letters read, 'Georgette, you are my life. Forever, Match.'

Georgette looked like a gypsy princess, high-spirited and exotic. The other two photographs on the mantel were of Clark surrounded by a bunch of kids under a softball champs banner.

Clark dropped into the swivel chair at the desk so I sat on the couch. His eyes followed mine to the nest of papers and the stacks of notebooks scattered across the desk and at his feet.

'I'm a teacher,' he said. 'Junior high math and music.'

'Tough job.'

I nodded toward the piano. It looked like the same one in the picture. 'Do you play piano?'

'I use it to teach and compose. The range of octaves lets you write for almost any instrument, even the human voice. For me, and I guess for most composers, it's just a tool. This,' he reached up and touched the glass case holding the clarinet, 'this is what I play.'

'Jazz?'

He smiled patiently.

'Everybody asks me that. I play classical music. It's what I compose, too.'

He cleared his throat, then fixed me with an expectant look, so I got right to the point.

'I'm involved in your father's case,' I began.

He nodded. 'My father told you who killed him, right? The police wouldn't tell me, but I appreciate your coming in person. I didn't know how to reach you myself.'

'That's what I came to talk to you about, but it's not what you think. Match didn't say anything before he died.'

'No?' He seemed surprised and disappointed.

'Who told you that he did?'

'Sharon told me. She said you knew, but the police wouldn't let you say who. I assumed . . .' His voice trailed off. 'Why are you here, then?'

'I was hoping you could tell me what Match did those years he wasn't playing, before his comeback.'

'You mean besides being strung out?'

97

I saw the pain creep into his face before he looked away. Somewhere down the street a small dog started yapping. Then a door slammed and the noise stopped. His gaze wandered to the photograph on the mantel.

'A big part of him died with my mother. I was just a kid so I didn't understand. I know now he was on heroin when he met my mom and he quit because of her. But he couldn't cope when she died. I went to a foster home and he went to live on the streets. His friends kept dragging him into rehab but it never stuck.'

'Until Sharon.'

He made a sour face. 'Did she tell you that?'

'Yes. Why? Isn't it true?' I played dumb.

'He stopped because the doctors told him he'd die if he didn't. And because Mary Elegius got religion and started a place for her fellow jazz musicians to kick their habits. Dad went there and that's when he finally was able to stick to a program. Sharon sent him, but really, Mary's the one who convinced him to stay for a whole year. Mary Elegius believed in Dad. Sharon was just coincidental to the whole experience. But she tries to take full credit because by then they happened to be married.'

'Why *did* he marry Sharon?'

'To be honest, I don't really know. I'm still as puzzled about it as I was the day they came back from Reno and told me they'd gotten married. The best I can come up with, having spent too many Sunday afternoons over at their house, is maybe she badgered him into it. She wasn't really his type.'

A thought occurred to me. 'Do you think she blackmailed him into it?'

For a fleeting moment, something crossed his face. Then his expression hardened.

'That presupposes there was something to blackmail him about,' he said coldly.

'Was there?'

'Of course not. And I resent your asking. My father might have had some weaknesses, but he was only human. And he was honest about them. He acknowledged them, took responsibility, and eventually conquered them.'

His response was clipped, annoyed. A less polite person would have asked me to leave, but I was banking on his good manners.

'Tell me about your half-sister.'

'Yvette? What's there to say? She's only interested in money. My father and I never heard a word from her until she found out he was planning a comeback. She assumed he'd start pulling in some money if he got back into the jazz scene again so she started calling him and seeing him again. I can't say her shortcomings are all her own fault. I've thought about it a lot and I think people like my father shouldn't have kids. They just don't have what it takes, you know what I mean? He was a great musician, his friends say he was the life of the party, but he was a lousy parent. She was there Saturday night.'

'I know. Were you happy about his comeback?'

He shook his head and looked away.

'Why not?'

'Sharon. This comeback was completely orchestrated by her. Dad didn't want to go out there again but Sharon pushed him, kept after him, forced him into detox, then rehab. Kept sending him back.'

I guess what I was thinking showed on my face because he stopped abruptly and explained.

'Regardless of what the doctors told him, he was okay on heroin. He'd found his maintenance dose and he was fine. A lot of people don't know this but you can be addicted to heroin your whole life and it won't kill you. Being straight didn't help him necessarily. Off it, he worried all the time. Then she started nagging him into playing again. She wanted him to compose. I didn't think he'd go for it – he told me he couldn't. Then suddenly there he was, playing new songs again. I couldn't believe it. But he was better off without her.'

'Don't you think he wanted to be productive?' I asked gently.

'You don't understand. She was forcing him to live a lie.'

'What do you mean?'

His gaze went to the picture on the mantel again. 'Saturday

night? That wasn't the real Match Margolis,' he said. 'That was all a lie.'

The interview was starting to feel a lot like a therapy session. It was pretty clear I wasn't going to sort his jumbled and complicated feelings out. Besides, I didn't want to. Sometimes it's best just to let things from the past stay in the past.

'Do you have any idea who would want to steal your father's saxophone?' I asked.

'*What*?' He looked horrified. When he spoke again, his voice quavered. 'My mother gave him that sax. Nick DuPont kept it for him all those years. Jesus, when did this happen?'

His reaction wasn't feigned, so my best guess for the person most likely to want Match's stuff went out the window. I told him about the burglary at Sharon's house and, even though I doubted they'd ever turn up anything, assured him the police were investigating.

'Who do you think killed your father?'

He shrugged. 'I couldn't even begin to guess.'

'How about his friends? DuPont, Malone, Tobinio, or Teagues?'

He shook his head quickly. 'Those four men? I'd vouch for each and every one of them in a heartbeat. They'd no sooner hurt Dad than themselves.'

'You seem pretty sure about that.'

He nodded for emphasis. 'I'd stake my life on it.'

28

'You calling it a total wash?' Blackie asked, wheeling his ancient Buick down a side street.

We were on our way to Match's tribute concert down at the

musician's union hall in the Tenderloin and I'd just told Blackie about my trip to the bank – they'd refused to clear Sharon's check. When I broke the news to Toby and Hakim, I promised to get them the money before the week was out. Now I just needed to figure out how.

'Not a total wash,' I said to Blackie, keeping my eyes on the road spinning in a blur in front of us. 'I'll get something out of her.'

I'd hate to end up evicted, house-sitting in Marin for Mitch, all because of Sharon Margolis.

'Fuck her,' Blackie said. 'Go for the reward.'

'Looks like I'm doing that anyway,' I said.

It was the first time I'd seen Blackie beam.

'Fuck Post,' he said, pleased.

I told him about the stolen saxophone, the routine autopsy report, and my visit with Clark.

'You been busy, doll. That bitch reporter still on your case?'

'Abby? I haven't seen her since I read her the riot act. Maybe she listened.'

'Fat chance on that one, doll.'

He angled the big Buick into a yellow zone outside the hall, then lit a cigarette. When we got out we could hear the band from where we stood on the street. They were doing one of Match's standards, an upbeat swing number that sounded different somehow.

'Hear that, doll?' Blackie paused at the curb and cocked his head. 'Listen.'

After a few measures, I figured out what was so different. A trumpet was blowing the lead.

'Where's the sax?'

'Not tonight, doll. The sax on that song was his.'

I started for the door and Blackie followed.

'This ought to be a show,' he muttered with a chuckle. And as soon as we stepped inside, I understood exactly what he meant.

Every jazz name on the West Coast was there: Duddy Canuto, Fred Pilfoger, Spode Holcum, Mary Elegius, and about fifty others. There were singers and actors and tons of people I didn't recognize but who acted like I ought to. I guessed they were behind-the-scenes people – producers or agents or technicians who'd all worked with Match years ago. A lot of old-timers.

Then, of course, huddled at one end of the room, were my old friends, Teagues, DuPont, and Malone. DuPont was surrounded by monster-sized goons in sharkskin suits who had to be bodyguards. Next to them, DuPont looked more elfin than ever, but I got the feeling the big boys would probably lick the floor if he told them to.

The band was on a raised platform at one end of the hall. Behind them, draped against the wall, hung a blowup of Match's last album cover. The picture of Match was fifteen years old – vintage. He looked good back then. It was probably his best picture, taken before Georgette died, before he fell into the heroin trap and hit the downward skid that cut him off from the music that was his life.

Just off to the right side of the stage stood Sharon Margolis, flocked by a mob of reporters – Abby Stark and Glen Faddis among them. Media hounds. Sharon seemed an unlikely center of attention in this room full of jazz celebrities, squat and no-class as she was, but the press seemed to love her. The TV cameras whirred, taking it all in, like maybe her inane pronouncements were significant in some way. She obviously didn't mind talking to reporters tonight.

If nothing else, Sharon at least had the class to wear black, even if it was a low-cut miniskirted outfit with a fringed hem. The heavy-duty makeup was plastered on like a ceramic mask, but it didn't look so bad anymore. Maybe I was getting used to it. I watched her for a minute or two, then started to get annoyed all over again. Not only had she written me a bad check, she'd lied to me about starting the rumor about Match's dying words.

I looked around and realized I'd lost Blackie to some dark-haired conchita. She looked wholesome enough in a vampish sort of way, so I let him go, and ran straight into Clark Margolis. He was seething so bad he didn't even say hello.

'Look at her,' he muttered. 'What does she think she's doing?'

'I think it's called PR,' I said mildly.

'That's all she ever thinks of. She just announced a deal with the museum. I thought you told me Dad's saxophone was missing. Did it turn up?'

I shrugged and he continued.

'She's a bitch. All for money. Doesn't she ever quit? For God's sake, the man is dead!'

'It's tough,' I said, then took his arm and steered him to the bar. If ever a man needed a drink, it was Clark.

As we physically put distance between her and us, his anger seemed to dissipate. At the bar, his expression cleared and he looked at me with Match's wise old eyes.

'I'm sorry,' he said. 'She's not worth it, is she?'

'Nope.' I pointed to the bartender hovering across from us. 'Tell the man what you want.'

'What? Oh.' He took a second to focus. 'Gin and tonic.'

'Anchor Steam,' I said. When our drinks came, I said, 'What about this museum deal? What exactly did she say when she announced it?'

'The reporters all seemed to already know about it. She just told them she wasn't sure she was going to sell the sax. Christ, I bet she doesn't even have it. And I told her yesterday that's the most important thing that should go to any museum.'

I followed Clark's gaze across the room to the tight little group of five on the bandstand: Match's band minus the sax. They'd just announced they were going to take a twenty-minute break.

I said, 'Do you know the band?'

He nodded absently.

'How about if you introduce me?'

'They can't tell you much; they hardly knew him.'

'Why did Match use a bunch of new guys? Weren't there more established musicians he could have used?'

'You've got me.'

He picked up his glass and followed me across the room to the band. On the way, I caught sight of Sig Malone. He was alone.

I passed by close to him and I could see he'd washed the grease off his face and put on a clean shirt. Even the scab on his chin had healed. It didn't make a bit of difference, though. He still looked as unappealing as a ground slug. And I wasn't the only one to think so to judge from the wide empty circle around him. Nobody was breaking his neck to make small talk with the guy, and I couldn't blame them.

Malone watched as Clark and I forged through the crowd. I waved to him, but his expression didn't change. His eyes just seemed to get colder.

29

If you'd seen them one at a time on the street you never would have pulled them all into one single category. They were an odd assortment, but talented as hell. They all showed promise, even if they weren't as polished as Nick DuPont, Sharon, or Clark thought they should be.

The one that intrigued me the most was the woman – the bass, Rochelle Posner. She had to be almost six feet tall and she was black, built big – not fat, but large and thick and solid, like a longshoreman. When she wrapped her arms around the bass, there was no doubt in the world that she owned it.

Clark introduced me to her first, and her finger-crushing handshake almost sent me to my knees. I grinned up at her to keep from crying out. She regarded me with narrowed, expressive yellow eyes beneath an African-print turban.

'You the woman he fell on. That night.'

We both knew who 'he' was, and what night she was talking about.

'That's right,' I said.

Her lip curled back.

'And you seen nothin'? Girl, what *were* you lookin' at?'

She sounded angry.

'Actually,' I said, 'my back was turned. I didn't even know Match was behind me. Did you happen to see anything?'

'Listen to that! Did *I* see somethin'? Hummmph!'

'Rochelle thinks somebody knows who did it but isn't talking.'

Rochelle frowned at Dickie Almaviva as he popped out from behind her. He'd just drained his trumpet on the floor behind the stage and was wiping it dry. Next to her, he seemed about the size of a jockey, but that was just an optical illusion. Rochelle's clothes were loose and bulky and his were tight. They both were actually about the same size.

'Have I got it right, Rochelle?' he goaded.

Dickie looked different tonight than when I'd seen him Saturday, snuffling and miserable over Match's death. Gone were the long face and the tears. Tonight he offered the world a ready, almost cocky, smile.

Rochelle dismissed him with a sneer.

'Fool,' she said.

Dickie set his trumpet down tenderly on a table between us and the bandstand, then offered me his hand.

'It's a pleasure to meet you.'

Somebody jostled me from behind so I stepped in closer. Dickie sobered and turned to Clark, who was still standing next to me.

'Your father,' Dickie said. 'He will be missed.'

Clark nodded absently, took Dickie's extended hand, then quietly excused himself and disappeared into the crowd. The murmur of the crowd had grown to a low roar. I had to raise my voice to be heard.

'Your last number was really touching,' I said to both of them. 'It was one of Match's new songs, wasn't it?'

Dickie shrugged. 'It's tradition to play without him tonight.'

I glanced from Rochelle's smooth face to Dickie's sharp, Latin one.

'Has the band made plans?' I asked. 'Do you think you'll stay together and keep playing Match's stuff?'

'Plans? We ain't got no plans, girl. I was set to do a month-long gig. Now I got nothin'. That's all I know about plans. Hmmph!'

Rochelle crossed her arms and glared at me like she thought Match's murder – or at least her sudden unemployment – was all my fault.

'We haven't talked about it really,' Dickie said, edging in closer to be heard. 'But we're all pretty independent. Wouldn't you say, Rochelle?'

She just glared back at him.

I said, 'Clark told me Match pulled all of you together just a few months ago.'

'Somethin' wrong with that?' Rochelle demanded.

In case her defensive tone wasn't enough, she shifted her weight impatiently from one foot to the other and fixed an expression of absolute unveiled boredom on her face. Dickie ignored her so I followed his lead.

He said, 'I met Match six months ago.'

Rochelle snorted loudly. 'We all did, pretty boy. Don't make yourself sound so special.'

Dickie's smile became strained.

'Rochelle can't decide whether she wants to love me or hate me.'

'I decided all right, pretty boy. You sorry—'

'Ahem!'

Clark appeared at my elbow and said, 'I'd better introduce you to the others before they get away. Rochelle, Dickie, if you'll excuse us.'

Firmly, he steered me around them to where the rest of the band were stepping down off a platform behind the bandstand. Dickie followed us, but Rochelle took off toward the bar, her stately figure parting the crowd gracefully like an ocean liner slicing through the Atlantic.

'Les Barton,' Clark said, introducing me to the curly-haired, gold-chained piano player.

I'd seen him before, away from the band, but I couldn't remember where. The hand Les offered me was limp and his smile lukewarm. I couldn't help but wonder how he could pound out such great rhythm with such weak wrists.

'Pretty good turnout,' Les mumbled. I had to strain to hear over the noise behind me. He said more, but I didn't catch it.

'And here,' Clark continued. 'This is Cheese Herman.'

I remembered the trombone player, a pinched-faced old man who'd played with Match twenty years ago. He somehow managed to look morose even when he smiled.

'Ain't it a damn shame about poor old Match? I'm gonna miss him. I know you will, Clark. Why, I remember when you were just a button and Match used to show up at rehearsal with a batch of new numbers. Then he'd—'

Clark pulled me away.

'Hank! Over here!'

The drummer was trying to slip away behind Cheese, but Clark called him back. Hank was blond, fortyish, and seemed eminently satisfied with himself.

'Hank, this is Ronnie Ventana.'

Hank smiled at Clark, dismissed Dickie with a contemptuous glance and started to offer me his hand, then froze.

'Wait a minute. You're that private investigator Sharon told me about. Are you investigating Match's murder?'

At that, they all stared at me with a new interest. Les Barton and Herman looked both surprised and annoyed. Hank seemed curious and Dickie appeared detached but amused, like he was above it all.

'Investigatin'?' Rochelle was back, a frothy pink drink in her hand. 'Shit, Match done fell right on top of her sorry little ass and she didn't see nothin' or hear nothin'. What she gonna investigate?'

My guess was I hadn't made much of an impression on Rochelle.

'I'm . . .' I began.

Hank made a big show of retreating. 'We already talked to the police.'

They all looked at one another and nodded.

'Do you think one of us killed Match?' Dickie asked. He was playing the bad boy and he knew it.

The whole group recoiled. I could have clobbered him. If there'd been any rapport at all to salvage, it vanished with his question.

I studied their faces: alarmed, angry, tense. Each and every one of them seemed worried. Did somebody have something to hide? I tried to picture each one of them behind a Richard Nixon mask, or stabbing Match in the dark.

'Don't be lookin' this way, girl,' Rochelle said. 'We done talked all we gonna talk.'

She steamed away again without another word.

Cheese Herman came into the circle and they sort of spread out to let him in. His thumbs were hitched inside his belt and his chest stuck out. He looked a little like Gary Cooper in *High Noon*. He acted like he had something important to say.

'I wasn't lookin',' he announced with a significant nod to me and the others. 'I wish to God I was, but I wasn't lookin' when it happened.'

'Me, neither,' Les piped in.

Dickie and Hank just stonewalled. I focused on Cheese.

'How about beforehand? Where were you before he fell?'

Cheese shook his head without answering. Nobody else volunteered anything, either. I pressed on but I knew the ship was sinking fast.

'Was Match different on Saturday? Did he seem nervous to any of you?'

Cheese set his jaw and glowered at me, still without answering. Dickie opened his mouth, but Cheese cut in before he could speak.

'Shut up, Dick.'

Cheese Herman's old eyes had turned wily.

Dickie looked surprised. 'All I was going to say was, we don't have anything to hide.'

'That's just the point,' Cheese said. 'We don't need to be talking to her. This is eating into our break. Come on, boys. You, too, Dick. See you later, Clark.'

I let them go. It was obvious I wasn't going to get anything out of them as a group. But before they left I passed my card out to each of them and asked them to call if they thought of anything. I knew I'd probably never hear from any of them, but somebody might surprise me and call. Stranger things had happened.

'Not a real friendly bunch,' I said to Clark as we made our way back to the bar. A new band was just starting up on stage.

'They were counting on work for the month, it seems.' Clark sounded disappointed.

'They were counting on Match, too.'

I glanced back at them over my shoulder.

'Sharon said Dickie's the one who got your father back into music. Is that true?'

Clark shrugged. 'That's what Dad told me. He said Dickie had enough enthusiasm for both of them.'

'Any idea why the rest of the band don't like Dickie?'

'What makes you think they don't?'

To me, it had been obvious. He didn't fit in with them, either because he didn't want to or because they didn't want him to, I couldn't tell which. But I was sure he wasn't one of them. And because of that, maybe, if I got him alone, I could get him to talk.

30

Clark Margolis wandered off into the crowd and left me at the bar. I looked around for Blackie and saw he was still making time with the black-haired conchita. She was acting like every other woman acted around Blackie. She was all over him, trying to keep the other women – who were drawn to him like a magnet – away. She wasn't having much luck. I gave him the high sign, then went to pay my respects to the widow.

I didn't get much of a hello out of her. Before I could bring up the bad check or ask her why she'd fingered me to Clark, she grabbed my arm and hissed at me.

'We can't talk here, honey. The *reporters!*'

I didn't care about the reporters and told her as much.

'Your timing's real bad, honey.'

I smiled. 'I know.'

She gave me an exasperated look, then said, 'Oh, all right. We can talk in the ladies.'

Sharon's tight, black satin miniskirt rode up when she walked, so every few steps she'd have to smooth it back down with a leopard-spotted-bangled hand. Her shoes and earrings matched the bracelet, but otherwise, she was done up all in black. She put off a couple of reporters on her way to the john – mostly, I figured, because she knew I was right behind her.

Once inside, Sharon checked both stalls to make sure they were empty, braced her back against the door to keep every-body else out, then said, 'What's going on here, honey? Are you trying to wreck my deals?'

It was an accusation, but all I could think was, *So what?* I pulled the bad check out of my back pocket and handed it to her.

'I want cash.'

She didn't even glance down to see what I'd given her. She knew.

'Oh, honey, I'm so sorry. I realized the minute you walked out the door, but I just couldn't get to the phone. That's the wrong account. I'm so sorry, honey. This whole thing's got me so turned around, I don't know what I'm doing half the time. I goofed. Let me write you another one.'

She whipped a checkbook out of her purse and held it up for me to see.

'This one's the mother lode.'

'I don't want another check. I want cash, Sharon. The job's done. I want the whole payment in cash.'

'Sure, honey, sure. I'll take care of it. I'll go down to the bank first thing and get it for you. I—'

'I'll meet you at the bank at ten.'

'Anything you say, honey. Just, please, please don't talk to me anymore out there. I can't—'

'I know,' I said, not keeping the disgust out of my voice. 'The reporters.'

She mustered a smarmy smile. 'Thanks, honey. You're a princess.'

She put her hand on the door, but I stuck my foot out and jammed it shut.

'There's more, Sharon. I want to know why you told Clark that Match whispered his killer's name in my ear.'

'Did Clark tell you that, honey? He's lying. I never said anything like that. Besides, I heard it from the bartender. But I never told Clark. We didn't hardly speak that night.'

I couldn't be surprised. I was way past realizing that Sharon's reality was eminently relative to her interests. But I didn't want to give up. Not yet. She wanted out so she could schmooze with the reporters. Motivation, sometimes, is everything. I pressed her again.

'I want to know about this insurance policy on Match.'

'Who told you about that?'

'Mr Teagues happened to bring it up.'

She scowled. 'Buddha. Listen to me, honey. Buddha Teagues is an ass and don't you forget it. He doesn't know what he's talking about.'

'Are you saying there's no policy?'

'I'm not saying that at all. But I didn't get it, Match did.'

'I asked you to be straight with me, Sharon.'

'I *am* straight, honey. I just don't appreciate you jumping on every single rumor you hear. This is no way to work for somebody.'

I plucked the bad check out of her pudgy fist.

'Neither is this. If you don't mind, I'll hold on to this until you give me the cash tomorrow.'

I stepped away from the door to let her pass. She threw it open and clattered out into the crowd.

I stood for a moment in the relative quiet of the empty bathroom, wishing Match had had better judgment picking his wife, his friends, his band, and his enemies.

I pulled a cup out of the dispenser on the wall, filled it at the sink, and drank.

My back was to the door when it whooshed open in a rush of sound – crowd noise and music – and smoke. I turned and there was Rochelle Posner, looking as surprised as I felt.

'Hummmph!' she said, and slid her boot backward to wedge her heel against the door. Nobody else could come in. People were going to think I'd set up an office in here.

'Rochelle,' I said, and nodded.

Her expression seemed just a shade less hostile than it had earlier, but I wasn't sure. Turned out I was wrong.

'Ain't you something?' she huffed.

With angry people it's usually best to be friendly and calm and civilized. I pulled out a business card, crossed the room and offered it to her.

'You might not feel like talking now, but if you change your mind, here's my card. You can call me day or night.'

She eyed the card, but didn't take it.

'You got questions?'

It sounded like a dare.

'A few.' I returned the card to my pocket. 'Have you got answers?'

'Those police wasted enough of my time.'

'Maybe you haven't heard my questions before.' Her curiosity hadn't got the best of her but she was still there and still engaged, so I carried on. 'Did anybody in the band ever have any disagreements with Match?'

She crossed her long bare arms over her chest and scowled.

'You don't know nothin', girl, do you? Match was all class, understand? He was good, always askin' to hear what you had.

112

Always. Anybody, anytime. Not just us. Any young blood jazz fool could come in and Match'd say, just like they was somethin' special, "Let's hear what you got!" That was his rep, girl. Good to the bone.'

I thought of the twenty thousand he'd borrowed from Malone just before starting up the band.

'Did he ever buy any songs?'

'Buy? Did you say *buy*? I'd pay *him*. It's an honor to have Match play your stuff, girl. He announces to the audience he's doin' one of yours and everybody hears your name. Then he rips into your song and brings the house down with it. You hot shit, all 'cause you got to be somethin' special for Match to do your stuff.'

'I didn't hear him say he was playing anybody's songs Saturday night.'

'Thing about Match, he let you down easy. Left you respect so you didn't feel so bad if he didn't take up your stuff.'

She closed her mouth and eyed me up and down.

'What you think you gonna find, girl, asking these things?'

'I don't know,' I answered honestly.

That's the problem with questions: you don't always get answers and sometimes, if you do get them, they're not the ones you want.

Somebody knocked on the door. Rochelle hesitated, slid her foot to the floor and let in a couple of been-around-the-block brunettes in black tights and leather jackets. They both stared at me, then at Rochelle, then made a beeline for the stalls. Rochelle kept her hand on the door knob. She'd had enough. But I hadn't.

'One last question,' I said.

She touched her turban and huffed loudly to let me know she was doing me a big favor just by being there.

'Who was in charge of the band if Match wasn't there? Was it Dickie?'

'Dickie?' she repeated incredulously, then threw her head back and laughed. 'Go back to your planet, girl, 'cause you ain't doin' nobody no good on this one.'

113

She shot me one last derisive glare before steaming out the door.

I waited a few minutes just to give her enough room to get clear of me and followed the brunettes when they left. As it turned out, I should have gone out with Rochelle. Not five feet out the door, I ran right into Lieutenant Philly Post.

He was the first person who actually said hi to me tonight, but his heart wasn't in it. He backed me into a corner to the left of the bathroom door and lowered his voice. His big white teeth flashed while his eyebrows twitched at me.

'Didn't I tell you not to jack around with me on this one, Ventana?'

'What are you talking about?'

'Don't pull my chain. Didn't I tell you to keep out of this? Didn't I *specifically* say "hands off?"'

'Sure, I remember.'

'So?'

'So what?'

'So why can't you listen to me?'

His face flushed that darkened tinge of scarlet that made me worry about his blood pressure.

'Listen, Ventana—'

'No. You listen to me, Post. And this is important. You won't get anywhere bullying me.'

'Aw, can the tough talk, Ventana. I know . . .'

A shadow bobbed up behind Post. I craned my head to see, then smiled.

'Hi, Blackie.'

'Shit.' Philly Post dropped his arm, the one blocking me in, and pivoted. 'What do you want, Coogan? This is official police business.'

Blackie ignored him. 'You all right, doll?'

I was still smiling. 'Sure. Philly Post and I were just having a little heart-to-heart, that's all.'

Blackie studied my face, then Philly's. 'Yeah?'

Post gave him a nasty, vitriolic stare. 'Beat it, Coogan. This is police business.'

I stepped out of the corner. 'Did you come back here to say goodbye, Blackie?'

'As long as this asshole isn't fucking with you.'

Post bristled. 'Who's an asshole, asshole?'

I wedged myself between the two of them and gave Blackie a warning look.

'Go ahead,' I told him. 'I'll catch a ride home.'

'What do you see in that old man?' Philly asked after Blackie left.

'He's all right.'

'Maybe you ought to give him lessons on how to act in public.'

'You're not such a lord of gentility yourself, Post.'

'I get by. Come on, Ventana.' He took my arm and started back into the hall. 'Let's go someplace we can talk.'

31

I hated to leave the jazz behind. The band was just start-ing up again, swinging into another one of Match's rousing numbers – trumpet growling into the plunger, piano echoing the melody, the trombonist doing things I didn't think could be done on a trombone, and the saxophone starkly silent.

When I suggested we hear one more set, I could have sworn I saw steam come out of Philly's ears.

'Not on your life, Ventana. Come on.'

And with that, he jerked me out the door.

The place where we could talk ended up being Coit Tower, the monument on Telegraph Hill named after a fireman's groupie. The official line says the tower's just a pillar and only happens to look like a fire hose nozzle. But every true San Franciscan know what it's really all about.

The night was clear and warm, typical Indian summer, with a slight haze that blurred the stars and made them look dreamy. Too bad I was stuck with Philly Post and the grating cackle of his babbling police radio.

When we pulled up and parked in the circle plaza atop the hill, I blocked everything out but the view: the Golden Gate Bridge; Berkeley and Oakland, sparkling their city lights from across the Bay; Fisherman's Wharf; the old ship *Balclutha* down below; and the long, deep span of the Bay Bridge, outlined in little party lights the city had strung along its cables on its birthday. I'd seen it all from here a hundred times, but it never failed to take my breath away.

'So what about it, Ventana?'

We were being watched furtively by a few curious tourists who'd overheard the radio chatter through our open windows.

'What about what?'

'Didn't you hear what I just said?'

I quit staring at the sparkling lights down on the wharf and looked at him in the dusky light. He wasn't smiling.

'I guess not.'

'Shit.' He took a deep breath. It was pretty obvious he was losing his patience with me and that worried me. We hadn't even started our little chat yet.

'I'll cut right through the bullshit, Ventana. Now listen, or I'll take you down to the Hall so you *will* listen.'

'Hey, that's major bullshit right there. You can't—'

'Shut up.'

'*You* shut up.'

We sounded like a couple of brats fighting in the back seat of our parents' car. Or like a badly matched couple who never should have gotten together in the first place.

Post must have been thinking the same thing because he took the heat out of his voice. 'The chief's all hot again, Ventana. Because of you.'

'Me? I haven't—'

He held up his meaty hand. 'Listen. You've been poking around, talking to people. The wrong people.'

'Who?'

'I told you to keep out of this, didn't I? I said it was high profile. If you can't leave it alone, why don't you take a trip, pack up and get out of town for a while? When's the last time you had a vacation?'

He was serious. 'Who are the wrong people?' I asked.

'You know who I'm talking about.'

'Give me a clue.'

'DuPont. Malone. Teagues. Any bells ringing for you, Ventana?'

How could he possibly know? 'You're having me followed.'

'No.'

'Then how . . .?'

He blinked but didn't answer. Then it hit me.

'You're watching *them*.' Shit. What did the SFPD know that I didn't? 'You told me this morning you didn't have any leads.'

'And you told me this morning you weren't working the case.'

'Why didn't you warn me off this morning? Before I saw DuPont?'

'I work in a bureaucracy, Ventana. I just read the report tonight. Your license plate's on every other page. Cough up. What's your business with these guys?'

I thought of the bad check. I thought about Sharon setting me up for Match's killer by telling Clark I knew who killed Match. I thought about how Sharon admitted to sending me in blind to talk to presumed murderers and how she hadn't once played straight with me. I'd hung in with her this long because she was Match's widow. But if I'd felt any shred of loyalty to her at all, it had vanished tonight.

'They all loaned Match money,' I said. 'The little missus hired me to chill them out. She sort of set me up.'

'Christ, Ventana.'

'It turned out okay. They're all cool with Match. Kind of like a family.'

'Right.' Post didn't sound convinced.

117

'Why are you looking at these guys? What makes you suspect them?'

'They're underworld.'

'That's it? Whatever happened to means, motive, and opportunity?'

Post scowled. 'We got a tip. That's all I'll say. I've done more than—'

He stopped, cocked his head to one side and listened to the crackling voice breaking in over his police radio. It sounded pretty garbled to me but he was obviously getting something out of it. The only thing I heard clearly was at the end when they gave out the address. That, miraculously, the dispatcher said clearly. 855 China Basin. The Riff Club.

Philly glanced sideways at me as he picked up the mike and told them in police-ese that he'd be right over.

He wound the car down Telegraph Hill and started in the direction of the Quarter Moon Saloon and my apartment. I knew he was going to dump me on the way.

I couldn't remember if I'd ever begged anything from Post before, but there's always a first time for everything. I begged him to take me along. I started talking deals. I wouldn't have to make full disclosure, I told myself, but I was willing to drop him a lead or two in the future.

'No deal,' he said. 'After this morning, I don't think you'd shoot straight with me anyway, Ventana.'

It was a pretty low blow but he wouldn't budge. He made a few turns, then stomped on the brakes. We were in front of the Quarter Moon. He scowled at me.

'Out!'

I didn't move.

'Come on, Philly. Maybe we could work together on this like we did the Fort Point murder.' That was the last thing I wanted, but my mouth was working on staying with him, not thinking. 'Two heads and all that?' I smiled my most fetching smile.

'Out.'

'Dammit, Post. It's times like these when it gets hard to think of you as a decent human being. Come on.'

'No way. Out.'

'*Please.*' I whined at him like a teenager pleading for a later curfew.

He reached across me and opened the car door. 'I told you, it's too high profile.'

'But you're not getting anywhere. You said so yourself.'

'Did I say that?' He showed his big white teeth and revved the engine. 'Well, Ventana, I think my luck just changed.'

32

I watched Philly Post's car disappear around the corner, then made a dash for my Toyota. I'd just cranked the engine over when my cell phone rang. It was Mitch.

'I gave notice today, Ron,' he said.

'Good.'

'Good? You said it was a bad idea. You told me not to do it.'

'Right.' I pulled out and made a U-turn to head south toward the Riff Club.

'So what changed your mind?'

'Listen, Mitch. This isn't a good time. I'll call you later.'

'You never want to talk anymore, Ron.'

'There's a reason for that, Mitch. We're not married anymore. We don't *have* to talk.'

He kept chattering like I hadn't said a word until I finally hung up. That was Mitch – no matter how direct or rude I was, nothing ever blunted his single-minded need to 'talk.'

When I came up on the Riff Club, there were enough police cars for a John Gotti takedown angle-parked in front of it. In the center was Philly Post's unmarked sedan.

I parked down the street and wandered over. There were clusters of uniformed cops dotting the street in front of the club but I knew none of them were going to tell me anything – I needed to find one alone. I looked around and spotted a guy, a civilian, across the street. He seemed to be taking it all in, an eager and curious expression on his face.

I crossed the street and said, 'Hey.'

He smiled and nodded.

'What happened?' I asked.

'They all just showed up. Five of them at once. They just kept on coming. I think it's something inside the Riff.'

'What?'

He shrugged. 'Dunno. I think they found something.'

I kept walking down the street and dialed Lucius on my cell phone.

'Yeah?'

'Lucius?'

'He's busy. Who is this?'

It was a cop. Great. 'It's his sister,' I lied. 'Tell him not to forget mom's birthday.'

The guy kind of grunted into the phone, then hung up.

I kept walking and went around the corner to where the alley behind the Riff Club hits the street. My thought was to stroll down the alley and maybe peek inside the back door. But instead of an empty alley, there was a beehive of activity around the dumpsters in the back. And Philly Post was at the center.

I started toward them like I was just a regular Joe Blow citizen out for an evening stroll, but before I took ten paces, somebody shouted at me. The whole crew of cops turned and looked at me. Post made an ugly face, said something to Johnson, who was standing beside him, then rushed up the alley to meet me.

'Get out of here, Ventana.'

'It's a free country. What's down there?' I craned my neck to see over his shoulders. 'Is this tied to Match's murder? Did you find more evidence? What's in the dumpster?'

'This is a crime scene. You're interfering with an investigation, Ventana. If you don't leave – right now – I'll have one of the guys take you in.'

'Come on, Post. Twenty minutes ago we were conferring. Now I'm public enemy number one? Make up your mind here. It's more evidence in Match's case, right?'

Post turned and beckoned to one of the uniformed cops. As the guy came toward us, Post turned back to me and said, 'Last chance.'

The fact that I didn't immediately bolt seemed to strengthen his resolve against me.

'Officer Ruben, I want you to escort Ms Ventana to her car and make sure she leaves the premises. If she doesn't, hold her in your car till we're done here.'

I said, 'Come on, Post. You know I'm going to find out anyway. What's the big intrigue? Give me a break.'

The beefy guy, who had the thickest mustache and widest shoulders I'd ever seen, looked around thirty years old, twenty-nine of which were probably spent at the gym working out and lifting weights. He nodded, first at Post, then at me. Then he took my elbow and gently steered me toward the mouth of the alley. I knew better than to resist.

The uniformed cop didn't say anything until we were past his colleagues loitering in front of the Riff, and had almost reached my car. Then he said, 'You Cisco Ventana's daughter? The cat burglar?'

He gave my father's name the Spanish pronunciation: *Cees*-co Ven-*tahh*-na.

When I nodded, and said, 'That's right,' he offered me a shy smile.

'My dad used to play pool with yours.'

'Was he a cop?'

'Yeah.'

'That's great. Where did they play, at that bar off Valencia?'

I kept him talking and reminiscing about his father, then steered the conversation to the scene behind the Riff.

'So what's back there?' I asked.

'Tell you the truth, I just got here. The radio call said it was a homicide but I didn't see any body back there.'

He glanced over his shoulder.

'No ME truck. I think it's a probable related incident to the earlier homicide, the one last weekend. I think they found something, you know, some piece of evidence or something.'

'Like what?'

'I don't know.'

I held his eyes, smiling encouragement, but he just shook his head and laughed.

'I'm serious. Like I said, I just got here. Really. I'd tell you if I knew. Honest.'

'Are you going back there?'

He laughed again. 'As soon as you leave, I am.'

'Okay, I'll take the hint.' I reached into my back pocket and handed him my card.

'Will you let me know what's back there?'

He glanced down at the card, then looked at me.

'One condition,' he said. 'Come by and see my old man sometime. He retired last year and spends a lot of time in the garden. He'd probably get a kick out of talking to you.'

'That's the best offer I've had all week,' I said, then jumped in my car and left the scene of the crime.

33

I was back at Match's tribute concert twenty minutes later. There were about a hundred more people there than when I'd left with Philly Post over an hour ago. And the band was really hot now.

It wasn't just Match's guys up there anymore. Some of them

were still playing, but now Slocum was on deck with his alto sax, Neal Reams and Johnny Bonaventure were working their horns, and Julia Puliko was belting out answers to the calls of the brass and reeds with the voice of a dove.

All the reporters, including Abby Stark and Glen Faddis, had put away their little notebooks. They were as spellbound by the jam session as the rest of the crowd. Everybody in the room was mesmerized by the magic they were making up there: hard bop, scat singing, mellow, big band. They even got some electronics up there and got around to some fusion before they finally broke off the set.

Then I remembered business and scouted around for the band. If Rochelle had talked to me alone, maybe the others would, too.

Hank Nesbitt and Cheese Herman were still onstage, tinkering with their instruments and shooting the breeze with the old-timers from Match's first time around. I approached them but they cold-shouldered me in spite of my most polite and charming smile. Les Barton and Dickie Almaviva were nowhere to be found. I scanned the room for Malone, DuPont and Teagues and realized they were gone. So was Clark. Sharon's head was bobbing in the crowd, but I didn't want to speak to her anymore. Just the sight of her made my blood boil. Abby Stark tried to talk to me, but I sneered threats at her and she went away.

Feeling defeated, I made my way to the bar and tried to catch the bartender's attention.

As I waited, I heard somebody behind me say, 'You a friend of Sharon's or Clark's?'

I turned from the bar and found myself face to face with Dickie Almaviva. His smile was tentative.

'I know you can't be both,' he said.

'Does it matter?'

I still hadn't forgiven him for blowing things for me earlier with the band.

'Ronnie – can I call you Ronnie?'

I turned back to wait for the bartender. Dickie slid into the seat beside me.

'You're angry with me because of what I said in front of the others.'

He held my business card in his hand and flicked the fleshy part of his thumb back and forth across the edge of it.

'They wouldn't talk to you anyway, Ronnie. They're too scared.'

'Of what?'

'Jazz is a small world. People talk. Someone said the Mafia killed Match.'

'That was you, wasn't it?'

He laughed glibly. 'I only said his friends were gangsters.'

'I guess that's all it takes. Why aren't you afraid?'

'What happens, happens, eh? Why live in fear?'

He watched an anorexic-looking woman in her forties sidle by. 'How is your investigation coming?'

The bartender suddenly appeared, so I ordered. Dickie ordered the same.

While we watched the bartender fetch our bottles, Dickie said, 'If I was investigating, do you know who I'd look into very, very closely?'

The bartender set the open bottles in front of us. I picked mine up and drank.

Dickie said, 'Sharon, that's who.'

Naturally. I was talking to the man she'd tried to get fired. Dickie went on.

'She was an embarrassment to Match. Do you know why? She tried to seduce everybody in the band. Did you know that? Everybody. Even Rochelle.'

'Any success?'

'Nah. We all had too much respect for Match. But do you understand what I am saying? This Sharon, she wasn't happy in the matrimony. She no longer wanted to be with her husband.'

'So she killed him in a room full of people while she was standing on the elevated bandstand?'

He smoothed his black hair back and his expression turned rueful.

'Perhaps she didn't kill Match. But in my opinion, it would be a fair and just world if Sharon went to jail.'

I laughed. He looked at me and shrugged.

'Just and fair, but impossible, eh?'

He knew he'd redeemed himself for screwing me over in front of the band. I asked him how long he'd known Match.

'About six months.'

'You just showed up on his doorstep?'

He nodded.

'Why?'

His face filled with grief. 'I liked his music. I have talent. I wanted him to perform again. So . . . I took a chance. Very quickly we became true *compadres*, you know, musically. I worshipped him.'

His voice quavered and he looked away quickly, but his hands, wrapped loosely around his bottle of beer, trembled. I watched him without saying a word. After a moment, he turned back to me, his dark Latin eyes intense, on fire. His rage burned right through me, raw and pure, like something he'd been handed and didn't quite know what to do with.

He said, 'I get angry every time I think about it.'

Then he drained his beer and set the empty precisely in the center of the napkin on the counter. His hands had quit shaking.

'I learned a lot from Match,' Dickie said. 'Things I shall never forget as long as I live. But a lot of good that does me now, eh? Do you know what a Marielito is, Ronnie? Everyone says it's when Castro emptied his prisons and sent the convicts to these shores. But I am a Marielito, Ronnie, and I will tell you that we were not convicts. We confessed to crimes we did not commit in order to win passage to America. Our crime was wanting to leave Cuba. But here, no one wants to know the truth. They only see that I was a convict. But Match, he was the only one who ever asked.'

Dickie had seemed close to tears while he spoke but once he'd finished, the fury and hurt disappeared from his face, like he'd closed up his hurt feelings in a little box and put them away.

'Life,' he said, then raised his empty bottle and touched it to mine. 'To jazz.'

As if on cue, the music started up again. I raised my voice and leaned in closer to be heard.

'Tell me about the band. What are they like?'

He glanced at the two jamming with the group onstage and hesitated. 'They're all pretty great musicians, you know. But we limit our talk to music and that's it. I don't know much about their day jobs. Hank Nesbitt sells furniture in Marin and Rochelle is a floor manager at some kind of warehouse in Richmond.'

'What about Les Barton and Cheese Herman?'

The bartender had brought us fresh beers, so Dickie took a gulp and said, 'Les does actuary work – I think that's what he said – for an insurance company. And Cheese, he's retired from the Post Office and hustles pool at the Corner Pocket most afternoons. He doesn't work at all.'

'What about you?'

'Me? I work in a ceramics factory in South City. Big deal, huh? Well, it pays the rent and lets me play. That's all that matters to me.'

'Did you talk among yourselves about Saturday night?'

'Not really. Nobody saw anything, if that's what you want to know.'

'What about you? Do you remember what Match did after he finished that last set? He turned around and said something to somebody, didn't he?'

Dickie wasn't listening. I followed his gaze to the corner of the bar. Rochelle Posner's yellow cougar eyes were trained on us. Her lips tightened to a narrow line and her face seemed to say, 'Don't you dare.' She was concentrating all her energy on Dickie, like some high priestess of voodoo or something.

Dickie turned back to me, obviously unnerved.

'That's . . . uh . . . right. I–I'd forgotten.'

'Was it you?'

'Yeah.'

126

My heart jumped. 'What did he say?'

Dickie shrugged. 'Nothing. I couldn't hear him over the crowd. They were clapping, you know.'

'No. Wait. Think back. He blew out that last note. Then he set the sax down in its stand. The spotlights went down, then came right back up again. Then what?'

He thought for a moment, glanced nervously in Rochelle's direction, then shifted slightly in his chair so I blocked him from her line of sight. Good.

'He talked to Sharon. He told her to pick up the scores and put them in the folder. Then he left the stand.'

'But when he laughed, what did he say?'

'I don't know. They brought the house lights up and we got off the stage.'

'All of you? The whole band?'

'Not Sharon and not Hank. They were picking up scores.'

'Who was the first to leave? Match?'

'Uh-huh.'

'And then who went after Match?'

'Uh, I don't know.' He squinted at me with one eye. 'Is it important?'

Just then my cell phone rang. I grabbed it out of my jacket pocket and said, 'Hello.'

A voice on the other end started talking but because of the music, I couldn't make out the words.

'Hold on,' I shouted into the receiver, then slipped off the bar stool and signaled to Dickie that I was headed for the door. Outside, on the street, the reception was better and the night was clear and quiet.

'It's Danilo Ruben,' the voice said. 'I just want to let you know I got called off the scene right when you left so I don't have anything for you. I'll ask around though, when I get back to the station. I'll call you tomorrow. Okay?'

'The sooner the better, Danilo.'

I closed the connection and looked up into the dark city sky. Stars sparkled valiantly through the night-time glare of the streetlights overhead and the brightness of headlights from passing cars. I thought about what Dickie had said about the impossibility of a just and fair world. Somewhere in the city, under this same glorious night sky, Match's killer watched the same stars I did.

34

I took the long way home – via the Riff Club.

The squad cars were all gone. Not a cop in sight. I drove down the alley to where the cops had been, left my headlights on and looked around. Nothing. Through the back door, the faint sound of jazz filtered into the alley. I pulled the car back on to the street, parked and went inside.

Lucius, the Riff Club's barman, was an average sort of guy, except for his eyes. They burned hot and black at you like he was on fire from the inside. A lot of people thought he was crazy just from the way he looked – dreadlocks and wild eyes – but if they took a minute to talk to him, they'd find out the only nutty part about him was that he was crazy about his three-year-old daughter.

'. . . so she says to me, "Daddy, I want to come, too!" Heh, heh, heh. What a girl! Is that kid smart, or what!'

I sat a few stools down from the man he was talking to, close enough for Lucius to see me, but far enough not to get sucked into the young genius stories. The music wasn't live tonight but it was hot. The group was into a horn solo and the trumpet player's licks burned the air.

Lucius finally excused himself from the guy whose eyes had glazed over by now, and came to my end just as the number ended.

'Howz about an Anchor Steam, *Miz* Ventana?' He plopped

a chilled glass in front of me, no foam. 'Sharon Margolis get you?' he asked.

'Yes. As a matter of fact, in a roundabout way, that's why I'm here. I heard the police were by earlier.'

He tossed his dreadlocks towards the back door. 'They found something out in the alley, some kind of trash or something. I don't know what it was.'

'Did you get a look at it?'

'Nope. The pigs covered it up. I asked around, but nobody got a bead on it. Sporty said it could've been a body, maybe a body part, but I guess they got outta here too fast for that.'

He trained his wild gaze on me. 'You sayin' you know what it was?'

'No. I think it could be tied to Match's murder, but who knows? I could be wrong. Let's talk last Saturday night. Tell me what you remember from that night.'

'Saturday? Shee-yut, what *don't* I remember? Man, that was grim. I seen fights in here before, but this was the first time I ever seen something like that – cold-blooded murder. Just like that!' He snapped his long, dark fingers with a *pop*. 'Dead. Nothing like it, man.'

His eyes wandered automatically over his domain while he talked. At the opposite end of the bar, one of the waitresses signaled to him.

'Back in a sec.'

He came back a few minutes later and picked up a towel to polish the empty glass in his hand.

'I'll tell you what I told the pigs. I was mixing drinks, see? Everybody always sets up another round after the show, so I was too busy mixing to be watching the crowd. I looked up when people spread out around you and Match. That's the first thing I seen that something was off. Match on the ground, Sharon over on the stand, and you bending over him like that.' He shook his head. 'Man, I couldn't believe my eyes.'

Another waitress waved at him. He scampered down to her at the end of the bar, mixed a few, took care of a couple of guys at the bar, then wandered back down to me, dreadlocks hanging like short, thick snakes around his head.

'So when you said call the cops, I did. You know the rest.'

I slid Sharon's list of Match's friends across the bar. 'Do you know any of these guys?'

He leaned in and stared. 'This guy here.' He laid a slender finger next to Nick DuPont's name.

'This guy, he's a fanatic. Plain, total crazy-nuts for jazz, man. He even blows a trumpet not half bad.'

'Did you see him Saturday night?'

'Yeah. But he cut out early.'

'You remember when he left? There were at least three hundred people here.'

'He tips big. Besides, good old Sharon was putting the moves on him. That coulda been parta why he split.'

'Sharon?'

'I know she's a widow and all now but she's still a skank. She'll spread 'em for anything in pants. She even put the moves on me a couple of times.' He pulled out another glass from behind the counter to polish. 'I let it go and she acted like she was just kidding. She's like that, you know. To tell you the truth, when she came around to ask about you, I figured it was just another pass.'

He set the glass down, then folded the towel. 'I'm sure glad I was wrong about that.'

I thought a moment. 'Would you have noticed if DuPont came back that night?'

'Only if he ordered another drink.'

'What about these other guys?'

When he shook his head, I described Teagues and Malone.

'Yeah. I seen a fat man and a slob with the little guy. They all cut out the same time.'

'Did you see them hanging around Match at all?'

'Early on, yeah. Looked like they were having a great time. Brought in some champagne, even. Had me pour it.'

'And they all left together?'

'Yeah. But like you said, if they came back, I didn't see 'em.'

I pocketed the list and said, 'What about Match? How well did you know him?'

He lifted a hand and tilted it back and forth. 'Had a lot of respect for the talent and all, but mostly I tried to avoid him. I don't get next to dudes with wives like that. Ain't no point.'

'What about his band? What do you know about them?'

'They were like sheep, man. They were lucky and they knew it. Match tell 'em to walk over a cliff, they'd do it. They'd even fight over who'd get to go first.'

He trotted down to pour a few for the waitresses, then came back with a fresh beer for me.

'Tell you what, Ron. That old man, Cheese, hangs at some pool parlor on Franklin.'

'The Corner Pocket.'

'Yeah. And you know Hank Nesbitt, the drummer? You talk to him? He's in here sometimes, even gigged with a couple of bands here. He's the one warned me off on Sharon. He shows up, I'll call.'

I didn't have the heart to tell him I'd already had my chances with Hank and Cheese, and blown it.

'Thanks, Lucius.'

He winked one hot, burning eye at me. 'You bet.'

35

The ringing phone woke me up. Again. I tipped the clock toward me and squinted. Seven A.M. It had to be business. It had to be Sharon.

'Ronnie? This is Sharon – Sharon Margolis, honey.'

She sounded out of breath and frantic, as usual.

'What is it?'

I didn't bother to hide my annoyance. I knew she wasn't calling to tell me she had the cash for me and I was getting tired of her hysterical early-morning calls. I'd pretty much given up on getting any truth out of her, but I guess I wanted her to ask if she woke me up. I wanted her to say she was sorry to bother me again, even if she didn't mean it. I wanted to hear something polite come out of her mouth, just once.

'The police just phoned me, honey. They found the sax! And they want me to go down and look at it. Can you meet me at the Hall of Justice in twenty minutes?'

I'd decided last night that I was done holding her hand, that I was fed up with her, that as soon as I got the cash she owed me, I'd wash my hands of her. But this was Philly Post's Riff Club call. This changed things a bit. If I went, it meant I'd miss my morning run, but it'd be worth it just to see Post's face when I walked in with Sharon.

'I'll be out front,' I said, smiling. 'Top of the stairs.'

When she huffed up the Hall of Justice's front stairs, Sharon looked good – still cheap and brassy, but she looked better than I'd ever seen her. Maybe the reporters at the memorial last night had done her good. Maybe the prospect of seeing Philly Post put a twinkle in her eye. Or maybe she was just feeling like things had finally turned her way with them finding the sax – the prospect of a hundred grand could do things like that.

Whatever it was, she seemed almost perky in her tight yellow sweater and tighter black skirt. She'd even used a lighter hand on her makeup today.

In the elevator on the way up to Homicide, Sharon practically glowed.

The usual bustle was on outside Philly Post's office. He was on the phone when we stepped inside. With the receiver to his ear, he scowled at me, then motioned for us both to sit. While he listened to the voice on the other end of the line, he pawed tirelessly through the stack of folders and bureaucratic debris on his desk like he was searching for gold. We waited what seemed like thirty minutes, but was really probably three, while he wrapped up whatever was so urgent and vital over the phone.

As usual, the room smelled like dirty gym clothes. The Pirates baseball pennant – the only personal item in the closet-sized office – had lost a tack off the tip of its long end so it hung curled in a felt ringlet against the drab wall. A rumpled morning edition of *The Explorer* was folded open on a corner of his desk. Abby Stark's story didn't get the front page, but Post had found it all the same: DETECTIVE WORKS TO CLEAR MUSICIAN'S DEATH.

Post was still on the phone but I glanced over to see if he'd noticed that I'd noticed the piece. His hard black eyes met mine. *Damn.*

'Yeah . . . yeah . . . I got you.'

He scribbled something down on the back of a printed form stapled to a folder, then tore the page in half and stuffed what he'd written into his breast pocket.

'Yeah. Got it. What else? Yeah. Okay. I'll check it out.'

Loose sheets of pink and blue paper drifted off the pile of junk on his desk and settled on the scarred linoleum floor. He didn't even bother to pick them up. The cleaning people probably had nightmares about Post's office like I had nightmares about Post.

When he finally hung up, he ignored me, forced a smile at Sharon, and said, 'Thanks for coming down, Mrs Margolis. I'm glad you could make it down so fast. We found what we believe is your late husband's saxophone last night.'

He was being positively solicitous. I glanced over at Sharon, then back at Post, and wondered what had happened since I'd seen them both together at her house after the break-in.

'Thanks, Lieutenant. You're a real prince.' She smiled a tight, barfy little smile, then scanned the office with her eyes. 'Where . . . where is it?'

Then she noticed Philly's cold glare in my direction. She said, 'You know Ronnie Ventana, don't you?'

'We've met.' It sounded like an indictment.

'So where's the sax?' I said.

'Yes, please. I'll feel better once I get a look at it.'

Post made an odd face. 'We're not one hundred percent sure this is it, Mrs Margolis. That's why we asked you to come down and ID it. It looks a little different now.'

He muttered something about damage and engravings, cleared a spot on his cluttered desk, then reached down behind his chair.

'Like I said, Mrs Margolis, we're not one hundred percent on this.'

He straightened and set a flattened, brass-colored mass of twisted metal in front of us.

It took a second for it to sink in. I glanced quickly at Sharon. She looked baffled at first, then gasped and shot out of her chair.

'No! I . . . I don't believe it.'

From the look of it, somebody had pounded on the sax for a long time with a big hammer. Nobody could have done that much damage with just a couple of simple whacks. The whole thing looked like it'd been stomped on, then steamrollered. A crime of passion.

'The patrolman on the Riff Club's beat found it last night, thought it looked like a saxophone. Then he remembered the murder and called me in. What do you think?'

Sharon had blanched. 'I don't believe it. The museum . . .'

Post cocked an eyebrow at me, then turned back to Sharon. 'Any idea who'd do something like this? Or why?'

He was asking Sharon, not me. His eyes were trained on her like he expected her to solve the whole thing for him right then and there, but poor old Sharon was someplace else entirely. She couldn't seem to take her eyes off the smashed chunk of metal in front of her.

'Mrs Margolis?' Post said, then raised his voice. 'Sharon!'

That reached her. She lifted her eyes and wailed, 'What am I going to do about the museum?'

Then she slumped into her chair and started to cry.

Post mouthed the word *shit*, ran his hand across his forehead, and shot me a desperate look. Then he pulled a handkerchief from his back pocket.

'Here,' he said gruffly, then rolled his eyes at me when Sharon buried her face in it and made snorting, hiccuping noises.

We sat there for a few uncomfortable moments while she sniveled into the hankie, thinking she'd pull herself together, but instead of easing up, she just got louder and messier. Blue mascara stained her cheeks and Philly's plaid handkerchief.

'Look, you want some water or something?' I finally asked. 'Can she have some water here?'

'Yeah, yeah. Water.' Post picked up the phone and barked a terse command into it. 'That's right, Kendall, *water.*'

Ten seconds later the obsequious Kendall showed up with a tiny styrofoam cup in his hand. He knocked timidly at the door, then waited for somebody to tell him what to do next. There was no place to put the cup – Philly's desk was a rat's nest of papers except for the cleared spot where the saxophone lay – and nobody told him who the water was for. I guess it was too much to expect him to figure it out.

'Give me that.'

Post grabbed the cup, splashing water on the dirty linoleum, then shoved it under Sharon's nose. She kept sniveling until Post set an awkward hand on her shoulder to get her attention.

Kendall hovered unassumingly by the door, then cleared his throat softly.

'Anything else, sir?'

Post waved him angrily out of the room while Sharon sipped water, wiped her face with the soiled handkerchief, and tried to compose herself. All I could think was it was too bad she couldn't work herself up like this over Match instead of over some damned piece of metal. Sure, it was *his*, but why couldn't she break down like this over him?

'The museum,' she mumbled. 'I just . . . I just . . .'

Her solid little shoulders shuddered and tears welled up in her eyes again. If somebody didn't say something fast, she was going to go into it all over again.

'Where'd you say they found it?' I asked Post.

He glared at me at first, then seemed to catch on. 'Outside the Riff Club, in the alley out back. Last night.'

I turned to Sharon. 'What do you think, Sharon? Any ideas who could do something like this?'

She lowered her eyes and dabbed at them. 'They must be doing this to get to *me*,' she said, almost to herself.

Post was on her in a flash. His heavy eyebrows lifted for a split second, just long enough to show his fox-like eyes.

'Who're *they*, Mrs Margolis?'

She seemed bewildered by the question. Obviously she hadn't realized she'd spoken out loud. 'W–w–what?'

'You said "they" just now. Who are you talking about?'

Sharon shot him an exasperated look.

'Who do you think, Lieutenant? The jerks who're doing this to me.'

She sniffed indignantly and wiped at her nose. 'I wanted this comeback more than anything I've ever wanted before. They took that away from me. Now the museum . . .'

Somehow, I could have had more sympathy for her if she would have said, 'This would have killed Match,' or something like that. But all she was worried about was the damn museum deal. I watched her stuff Philly's hankie into her purse, then sit up.

'I don't know what I'm . . .'

She trailed off while her eyes lingered on the mangled saxophone. I could almost see the wheels turning. After a moment she glanced over at me, then at Philly Post, and finally back to the instrument.

'Unless . . .' she began, her voice sounding stronger. 'I *could* be jumping to conclusions.'

Post looked alarmed. 'What do you mean?'

Sharon suddenly leaned forward and stared hard at the saxophone.

'Lieutenant, I'm just not sure.'

Philly circled back to his chair and shot me a what's-she-up-to? look. I shrugged. She caught the movement and smiled uncertainly.

'What's the matter, honey? Do you think you know Match's sax better than I do? I'm too worked up over this to think straight, that's all. Nothing wrong with that, is there?'

She hefted herself out of her chair, then leaned over the banged-up instrument like she was really giving it the once-over. Then she smiled up at Post.

'This isn't Match's,' she announced.

'What?' I shot out of my chair and grabbed the mangled sax. 'Look at this detail here. And this. Look at how this M fits in right here. This has *got* to be Match's.'

'That's not an M, honey. Look at it.' She glanced at Post. 'Is that an M, Lieutenant? It *could* be a W if it's upside down. And you know what? I think it *is* upside down.'

I looked over at Post for help.

'Well?' I demanded.

'It fits the description you gave us, ma'am,' Post said, but he seemed weirdly unperturbed.

'I ought to know,' Sharon said in a tone that dared him to question her further. She scooped up her purse and glanced around the room like she was getting ready to leave. 'Call me when you find the right one.'

She started for the door. I watched her retreating back, then turned to Post.

'Aren't you going to stop her?'

'For what? She's not breaking any law.'

I ran out the door and followed Sharon.

'What are you *doing*?' I demanded once we were alone inside the elevator.

'What do you mean, honey?'

'You know as well as I do that saxophone belonged to Match.'

'Don't be ridiculous. I know what Match's saxophone looks like, honey, more than anyone else. That wasn't it.'

The elevator doors swished open and she swished out.

'You're not going to find a replacement, Sharon, not in two weeks.'

She'd told me on the way up that the museum wanted to take possession in two weeks.

'You act like I'm tryin' to pull something over, honey. You ought to know me better than that.'

The sad thing was, she was right. I *should* have known her better than I did. I shouldn't have been surprised.

36

Sharon went with me to her bank to make good on the bad check and acted like she'd been monumentally blindsided when the manager declined the transaction. Between her sputters of indignation, I made her give me – in cash – the $237.45 the manager said *was* in her account, then drove over to Toby's and gave it to him. Hakim, my landlord, would have to wait.

Being a business owner, Toby'd been through it all before, so he already had all the papers for a mechanic's lien, which he filled out and gave to me to record at City Hall. Forty-five minutes later, we had it covered. If we couldn't convince her to cough up the rest of the cash, we'd eventually get paid principal and interest if Sharon ever sold her house.

Outside City Hall, the news rack offered today's copy of *The Explorer* for twenty-five cents. It was a cheap rag and a gip at a penny, but I plunked in a quarter to read Abby Stark's lies.

Her story was exactly what I thought it'd be: a misinformed, garbled account of something she'd imagined. No wonder Post was fuming. It would have been laughable if I didn't know the killer most likely would read it, too.

Abby wrote that I had 'vowed solemnly' to track the killer of my 'father's dearest, closest friend.' Then she said that I'd refused to comment about the possibility that Match had whispered a clue to me before he died. Great. She should have just drawn a bullseye on my forehead.

I tossed the paper in the garbage can on the corner and headed for my car. As much as I wanted to, I had better things to do than hunt Abby Stark down and pound some sense into her.

37

My first stop was Pear-face Barnes's apartment above the tailor shop on Market Street. On the way over, my cell phone rang. It was Danilo Ruben, the cop from last night, telling me the secret find behind the Riff Club was a banged-up saxophone tied to the murder.

'Did anybody know why it was there? Why it was banged up?'

If Philly Post wasn't going to give me information, I'd get it second-hand.

'Nobody figured a bead on it, Ronnie. It's weird, huh? Somebody could have made some money off it. A good saxophone's not cheap and this one's got history. It's a collector's item, right?'

He offered to let me know if he heard anything else and asked me again to come see his father, promising me home-grown tomatoes from the garden this time. By the time he hung up I was standing outside Pear's apartment door.

I could smell the garlic wafting into the hallway from their kitchen, and got a solid blast of it when Mabel opened the door. She was very pregnant and glowing with a smile as big as the sky.

'Ronnie! Come in!'

Mabel Barnes was living proof that there's somebody for everyone. As young and as pretty as she was, it was hard to believe she was so madly in love with Pear – black Brylcreemed hair, pot belly, chewing tobacco, weird clothes and all.

'Come in! Pear didn't tell me you were coming!'

She was a hearty redhead – big boned, big chested, and big hearted. Now she had a big stomach, too. Her loose smock swirled when she pulled me inside to give me her usual greeting – an arm-clenching bear hug.

As far as Mabel was concerned, I was the only person who ever gave her husband an even break. Why she thought this, I didn't know.

'Did you come over for lunch, Ronnie? I'm fixing pasta and there's plenty. Pear should have told me you were coming.'

'No, no, Mabel. Thanks. It's just business this time.'

'You're sure, now? It'd be no trouble, Ronnie.'

She drew me into the living room, a good-sized space filled with elegant furniture. They had a couple of original oil paintings and a collection of crystal to rival a queen's. All the furnishings matched perfectly – bronze here, eggshell white there, and polished wooden pieces all from the same period. Pear – and I guess Mabel – had done a good job putting it all together.

'Pear's in the office,' Mabel said. 'I'll ask him to come up.'

She lifted the phone, pressed a couple of buttons and murmured something into the receiver. Two minutes later, Pear came charging in from the back of the apartment.

'Ronnie – babe! So good to see you, again!'

He put his arm around Mabel and patted her belly, then looked up proudly.

'Still think it's gonna be a boy, Ron? What's the word? Now ya seen her, you got any feeling about this kid?'

Mabel blushed, laughing. 'Isn't he silly? I need to see the doctor about that sonogram just to put an end to this foolishness.'

'Listen to this dame! You hear that?' He shook his head in mock disgust. 'She wants to ruin me. Everybody – I mean *everybody* – has got simoleans on this kid. You find out what it's gonna be, sweetie, and I'm ruined for life! I gotta cancel bets and blow my whole reputation.'

Mabel patted his Brylcreemed hair and kissed the tip of his pointed nose.

'Poor baby.'

Then she giggled when he slapped her behind and murmured something to her about letting us talk business. She vanished into the kitchen without a sound. Pear watched her go, beaming like he'd married her yesterday.

'Ain't she something, Ronnie? I never thought a man could be this happy.' He slicked his hair back with both hands, then looked at me and sobered.

'I guess you want to know what I got for you, huh? Well, let me tell you, I been busy, hon, since we last talked. Checkin' out this DuPont dude rattled a lotta cages.'

He sauntered over to the side table where he'd set up a small bar. 'It's past noon. Can I talk you into some Scotch?'

I accepted and he poured us two stiff ones. Then we sat down to talk.

'This guy DuPont,' he began. 'He's pretty weird.'

I glanced at Pear's green and orange plaid pants, his bow tie and wire-rimmed glasses and tried not to smile.

'Really?'

'Listen to this, hon – he's a jazz buff. Total loco. And guess who's his fave?'

'Match?'

'You got it, babe. He put Match on H way back when. I guess when his old lady croaked – the first one. Maybe he figured the guy needed it. I don't know. Anyway, my source says DuPont gave – *gave* – horse to Match for free.'

'Free heroin to a junkie for fifteen years?'

'I said weird, didn't I? I couldn't believe it myself, either, but there you have it. An' this revenge bit, he's serious as hell about it. He's outta joint 'cause Match got popped right when he was startin' up again.'

'That's real heart.'

'Sure. Fifteen yearsa feedin' a hype and right when it's about ta pay off in music, somebody croaks the goose. I'd be teed, too.'

He swigged some Scotch, threw his head back and said, 'Aaaaah!'

'What about the other guys?'

'We're not done with DuPont yet. Word is he was puttin' heavy duty pressure on Margolis to pay him back.'

'For the heroin?'

Pear nodded. 'If that isn't nasty, I don't know what is.'

'But why?'

'Got me. He really turned it on serious-like after Match put the band together.'

Pear swigged more Scotch and said, 'Anyway, that's DuPont. Didn't get much on the others. Teagues gave him free booze and free bets – paid him if he won and ate it if he lost.'

Teagues had told me as much himself.

'Malone Junk, he took over and ran the place while Malone did time. That's how he got a twenty-percent piece of it. Legit.'

'What about Tobinio?'

'The Mafia guy. Shit. *He* gave the hype free meals. That's what that's all about. This Margolis was some kinda humdinger, you know that? He had some of the biggest creeps in town eating out of his hand.'

'It doesn't make sense, Pear.'

'Sure it does. You like somebody, you take care of 'em.'

'Things aren't ever that simple.'

Pear said, 'You're thinkin' too hard, babe. Here, try some more of this Scotch.'

Before Pear could pour, my cell phone rang. It was Mitch.

'I can't talk right now, Mitch. Let me call you later.'

'It's just a quick question. Are you sure you won't come house-sit for me while I'm in Tahiti?'

'Yes.'

'Positive?'

'*Mitch.*'

'I'm only asking 'cause I ran into Myra—'

'My *cousin* Myra?'

'Yeah. She's going to do it if you don't.'

'Go for it.'

'It's a go?'

'Absolutely. Goodbye, Mitch.'

Something clanged from the kitchen. Pear looked in the direction of the noise and, smiling, said, 'You know, Ron, I'm the luckiest man on earth.'

I saw the love in his eyes and thought of Match and Sharon's marriage. Had some mysterious quality drawn Match to Sharon just as Mabel had seen something in Pear, something compelling enough to make her want to have Pear's child?

I thought back to the few minutes I'd seen Match and Sharon together and tried to remember how'd they'd interacted. She'd seemed solicitous of him and I'd assumed it was because she cared. Now, I knew he'd just been a commodity. A commodity who, it turned out, was worth more to her dead than alive.

38

I spent most of the rest of the day tracking down Nick DuPont and finally found him at home. His Financial District apartment, a few blocks down from his Montgomery Street office, was impressive. He was into dead animal skins. The zebra-skin rug, the polar-bear-skin rug and the cheetah-skin rugs dotting the warehouse-sized living room made me wonder if he had their carcasses hidden somewhere in the back room. He even had sheepskin covers on some of his chairs. And leather couches. The place was enough to make a vegetarian squirm.

Buddha Teagues had given me DuPont's home address and from the look on the little man's face when he opened the door and greeted me, Teagues had phoned ahead to tell him I was on my way.

'I was just having coffee,' DuPont said. 'Would you care for some?'

His brilliant white teeth flashed in a smile at me as he motioned to one of the black leather couches in front of a huge wall of glass. I sat down and saw the city twinkling in front of me. Beyond, the bay glistened like a black mirror in the waning light of the evening. Things seemed quiet and peaceful up here.

DuPont served us coffee from an ornate silver urn with all the skill and decorum of a trained butler. Then he sat down in a chair angled by the glass wall in front. Just like in his office, he was framed by the magnificence of the city behind him.

He stirred two lumps into his coffee, then, as he started to lift the delicate china cup to his lips, I said, 'I understand you supplied Match with heroin.'

He coughed, set his cup down abruptly, and turned to me. His expression was chilling.

'I don't know what you're talking about,' he said.

'I think you do. I'd like to know why.'

He stood. 'I'm afraid you'll have to leave.'

I didn't move. 'Mr DuPont, if you're sincere about wanting Match's killer caught, you'll cooperate. I'm not the police. I'm not working for the police. I'm not going to arrest you and I'm not going to turn you in. What you say here, now, goes no farther than your front door.'

He just stared at me, so I launched into a long spiel about my father and integrity among thieves and codes of honor. I doubted my father would have thought much of Nick DuPont, but I kept talking and talking until I sensed he was starting to thaw.

'If you cross me, Miss Ventana, you won't live long enough to tell me how sorry you are.'

'I understand.'

He gestured for me to stand and, from out of nowhere, a huge thug stepped into the room and stood in front of me.

DuPont sat back down again and said, 'I must take precautions, you understand.'

I raised my arms and let the lug pat me down. When he

144

finished, he nodded at DuPont and vanished around the corner like he'd never existed.

I dropped back down onto the leather couch. DuPont was sipping his coffee again, and mine was getting cold on the low glass table between us.

'What is it you want to know?'

'Why were you supplying Match with heroin?'

'If I hadn't he would have gone to the street. I don't know if you're aware of this fact, Miss Ventana, but a person can use heroin many, many years. The product on the street, adulterated, stepped on, can be lethal. I protected Match from that. I made sure he was never in danger. Maybe it wasn't wise, maybe some would say it wasn't helpful, but I believe that Match lived as long as he did because of me.'

That was one way of looking at it.

'So you did him a favor?'

He nodded imperceptibly.

'If it was a favor, then why pressure him to pay you back once he'd quit?'

He pressed his lips together in a thin line, just enough to let me know he didn't like the question and he didn't like answering it.

I pushed. 'He did quit, didn't he?'

'Yes, yes, of course.'

'Then why ask for the money?'

'It was obvious the other way hadn't helped him.'

'Helped him what?'

'Get back into his music.'

'Or you could say once he quit heroin, you didn't have a hold on him anymore.'

'You've got it wrong, Miss Ventana. I gave him incentive. And it worked.'

'How much did he owe you? How much did he return?'

'That's irrelevant.'

'Why?'

'Because I wasn't serious. I never expected him to make good on the debt. I only wanted him to start writing and performing again. That's all. I gave him heroin all those years because I thought it might feed his muse. But it turned out what he really needed was something else. As soon as I saw that, I took another tack. And it worked.'

He set his now-empty cup of coffee down on the table in front of him and leaned forward in his chair. His voice turned deep and hoarse with passion.

'Match was a complicated man. He had his demons, yes. But the bottom line was the man had a genius for music. He was wasting his life.'

I looked at the rich, powerful little man in front of me, manicured and massaged, clothed in a suit that probably cost him what I pay for half a year's rent on my apartment, and all of a sudden, I understood. Match had the gift but not the drive. DuPont had all the determination in the world but none of Match's talent. Some dreams money can't buy.

'You play trumpet, right?'

He nodded.

'Did you ever play with Match? Professionally?'

DuPont turned his head to watch the little red lights on a boat crossing the bay.

'Not really. I don't . . . uh . . .'

'Did you ever show him your compositions?'

Something flickered across his face. I hadn't known he'd written anything when I asked the question.

'He saw dozens.'

DuPont glanced at his Rolex.

'One last question, Mr DuPont. Did Match ever play any of your songs? Did he play any in his last set Saturday night?'

He looked out the window again, into the night, but there was no mistaking the tone of injury in his voice.

'Of course not,' he said. 'Every single one of those songs was his.'

I stood and took in the breathtaking city lights and the glistening view of the bay.

'I forgot to say it when I came in, Mr DuPont. Nice view.'

Then I turned and walked out the door.

39

I was starting to feel like I was on a merry-go-round as I drove out to Malone Junk. It was late, but I took my chances there'd be somebody there.

So much for chances. The place was locked up when I pulled to the curb. Even the derelicts on the street were gone. But when I peeked through the wooden slats of the fence, I saw lights inside the little shack. I whistled to see if Rover – if he existed – was around, and when he didn't show his snout, I picked the lock on the gate and let myself into the yard.

As I neared the shack, the murmur of voices filtered out through an open window. I glanced through it and saw two figures standing on the customer side of the counter: Malone and Sharon Margolis. From what I could tell, Sharon was coming on to him but Malone wasn't buying. Her hands were all over him and his body language and facial expression screamed, 'Hands off!'

I decided to give the slug a break. I walked over to the front door, rapped loudly, and raised my voice.

'Mr Malone!'

Things went quiet inside and, in the sudden silence, I heard something shuffling around in the dark behind me. *Shit.* I wheeled around and whatever it was stopped out there in the dark. The tiny hairs at the back of my neck stood on end. I could hear it breathing in the shadows, panting, heaving, but I couldn't see a thing. I rapped on the door again.

'Malone!'

Silence inside. Whatever was out there behind me moved again. I turned slowly this time – something told me to go slow – and what began as a low rumble erupted into a vicious growl. Rover.

A quarter into the turn, I froze. I'd seen enough. He was less than four feet from me now. Big gray wolf eyes, a neck the size of a bull's, black matted fur, and fangs to rival a vampire's. I tried to say 'nice dog' but it came out a constricted gasp.

Rover liked hearing the sound. He lowered his head, took a step in closer and snarled even louder. A thin string of saliva swung from the corner of his mouth.

A motion at the window caught my eye. It was Malone, watching. He looked like he was enjoying the show. I called out to him again, but he didn't budge.

I turned back to the dog. He'd noticed Malone, too, and went quiet for a few seconds, but when he saw my eyes shift back to him, he tensed and started growling all over again. I kept three quarters of my back towards him and wondered what to do next. If he jumped high enough, my whole head would fit right into his jaws.

Open the door, dammit!

My eyes flitted to the window. Malone was gone. I slid one foot forward, edging it closer to the door.

'Nice dog,' I said. I managed to get it out this time, but Rover didn't approve. His growl sounded like a subway train bearing down on me. I was cold, breathless and terrified, but I was starting to feel foolish. I couldn't stand here all night.

I'd just mustered the courage to knock on the door again when the growling suddenly stopped. Rover's eyes flickered and a second later the door opened to Malone's sadistic grin.

'What's up, hon?'

He sounded almost chirpy.

'Call the dog off, Malone.'

His nasty grin widened. I got the feeling this could turn into a long evening, but he snapped his fingers and spoke to the dog. It slunk away, tail between its legs.

My own legs felt like Jell-O. And for some stupid reason I felt like laughing. Instead, I tried a couple of tentative steps to test my legs, then forced myself to walk into the shack while Malone chased after the dog and put him on a chain outside.

Sharon popped out of a corner, looking guilty but managing to give me an icy stare just the same.

'What are you doing here, honey? Did you follow me?'

'The better question is, why are you here?'

'I'm conducting personal business,' she sniffed, and sidled toward the door. 'Not that it's any business of yours. I was just leaving.'

Malone appeared at the threshold, but Sharon nudged him aside.

'I'll call you later, Siggy,' she twittered, then stumbled out into the darkness.

Malone came back in and showed his putrid teeth when he stepped behind the counter, leaned his elbows on it and smiled at me.

'You like my dog?'

'He's . . . effective.'

My voice sounded higher than usual. I coughed, cleared my throat, and tried to regain my dignity.

'How'd you get in?'

'The gate wasn't latched,' I lied.

Malone cursed Sharon. 'I don't know how many times I told her . . .'

He muttered a whole string of obscenities under his breath, all directed at Sharon, then rubbed his stomach and eyed me with suspicion.

'What do you want?'

I noticed a flowered scarf Sharon must have left at the far end of the counter. Malone followed my gaze.

'Save your breath,' he said. 'I told her and I'm telling you: I'm not givin' her the money. If you tell me you're her muscle, I'm going to bust my gut laughing.'

'I don't work for Sharon anymore.'

'She didn't bring you?'

'I came by because I overlooked a few things the other day.'

'About that cunt? Don't worry. There's nothin' up between us. She was just doin' her usual thing – whorin'. Came looking for money.'

He laughed viciously.

'Thing she hasn't figured out is, these days, she'd have to pay *me* to fuck her.'

'Did she say why she needs the money?'

'Wouldn't be the truth if she said anyway.'

Malone had a point. Maybe I shouldn't have interrupted them. She could have been trying to get the cash she owed me.

'Actually,' I said. 'I'm here because I'm curious about your loan to Match. You said you loaned him twenty thousand dollars.'

He hesitated, unconsciously biting his lip, frowning at me like I was setting him up for some kind of trap.

'Look, Mr Malone. I need your help. And if you're inno-cent, you need mine. Your situation with Match left you with some pretty incriminating motives. If you help me find Match's killer, you'll be cleared. Otherwise . . .'

For somebody who looked like he only owned half a brain, Malone was quick.

'It was twenty K. All right? What's the big deal?' he said.

He absently picked up a pencil, made a circle with his thumb and forefinger and pumped the pencil back and forth through it. Ten guesses what was on Romeo's mind. The dog's chain rattled outside through the open door. I tried not to think about any of it.

'When did he borrow it?' I asked.

'About six months ago.'

'Did he say why he needed it?'

'Somethin' about buyin' himself a new career.'

'What did he mean?'

'Nothing. I didn't believe that crap for a minute. I can read between the lines, see? He was settin' up for a blow binge. Old Match told people he kicked, but I'm not so sure he didn't need that edge junk gives you to write those songs.'

'His dealer quit supplying him. He told me Match quit heroin. Are you saying he didn't?'

Malone shrugged. 'What else is Match gonna need twenty K for?'

But DuPont hadn't seen the money.

'Who would he buy drugs from if he didn't want his regular dealer to know about it?'

'Fella in the band.'

'Who?'

'The old fart.'

Cheese Herman.

I asked Malone a couple more questions, turned down his offer to take me out for a drink, and made a mental note not to come back at night again without a T-bone or a poodle in heat.

Some days I don't like the PI business. Today was turning out to be one of them.

40

The Corner Pocket was dark, except for big islands of light from the bare bulbs hanging above each of the six pool tables. Smoke turned the room gray, like the fog outside, and made the men's faces all seem pale, almost other-worldly. Everybody looked solemn and talked in a near whisper, like you would in a church.

The place was drab, colorless except for the shamrock-green felt on the tables and the particolored balls zipping around, bouncing off the sides and dropping out of sight after each loud *clack*. There was a makeshift bar in the back and a neon clock over the counter where the man took your money.

Nobody noticed me when I walked in – all eyes were intent on the tables where the action was – so I wandered through until I found Cheese Herman, perched on a bench in the shadows.

His entire aspect was morose: drooping eyes, sagging shoulders, a chewed-up stogie hanging from his downturned mouth and thin, narrow white hands hanging uselessly at his sides. He could've been dead except for his wily eyes taking in every movement at the table nearest him from behind a pair of thick, black-framed glasses.

He glanced over when I sat down beside him. He nodded, then watched a guy at the table sink the six and seven with a bank shot. The guy was using a custom-made cue and so was his opponent. They were good, solid and showy.

I sat through the whole game without saying a word, then, after the bank shot guy won and while everybody settled their bets, I reminded Cheese that we'd met.

'I know who you are,' he said. 'I was tellin' the truth last night when I said I wasn't lookin'.'

'I believe you. I've got a question about something else.'

He reached for the cue propped against the bench next to him, pulled a small cube of blue chalk out of his windbreaker pocket, and started chalking the cue. If I'd aroused his curiosity, he wasn't showing it.

'I'm up next,' he said, then left me on the bench while he broke a new game with the guy who'd just won.

Cheese was something to watch. His clothes were shabby, his face was covered with white stubble from a three-day beard, and his hands shook with an alarming palsy before and after – never during – each shot. His opponent was young, looked successful and self-assured, but Cheese trounced him soundly in under twenty minutes. I wished I'd bet on Cheese.

He came back over and sat down next to me after he won. Some of his tension was gone and I realized he'd been suffering pre-game jitters when I first sat down. But he still didn't smile.

'What's your question?' he said.

'Did Match shoot any heroin over the past year?'

'What kind of question is that?'

'It's important.'

'How am I supposed to know?'

'DuPont had cut him off. You were his alternative.'

'Huh.' He pulled the stogie out of his mouth and spat on the floor. 'Match kicked.'

'Could he have started up again? Once he formed the band?'

'He was in the room when I shot up about six months ago. I had a bindle and a bag for him but he turned it down. Said he didn't do that anymore.'

Cheese bit into the stogie, worked it to the corner of his mouth, then said, 'I'd say that's kickin', wouldn't you?'

41

All day Thursday was a total waste as far as Match was concerned, but for my pocket book, the day was good. I drove around serving subpoenas, and finding and interviewing witnesses on a hit and run. It was a good, solid sixteen-hour-day and I figured I was on my way to making the rent for the month.

While I drove around, I had plenty of time to think about Match's case. I kept coming back to the money and trying to figure out what he'd used it for. If he hadn't used it to pay Teagues back for his bets, or DuPont for the heroin, then Sharon had sent me on a wild goose chase. And what Sharon knew about any of it was anybody's guess.

I spent Friday morning writing reports, fielding calls from Mitch describing the boats he was looking at for his trip to Tahiti, and keeping Match's murder in the back of my mind. By two o'clock, I stuck the reports in the mail and found Blackie at the Quarter Moon.

Two beers into our liquid lunch, Blackie came back inside

from having his third cigarette, and said, 'The bitch hasn't fucking played straight with you once, doll.'

I couldn't disagree.

'I just wish I could figure her out. She's holding back on me, Blackie – I know that much. I'm just not sure if what she's not telling me matters. This insurance policy isn't exactly a secret. Teagues knew and so did Dickie. Is it important, or is it just more of her hyped-up business deal malarkey?'

Blackie drained his glass and belched softly. I continued.

'Then there's the sax. Whoever took it was out to ruin her deal. You'd almost think Match's murder and the theft of his stuff is aimed more at hurting Sharon than Match. But why smash it up like that and take it back to the Riff? Or did somebody just not want her to sell it? And now, I'll bet you a tall, cold one she's out there trying to buy a decorated saxophone on e-Bay.'

'What'd you say Sig Malone told you? More tricks than Houdini?'

'Exactly.' And then there was the money. I told Blackie about the unaccounted-for twenty grand Match had borrowed. 'There's got to be some kind of record to show where it went. Sharon says no, but I *know* there's got to be something.'

Blackie grinned. 'Sounds like you're goin' in.'

I nodded and waited for Blackie's usual objections. Instead, he said, 'You gotta trust your instincts, doll.'

He signaled Harry for another beer and pulled out his fourth smoke.

When he came back, I said, 'Why aren't you trying to talk me out of it?'

'Look, doll. She set you up. You gave her plenty of chances to square with you. Somebody's on to you because of Match. That bitch reporter's fried you by writing that crap in *The Explorer.* If you're a target and you think Margolis knows what's going down and she won't tell, how else are you gonna find out?'

I laughed. He could have been reading my mind. 'I'm going in tonight. Do you want in?'

154

His face fell. 'It's poker night, doll. Do it tomorrow.'

Harry set fresh beers on the table and took away our empties. The last time I'd seen Sharon, she'd mentioned the museum people were flying out from New York and she'd be meeting with them tonight. I couldn't wait. I didn't want to wait. In my head, a clock was ticking.

'No,' I said. 'Tonight's the night.'

'You know how you're going to do it?'

'Sure.' Right up until that very moment, I hadn't. But suddenly, I knew exactly what I was going to do. I'd built the system. I knew its flaws. And I knew its owner. Sharon was the biggest glitch in the system.

I left Blackie at the Quarter Moon and went upstairs to call Mitch. He sounded hurried when he answered.

'Find a sailboat?' I asked, then listened while he went on for five minutes about his three semi-finalists. Finally, I interrupted.

'I want to ask you a favor, Mitch.'

'Is it about the house-sit, Ronnie? 'Cause if it's about that, Myra's serious about it.'

'You're really going to go through with this?'

'End of the month.' He sounded almost giddy. 'Wesley won't dissolve the partnership. He said we can talk when I get back. I can decide then.'

'That's great. Listen, I called to ask how about if we switch cars tonight?'

There was a long pause.

'Mitch?'

'I'm here. Listen, Ronnie. I drove the Porsche in today. It's my baby. You know that, don't you?'

'Sure.'

'Can't you use the Beamer? How about the Citroën?'

'Come on, Mitch.' I didn't want to drive over to Marin to switch cars. 'I promise nothing will happen to it. I swear.'

He was silent.

'Just tonight,' I pleaded. 'I'll bring it back tonight when I'm done with it, okay?'

'I don't know . . .'

155

'Come on, Mitch.'

'If anything – I mean *anything* – happens to it, I'll never speak to you again.'

I could live with that. 'It's in your space?'

'Yes.' He sounded like a condemned prisoner.

'Embarcadero Three garage, B level, right?'

'You have to come up for the key. And hey, Ronnie, lock it up, okay? Even if you just stop to buy a newspaper. If Coogan rides in it, don't let him smoke. And no long-distance runs, okay? Keep it local.'

'Yeah, yeah, sure. No problem.'

42

It was ten o'clock and the neighborhood was quiet when I drove up. I'd driven over from the Embarcadero through parking garages and circling blocks and making impromptu U-turns just in case I was being followed. But I stopped to check my rearview as I pulled into Sharon's cul-de-sac just the same. A pair of headlights neared the intersection behind me, then continued past and vanished around the corner. I waited another full minute. Nothing. I was alone.

Sharon Margolis's house was dark and so was her neighbor's. I could kick myself now for having asked Rocky Peidras to keep an eye on the place, but three days ago breaking into my own client's home was the farthest thing from my mind.

I spun the Porsche into an open spot at the curb a few doors down past Rocky's house, under the broken street lamp. I shut off the engine, then pulled out my cell phone and dialed Sharon's number. It rang about fifteen times before I hung up.

My gym bag full of tools was in the trunk, but I wouldn't

need anything heavy duty – just my lock picks. So I got it out, rummaged out the little case and stuck it in my jacket pocket, then punched redial on the cell phone.

Sharon's car wasn't out on the street and I couldn't see into the garage, but when I reached the front door I could hear the phone still ringing inside. So far, so good.

I pulled out my little lock picks and went to work on the front door. The burglar alarm system's digital control pad was inside, ten feet down from the door, eye level on the left.

When I'd shown Sharon how it worked, I'd programmed a code into it, then told her to pick her own code and repro-gram it after I left. My whole gambit was based on her not following instructions. If I was wrong, just tinkering with the system would set it off. The guards would be on my tail before I could even make it back to the Porsche.

Luck was with me. Within a matter of seconds, I was inside and down the hall. I snapped open the little protective door to the keypad and started punching numbers. The phone was still ringing.

It went like clockwork, smooth as pie. The red digital display changed from 'on' to 'off' so I started to breathe again and looked around.

I wanted to start with Match's music room first, just to make sure the saxophone was really gone. It was. And so was the stand. I wondered if Sharon had found a replacement to pawn off on the museum or if she'd just called the whole deal off.

I scratched around for a few minutes amid the mess of sheet music on the floor, flicking my pen light here and there in the dark, paging quickly through notebooks and papers, and a set of original handwritten scores – Match's old songs – with the titles and dates inked in a tight little scrawl at the top of each sheet.

The museum would have fun with this stuff but I didn't see anything in Match's old compositions that would help me much now. I turned to leave the room. It was then that I realized the phone had stopped ringing.

I froze. Maybe I was just so hopped-up I'd missed the last

ring. I shut off my flashlight and listened. Silence. How long ago had it stopped? I pulled out my cell phone and listened. All I heard was a dial tone.

Something creaked down the hall. Then I heard a muffled shuffling, faint, but getting louder and closer by the second.

Damn. I fought a wild impulse to run screaming down the hall and out the front door, and forced myself to think. One millisecond was all I needed. There was no place to hide. No place to go but out. I made for the back window and fumbled with the latch.

It gave, silently, instantly, but before I could raise it, the blinding overhead light flooded the room. Behind me, I heard a gasp.

'Oh my God!'

I recognized Sharon's voice. The brightness just about blinded me when I wheeled around, but I managed to make out Sharon's stout figure in the doorway. The wide collar of her zebra-striped caftan sloped off one meaty shoulder and the hair on the right side of her head was smushed flat, like she'd been sleeping on it. She looked frazzled and trashed and only half awake.

I started to smile, but something caught my eye, something small and dark in her hand. My heart stopped. It was a gun. And it was leveled point-blank at my chest.

Sharon blinked groggily, then seemed to recognize me.

'Ronnie? What . . . what are you doing here?' Her voice sounded hollow and drugged. She didn't lower the gun.

Shit, my eyes hurt. I was tired of squinting and every cell in my body felt sharp and prickly. I wanted to say something smart, something that would diffuse her hostility and wake her up at the same time, but all I could think about was the gun. It was a Saturday night special. Cheap, black, and efficient.

'Put the gun down, Sharon.'

'When did . . .? You'd better explain, honey.'

She sounded coherent enough but the first rule Blackie taught me way back when was never argue with a gun – and never take a gun for granted.

'Explain,' she muttered.

So I did.

'Testing,' I heard myself say. 'I was testing your new system.'

'Testing?'

Her eyes drifted shut and she swayed against the doorframe, then snapped to attention.

'What . . . system?'

'Your burglar alarm system. Remember? I installed it for you. Monday. I always run a test after I put one in. It's routine. Hey,' I pointed at the gun, and offered her my most winning smile. 'You don't need that.'

But she still wouldn't put the gun down. I was starting to think Sharon and I didn't have the best client/detective relationship we could have. Her pupils were dilated the size of frisbees and her unfocused eyes swam. I watched her fat little fingers. One twitch, one unconscious spasm, and I'd be history.

'Honest,' I said. 'It was just a test.'

The slack muscles in her face tightened. It was obvious she didn't believe me.

'You wanna know what? I . . . You . . .' she trailed off in a mumble, then rallied. 'You helped, didn't you?'

'Right. I designed the system. The burglar alarm.'

'No, no, no.' She waved the gun back and forth, shaking it instead of her head. I held my breath and prayed it wouldn't go off, prayed it wasn't loaded.

'The break-in,' she said. 'You helped . . .'

'I—'

'You did, you little bish. An' Match's book – you helped steal that, too. An' his mushic, didn't you? Thought I didn't know?'

Her dazed, sloppy grin scared me almost as much as the gun did. I needed to say something before she added the Kennedy assassinations to the list of indictments and convinced herself to pull the trigger.

'Sharon, look at me. It's Ronnie. You know me. You *hired* me. I'm on your side. Remember?'

I don't think she did.

'Tell me who you're talking about, Sharon. Who broke in?'

I started toward her, my hand extended, the way you'd hold your hand out to a snarling pitbull.

159

'Put the gun down, Sharon. We're friends.'

I would have crawled if I thought it'd do me any good.

'Just stay calm, Sharon. I'm here to help. Now put the gun down so we can talk.'

I was creeping forward, one tiny step at a time, but there was still a good ten feet between us. My chest was the bullseye. It felt about to explode.

'You're my enemy,' she whimpered. 'Double cross . . . How . . . How could you?'

I forced myself to keep murmuring soothing things – anything I could think of that might bring her back to earth.

'Let's just go in the other room, Sharon. We can sit down, have a cup of coffee, and talk things over, all right? You look exhausted, Sharon. Are you tired?'

The hand holding the gun faltered. Sweat trickled down my forehead into my left eye and blurred my vision. I blinked and focused. Now the gun was pointed at my stomach. That was an improvement, but not by much. Sharon was talking again.

'Of course I look exhausted. The Seconals . . . the phone . . . that *damned phone.*'

I held out my hand. 'Come on, Sharon. Let's go in the living room and sit down and talk.'

I was about five feet away from her when she bristled and brought the gun back up to chest level.

'No,' she barked. 'I won't talk to you anymore.'

I held my ground.

'All right, Sharon. We don't have to sit down if you don't want to. But we should talk.'

She made some kind of snarling sound.

'You don't feel like it? That's all right. You can listen to me talk, then. You owe me that much.'

'Owe? I don't owe . . .'

She gripped the pistol with both hands and swayed. Her hands were trembling. My mouth felt dry and gritty, like I'd just swallowed a handful of sand.

'I can . . . shoot you,' Sharon said. 'You're a . . . a burglar. I'll . . . say . . . you broke in.'

'You don't want to do that, Sharon. Think about it. It's not a good idea.'

The gun hand wavered.

'Go away,' she whimpered. 'If you don't leave, I'll . . . I'm calling the police.'

'Bad publicity, Sharon.'

I took another step closer, hand outstretched.

'Go away!'

I took three more steps, shoved the gun aside and yanked it out of her hand. My own hands were shaking so hard, I turned my shoulder to her so she couldn't see them. I emptied the bullets on the floor, then tossed the empty gun on a chair and looked at Sharon. Her eyes were like a zombie's. I'd lost her again.

'We can do this one of two ways, Sharon: the simple way, or the ugly way. The ugly way, all that confidential crap you fed me hits the papers tomorrow morning and what's left of your deals go down the toilet. The simple way, we just sit down right now and talk like the two civilized people we know we are. What do you say?'

She stumbled over to one of the folding chairs in the middle of the room, sat down on it, and promptly threw up.

43

I'm probably the only person in the world who ever broke into somebody's house to clean up their vomit. I walked Sharon into the kitchen, wiped her face with a wet kitchen towel, then marched her into the living room.

I dragged the armchair in close to the couch and leaned forward so she'd know I was there.

'Why don't we start at the beginning, Sharon?'

Her eyelids drooped.

'Sharon! Wake up!'

'Uh . . . what?'

She sat up and blinked at me. I shouldn't have let her sit down.

'How many pills did you take?'

'Two . . . Five . . .'

'How many?'

She brushed the question away with a sloppy wave of her hand.

'I don't know, honey. Enough.'

Under the harsh light, the skin of her neck looked like parchment.

'The beginning,' I prompted. 'Do you know who broke in the other night?'

'Huh?'

By now my heart rate was almost back to normal, but her sluggish stupidity was making me lose my patience.

'Sharon, do you know who stole Match's things?'

'Said I did . . . told the . . .' she mumbled. 'Told them I knew when I called.'

'Who? Who did you call? Did you call the police?'

I glanced toward the front of the house and prayed the cops wouldn't come thundering through the front door.

Sharon's face was a blank. She stared straight ahead, lips slightly parted. Her breath was shallow and smelled of liquor and something sour. I was starting to think it was a miracle she hadn't fired the gun.

'The music . . . His . . .'

'Help me get this right, Sharon. Do you know who killed Match or don't you?'

'Ugh . . .' She was shaking her head.

'You don't know who killed him but you pretended to know? Is that what you said?'

I felt like I was playing some macabre game of twenty questions. Sharon's eyes blinked once, then she nodded.

'I told them . . . yes.'

162

'Who did you call? Sharon? *Sharon?*'

Her face looked just like the vicious little kid she'd spawned and left down at Malone Junk – stupid and soulless. I waited the better part of a minute for her to respond. But she nodded off instead.

I touched the gun I'd stuffed into my jacket earlier, just to make sure it was still there. Then I went to the roll-top desk in the corner and rummaged through it.

Nothing more exciting than PG&E bills, a stack of receipts from Frederick's of Hollywood and K-Mart, loan papers on the house, and a pair of checkbooks. The balance on one showed $103.02. The other one was the one she'd emptied to pay Toby for the alarm.

I went through all the drawers and found nothing significant. In the meantime, Sharon had slumped down on the couch and was snoring. It seemed safe to leave her and nose around upstairs.

There were two bedrooms – his and hers – connected by a bathroom. Again, nothing.

On my way back down, in the hall upstairs, I noticed a tall Oriental chest against the wall. When I opened the top drawer, I had to smile. Persistence pays. Always.

I was looking at important papers: tax returns, check stubs, marriage certificates, 1099s, Sharon's W-2s from before Sharon and Match married. And a copy of a mortgage insurance policy that covered the debt on their house. If anything happened to Match, the company would pay off the mortgage.

Granted, this was San Francisco, where property values had gone through the roof, but I couldn't imagine somebody would kill just to cancel a mortgage. Even no-class Sharon.

I didn't find an insurance policy on the sax, but I dug deeper in the next drawer down, under some yellowed papers, and found a thick bundle wrapped in brown paper and fastened with a rubber band. I knew what it was before I unwrapped it.

There wasn't time to count it all but there had to be at least two hundred hundred-dollar bills. Twenty thousand dollars. Great. Why did Match borrow it if he wasn't going to spend it?

I put the money back in the envelope, fastened the rubber band around it, stuffed everything back just the way I'd found it, and closed the drawer.

When I got back down to the living room, I tried to rouse Sharon, but she was slouched on the sofa like a slab of meat loaf, head lolled to one side, snoring as loud as a freight train.

I dumped the empty gun onto the table in front of her and didn't even bother to tiptoe on my way out.

44

Insult to injury. That's all I could think when I got home and found my apartment tossed. Whoever it was hadn't even bothered to try to pick the lock this time. He'd just pried the door open with a crowbar and left it ajar.

I don't own much, but the little bit of junk that is mine was scattered all over the floor – drawers emptied and boxes turned upside down. Even my box of stale Cheerios had been gutted and sprinkled across the room. The little round Os crunched under my feet when I walked in.

Standing in the center of the room, surveying the damage, I couldn't figure what I'd done to deserve such a rotten day.

Nothing I owned was worth stealing. The answering machine and the stereo were the only things anybody could possibly consider top-end consumer goods. They hadn't even been touched.

I checked the closet. Everything that had been on hangers was now in a pile on the floor, buried under the crushed boxes of office supplies I kept on the top shelf.

The minute I flipped the switch on in the bathroom, I regretted it. There was blood everywhere. The floor and the walls were smeared with it. My towels, bloodied, were strewn across the floor and the entire contents of my medicine cabinet was dumped in the toilet.

Abby's article from *The Explorer* lay on the floor, a thick blood-red X slashed across its face. I took it all in with one sweeping glance, then caught the reflection of something in the bathroom mirror.

I stepped gingerly into the bathroom, avoiding the stains on the floor, to get a better look.

The shower curtain was pulled back and there, scrawled in blood across the shiny white tiles, was a message, the reason behind the mess:

S T O P O R T H I S W I L L B E Y O U

A bloody arrow sketched on the tile pointed toward what had caught my eye in the first place. Dangling by a string from the shower spout was a dead rat, disemboweled, sad, nasty. My kitchen paring knife stuck out from his tiny belly. His lips, drawn back over narrow yellow fangs in a silent death scream, were bloodless and white. Something hung by a red thread from the corner of his mouth. I peered in closer, then recoiled. It was his tongue.

I heard a sick moan, realized it was me, then staggered backward, fighting the rising nausea as I ran through the debris to the window in the main room. I threw it open and gulped in the cool night air.

The shock of the cold sobered me and, after a moment, the awful squeamish feeling passed. I opened my eyes. Two stories below, on the sidewalk, locals and tourists wound their way from restaurant to bar to shop, seemingly oblivious to what was going on right over their heads.

Could it have been one of them? Was it the man in the Greek sailor cap looking over his shoulder? Or the tall man in leather crossing the street and heading south?

Then I saw it. The grinning face of Richard Nixon gazed up at me from the corner, down by the alley. As soon as he saw me glance his way, he vanished behind the wall.

165

Without thinking, I sprinted out the door, flew down the stairs and ran after him. It was late at night but it was Friday so there were a lot of people to dodge. They slowed me down, but he would have had to dodge them, too. But when I rounded the corner and kept going, he was out of sight. I kept running, circling the block, checking the back streets and alleys, even poking my head into some of the bars, but he'd vanished like a phantom.

I walked back to my apartment, soaked in sweat, and stopped in at the Quarter Moon.

'Harry?'

The bartender looked up.

'Did you see anybody go upstairs tonight?' I asked.

He smiled, then gestured at the packed room in front of him.

'They been keepin' me too busy, Ronnie. Is there a problem?'

I shook my head, thanked him anyway, then trudged back upstairs with every intention of cleaning up, or at least throwing out the dead rat, but when I saw the mess all over again, I changed my mind. I walked over to the phone and dialed the familiar number.

'Philly Post,' I said. 'Tell him it's important.'

45

I regretted calling Philly Post the second I hung up. He wasn't going to do anything except be rude and nasty to me and I would have phoned back and asked him not to come if I thought he would have listened.

So when he showed up and acted like a professional officer of the peace, I was shocked. My guess was his investigation had gone so stale that he was actually glad that I'd somehow managed to shake something loose.

The place was crawling with crime scene people photographing and dusting for prints and looking busy. None of them, however, was doing a thing to clean the place up. Now, on top of the mess, I had their oily black dust smudged over everything I owned.

Post and I were halfway through going over my day – I was telling him where I'd been and what I'd done and I'd already decided I'd tell him I went over to check in on Sharon, not break into her house – when he glanced over at my answering machine. The little light was blinking.

'Oh, no,' I said.

Neither one of us moved.

'You check your messages tonight?'

I shook my head.

'How long since you last checked them?'

'This afternoon.'

He stood and walked toward the machine. I jumped in front of him.

'Hey! That's private property,' I said.

I knew Blackie wouldn't leave a message asking how the break-in went, but all the same, I didn't want Post listening to my messages.

'I've got rights, you know. Privacy rights.'

'Forget it, Ventana. This is a crime scene.'

He reached around me and pressed the 'Play' button.

The tape rewound itself and the robotic voice announced, *'You've got five new messages. First new message.'*

Post leaned in closer. The fingerprint technician – a tiny, gray-haired woman with enormous hands and a permanent squint – was the only other person still in the apartment besides us. She stopped and tilted her head to listen, but I scowled at her and she went back to work.

Four-fifty-five P.M. 'Hey, doll. I'm at Elwin's tonight.' He rattled off a phone number. 'If you need anything, give me a call.' *Beep.*

Post glanced over at me.

'Coogan?'

While I nodded, message number two began. It was Hakim,

167

asking about the rent, again. Next came Sharon, telling me she might have more cash for me at the end of next week. The rest of the calls were hang-ups – probably the nasty guy who'd trashed my apartment. Once we'd heard them all, Post pressed save and looked over at me. The corners of his mouth were twitching.

'Sharon Margolis wrote you a bad check?'

He was fighting to keep from snickering.

'It's the cost of having your own business,' I said, then felt stupid for getting defensive and trying, however obliquely, to put him down for being a bureaucrat.

Post seemed impervious. I told him when he asked about the rest of my evening that I'd checked up on Sharon, left her sleeping on the couch and came home to find the mess and the Richard Nixon-masked guy down the block. I told him how I'd tried to catch up to him but lost him somewhere in the heart of North Beach.

When I'd finished, he scanned the room. The fingerprint technician was packing up her kit.

'What else?' he asked me.

I went over to the counter that serves as my kitchen. The intruder had knocked over my bottle of Scotch but he hadn't broken it. I waited until the tech left, then raised the bottle and offered Post a drink.

He raised his bushy eyebrows. 'This guy must have scared the shit out of you if you're offering me a drink.'

'I just want to know what you've got, Post. I want to know if you've run across anybody you think could be behind this. And if you have, I want to know who.'

I poured two stiff ones and pushed a glass toward him. He was still standing in the middle of the mess that was my apartment.

'Well?' I prompted.

He scowled. 'So you can go off on your own little hunt? Not on your life, Ventana. This break-in must have done something to your memory. Since you forgot, I'll tell you again: I don't share my police work with citizens. And I especially don't share it with you.'

'Malone,' I said. 'I can see him doing this. But the guy I saw was too quick to be him.'

Post was listening. I was starting to feel like Scheherazade.

'Or Tobinio,' I continued. 'He's too much of a big guy to junk the place himself—'

'Or catch a rat,' Post added sarcastically.

'Or Sharon.'

'I thought that's where you were – at her house.'

'Yes. But she could have somebody to do her dirty work.'

Post was shaking his head. 'Sharon Margolis likes money, Ventana, not power, not fear.'

Post was right. The message tonight was intimidation. And despite all her shortcomings, Sharon didn't seem like somebody who'd be behind something as creepy as dead rats and messages scrawled in blood.

'Does this match anything on any of the Riff Club's Saturday night guests' rap sheet?'

Post shrugged. He still hadn't touched the Scotch.

'You got anybody you need to visit out of town, Ventana? If I were you, I'd take a trip.'

'No, you wouldn't.'

I gestured at the mess around us. 'Somebody's left me a message. I'm going to answer it.'

46

I spent the rest of the night fixing my door and cleaning my apartment. The dead rat was the hardest part, but having to cut it down and stuff it into a garbage bag just made me angrier about the whole thing.

By the time the sun came up, the place was semi back to

normal. With sunlight streaming through my windows and the place smelling of disinfectant and soap, I dropped onto the couch and fell asleep.

47

The episode must have worn me out more than I realized because I slept the rest of the day. It was nearly six in the evening when I woke up. Twelve hours.

I checked my answering machine, thinking how odd it was that nobody'd called, but I must have slept through the phone ringing. The machine said four calls had come in.

On playback, the first message was Mitch, asking about his car. The next one was the office I'd done the subpoena and witness interview for on Thursday, calling to thank me for the reports and to tell me that they'd put a check in the mail for me. The last two were from Mitch, again, each call sounding more disturbed than the last.

I showered in my clean-as-a-whistle bathroom, found some fresh clothes in the closet, then picked up a couple of gyros at the Mediterranean place off Columbus, and drove Mitch's car out to Marin.

Afterward, I decided to hit the Riff Club. It seemed as good a place as any to consider my options.

As it turned out, it was Lucius's night off so I had to buy my own. Not surprising, given the luck I'd had lately.

Even the jazz was bad. The trio on the stand was painstakingly eking out a precisely discordant species of sound that made my temples ache and set my nerves on edge. Each scraping note lingered longer than it really needed to and the whole effect, sort of like getting a slow drill from a sadistic dentist, put me in a bad mood. There were only three of them – a piano, a trumpet, and a drum – but they were loud.

The gin I was drinking seemed to soften everything so I had seconds. The bartender knew his job well: he poured generously and minded his own business.

With my back against the bar, I scanned the half-filled room. Anybody who played the Riff knew he was playing mostly to his peers. On any given night, half the unemployed jazz musicians in town showed up to take in the tunes and sometimes, if they were good enough to be asked, to jam with the band up on stage.

Tonight, a lot of the faces looked familiar. I'd seen most of them perform at some time or another, and even knew the names of some. They didn't seem to mind the noise even though I knew they didn't play that kind of music themselves. I didn't see anybody from Match's band.

Five unsettling numbers and two gins later, I'd landed at a table of old timers who'd all known Match before he started chipping fifteen years ago. They were full of interesting anecdotes about the good old days, but proved worthless as far as anything remotely pertinent to the last decade was concerned. I talked to some people at a couple of other tables without turning up anything useful, then wandered back to the bar and sulked.

I was contemplating turning everything I had over to Post and taking him up on his suggestion to leave town, when I felt a tap on my shoulder.

'Still working for Sharon Margolis?'

I swiveled on the bar stool and found myself staring at Match's drummer, Hank Nesbitt. His weirdly stylish clothes – polyester in plaids and checks – hung off narrow shoulders and his coarse blond hair was combed back and up off his forehead, sort of like an overgrown flattop. I couldn't tell if he was overdue for a haircut or if he was pioneering some *très avant* hot style. High fashion's a tough read these days.

He didn't look like the kind of guy who'd string up a rat in somebody's shower, but you could never tell. I knew he hadn't followed me here. I was positive about that. Nobody could have with all the doubling back and U-turns and circling I'd done on my way over.

'Ventana? Isn't it?'

The band had just started up another agonizing song, so I had to shout to be heard.

'Right. And no, I'm not working for Sharon.'

'Good.'

I raised my glass. 'Can I buy you one?'

He hesitated, then leaned in close to my ear. He smelled of citrus.

'I'm with Barton,' he said. 'See that guy over there?'

He jerked his head in the direction of the door. The curly-haired man in a denim jacket who was slouched at a table near the door had the slick good looks of a gigolo. Les Barton, Match's piano player.

I didn't really want to talk to Hank Nesbitt in front of somebody else, but I got the feeling it was share him or nothing, so I bought drinks for both of them, then picked up my own glass and followed him over to the table.

'Les, remember Ventana—'

'Ronnie,' I said.

Les was too absorbed in the music to give me more than a cursory nod. Up close, his gigolo looks didn't seem so smooth. His features were coarse and his eyes vacuous. He had a big, flesh-colored mole protruding from his upper lip that made me wonder if he shaved around it or just mowed over it. *He* could have done the rat thing.

I sat and the moment I did, the music stopped. I clapped more out of gratitude than appreciation. When the band announced a ten-minute break, I clapped even harder. The silence was such a relief, I felt like somebody had stopped beating me over the head.

'They're pretty hot,' Hank said. 'Drum's good.'

'Sure is,' Les agreed.

'Where'd those guys learn to play like that?'

It was the only thing I could think to say about them that wasn't an insult.

Hank turned to me. 'You find out who killed Match yet?'

'Not exactly.'

'Getting close?' he asked.

'Forget it, Hank. Match told her who killed him the night he died. What's to figure?'

'That's just a rumor,' I said quickly. 'He didn't.'

'Yeah?'

Les's tone was full of doubt.

'Think about it,' I said. 'If it were true, the police would have arrested the killer that night. End of story.'

Les glanced from me to Hank, then sniffed and looked amused in a macho sort of way. Hank caught his attitude.

'Don't knock it, you chump,' he said. 'Ronnie here's a private detective. She does this crap for a living.'

'Yeah? So how come she hasn't cracked the case, huh?'

'She said "not exactly." That doesn't mean no. Right? Let her talk.'

Hank turned back to me. He seemed a lot more willing to chat tonight than he had in front of the whole band.

'That reporter said you'd just about got it figured. Was it the Mob?'

'What reporter?'

'Uh, I forget her name but she's the one with *The Explorer*.'

'Abby Stark?'

'Yeah. She said she's got an exclusive and you're gonna blow things open.'

I was starting to think Abby wanted me dead.

I said, 'She's wrong. On everything.'

'That figures.'

Neither one of them seemed surprised and I guess that was comforting. Not everybody who read *The Explorer* believed in its accuracy. That was probably the main reason I was still alive.

Hank Nesbitt dipped his finger into his drink and stirred it. He looked at me.

'You said you're not working for Sharon anymore, but have you talked to her lately? Man, she's gone off the deep end.'

'What do you mean?'

'She called me yesterday to tell me I ought to give myself up because she's got evidence showing how I killed Match. Me! The dumb broad was right up on stage talking to me when Match died. Then Cheese calls me a half-hour later. She's done the same damn thing to him. And Les here, too.

Les nodded, opened his mouth to say something, but Hank cut him off.

'You ought to talk to her, you know. I told her she was an idiot. Personally, I don't give a shit about her, but she could get her ass in some deep shit doing something so stupid.'

'Did she call everybody in the band?'

Hank shrugged. 'Wouldn't doubt it.' He shook his head in disbelief. 'Stupid broad. You see her, talk to her.'

I studied Hank for a minute. 'Do you think somebody in the band killed Match?'

He exchanged looks with Les. 'Not really. I mean, we were just talking.'

'I understand,' I coaxed, trying to keep the excitement out of my voice.

Les finally spoke up.

'There's nothing to it, really. I mean, Hank and I were just battin' around ideas.'

Hank said, 'We were talking about how Match and Dickie were always off doing stuff together, you know, like they were running the show together instead of it being just Match in charge. That never made sense. I mean, Dick's got a good trumpet, man, but we're every bit as good as he is.'

It sounded like sour grapes over favoritism, real or perceived.

I said, 'Why would Dickie murder Match if he was getting treated better than the rest of you?'

'It's hard to explain,' Hank said.

Bad logic usually is. Les seemed annoyed, but Hank kept talking.

174

'Then there's Cheese. I mean, I don't know if I should say anything.' He glanced quickly at Les, then continued. 'Match used. He kept telling everybody he was clean, but he was using.'

Cheese had pretty much sworn Match was drug-free. 'Did you see him shoot up?'

'He'd disappear into the back room all the time with Cheese. I figured they were taking care of business, know what I mean? Could have been Cheese had a problem with Match and the drugs. Hell, I don't know.'

It seemed pretty clear Hank was just spouting off to make himself seem important. I decided it was time to rein him in from fantasy detective land.

'Did Match ever mention any problems he was having?'

'Like what?' Hank asked, sitting up, attentive and earnest.

'Loans?'

'Nope.'

'Financial? Marital? Anything personal? Business?'

'*Match*? Match wasn't that kind of guy, was he, Les? He didn't air his problems if he had any. I don't think he had any.'

'How about the day of the show? Did he seem nervous or worried?'

Hank was shaking his head before I'd finished.

'Everything with Match was easy-going – sunshine and roses all the time, you know what I mean? He didn't let that kinda shit get him down.'

'I thought depression drove him to drugs after his wife's death,' I said.

'Yeah, well, that was before. I didn't know him then. I'm talking now.'

I glanced at Les and he nodded his concurrence.

'What about when he was on stage Saturday night, between songs? Did he act different or say anything that struck either of you as odd?'

'Nope.'

Hank slurped his drink, then swabbed the table with his

sleeve. Les just watched us both in silence, slouched in his chair. He could have been leery about talking, or maybe he felt a little left out. I looked at him but addressed them both.

'At the end of the last set Saturday night, Match turned around and said something to somebody, then threw his head back and laughed. Remember?'

They both stared at me, faces blank.

'Was he talking to either one of you? Did you hear what he said?'

They both shook their heads like monkeys on a stick.

'You know,' Hank said. 'It's a good thing somebody else is looking into this. That stone-faced cop that's supposed to be working on it's a real nobody. They'll never find the guy if that's all they've got to offer.'

Les suddenly came to life. New curiosity sparked in his feral eyes.

'Did you know something was going down? Is that why you showed up?'

'Hardly. I just went to hear Match play.'

'No shit? So it was just, like, coincidence?'

'Exactly.'

Hank was fumbling with a pack of Gitanes now. All of a sudden he seemed jittery. He could have been needing some nicotine or it could have been something else.

'Did you say you were on stage with Sharon when Match was killed?' I asked him.

Hank shoved the cigarette back into the pack, like he'd just remembered the no-smoking-in-clubs law. His green eyes narrowed.

'That's right.'

'Who else was up there with you besides Sharon?' I turned to Les. 'Were you?'

'Yeah.'

'Cheese Herman?'

Hank shook his head. 'Uh-uh.'

'Dickie said—'

'Dickie doesn't know freakin' shit.'

'Where were the other guys in the band, then?' I pulled out a pen and drew the Riff's floor plan on a napkin but when I asked them to show me where everybody was, they argued about every single person. I ended up without a single X on the drawing.

Seemingly out of nowhere, Les said, 'Don't forget Rochelle.'

'Where was she?' I said, ever hopeful.

Hank said, 'Doesn't matter.'

'The hell it doesn't! She—'

'Aw, she's just cranky, Les, that's all. She'd never kill anybody.'

'Why are you stickin' up for that cow?'

Les looked puzzled and annoyed. 'You don't owe her. Besides, we're hosed, man. No Match, no gig, no band. We're busted up for good.'

Hank ignored him, so Les turned to me.

'Rochelle's a pig. She hates everybody. Ev-er-y-body. Hell, she pulled a knife on me once. I'll never forget—' He started, nearly jumping out of his chair. 'Hey! What the . . .? Quit kicking me, Hank! Damn!'

Hank ignored him. 'I was there. It was nothing.'

'Nothing, hell! She threatened to cut my balls off.'

'Like I said, it was nothing.'

Les sputtered angrily, but Hank winked broadly at him, laughing and jabbing his ribs.

'It's a joke, you chump. I was making a joke.'

When Les didn't laugh with him, Hank shook his head, partly in disgust.

'You drink too much, Barton. You're so drunk you can't even get a lousy joke. Why don't you go home?'

Les did seem pretty looped. We'd been drinking steadily since we'd sat down, but he'd outpaced both Hank and me. I had a pretty good buzz on myself, but I was sober enough to see that Hank was nervous about Les.

We closed the place without me getting much more out of them other than the bit about Sharon's call and Rochelle Posner and the knife.

When Hank went to the john, though, Les confided that Cheese Herman was half blind and didn't like to wear his glasses onstage, so if Cheese said he hadn't seen anything, he was probably telling the truth.

When the bartender yelled out 'last call,' Hank tried to hustle Les out the door, but Les wouldn't have any of it. Then Hank tried to get rid of me. When that didn't work, he caucused privately with Les across the room. From where I stood, it looked like Hank was talking sternly to Les, giving him orders. Then Hank gave up and left the club without us.

It was two A.M. and I'd finally got Les all to myself.

48

We stood – not falling-down drunk, but wobbly – outside the closed-up Riff Club, watching people walking to their cars and driving off into the darkness.

'I know a great after-hours place,' Les said, looking more like a gigolo than ever. 'Jazz and some blues, too. How about it?'

I told him I wanted a cafe instead. Some place where we could sit and talk. He didn't miss a beat.

'I know a great place for that too. Parking's not great, but I can drive and bring you back here for your car after.'

He led me to a red Pontiac two-door and I asked him about Hank as soon as we were inside.

'Yeah, Hank. Good old Hank. You know, Hank's all right.'

Les was laboring clumsily to fasten his seatbelt, and I was starting to feel optimistic about how much information I was going to get out of him. Booze was the best thing I'd found to get people to spill their beans. He kept talking.

'We gigged together a while back, you know, before Match.

Two, maybe three years. Yeah. We played some fine stuff back then. You heard of the Jazz Beaus? That was us. Fine stuff, fine stuff.'

'Yeah?' I'd heard them. They were mediocre, at best.

'Sure.' He was still fumbling with the seatbelt.

'Look,' I said. 'Let's take my car. It's over there.' My brain was a little foggy but I was positive I could do better than he was doing.

'I got it,' he announced, finally giving up on the seatbelt and sticking the key into the ignition. 'I got it.'

I kept waiting for him to start the car but he just sat there and stared straight ahead. He was talking, though, and that's what mattered. Unfortunately, he seemed to be sobering up while he talked.

'I can understand how Hank would be loyal about being in Match's band. I was there, too, you know. But hell, we'd only been together a couple of months, since Match hired us all in. You know how long me and Hank played together before? A year and a half. Match's band only did one real gig and that was last Saturday night.'

He snorted. 'We hardly even finished.'

Les started the engine, then let it die. He tried again and gunned the motor once the spark caught. We rolled out of the parking lot, going about three miles an hour, and headed south on Third Street.

'So . . . I forget. What was the question? Oh, yeah, the band. Every band's got politics, you know what I mean? Everybody wants play time up on stage, solo breaks and all that, you understand what I'm saying?'

'Sure.' He was rambling, but I decided to be patient.

'Same went for Match's band. Inside, we're all fighting for the best spot, but to you, to the public, we were like this.' He held up his first two fingers intertwined.

'Inside, we'd eat each other alive for two extra minutes with Match. That's why Hank did Sharon. Thought it'd get him an in. Hell, I did her myself and look at me. It didn't do shit for me. Not even after he croaked.'

179

Les sped up to ten miles an hour and coasted through a stop sign.

'About Rochelle . . .?' I prompted.

From what I'd heard so far, I could easily picture her carving up a rat.

'Oh, yeah. She's one bad apple with a hard-on, you know? Pulling that knife on me. She never should have done that.'

'What kind of knife was it?'

'Girl knife.'

I wasn't quite sure what a 'girl knife' was, but it turned out that he meant a stiletto.

'But, man, a knife's a knife, you know what I mean?'

'What set her off?'

'Got me. That crazy bitch. We're talkin' one minute, next minute, I'm almost dead.'

Somehow, I didn't think I was getting the whole story.

I said, 'Hank thinks she's okay.'

'That's 'cause she put out for him. He's still grateful, I guess.'

I looked out my window and noticed we were heading deeper and deeper into the labyrinth of warehouses down around China Basin. We hadn't gone far, maybe five blocks. Like most drunks, Les was driving slower than he needed to and every movement of the car was exaggerated.

'Where's this cafe?' I asked.

'We're getting there,' he said. 'You never been to the Put Out before?'

'No.'

Les chuckled. 'Hang on, then, and I'll show you. I guarantee you're going to love it.'

He pulled into a warehouse yard and circled the car to park it with the passenger side – my side – boxed in up against a wall.

It all happened so fast it took me a couple of seconds to realize what had happened. By then, I was stuck. I couldn't open my door even if I tried. The only way out was through the windshield – or over Les.

49

'What is this?'

Every drop of booze I'd ingested evaporated from my veins – I was instantly sober.

Les smiled and unzipped his denim jacket. He didn't seem so wobbly any more.

'It's a date,' he said. 'Don't act so innocent. I know you've been on a date before.'

'This isn't a date, Les. It's an *interview*. I want you to cut the shit. *Now*. Let's get out of here.'

I didn't even see his hand move, but his open palm smacked my right cheek. I hadn't expected the blow or the force behind it. My ear seemed to explode. Tears sprang to my eyes and my hand flew up to my burning cheek.

I backed up snug against the door, scrambling to get away from his reach, but I was trapped. It was just me and him and the solid wall of brick behind me.

'Don't talk to me like that,' he said, and grabbed my wrist.

The memory of the dead rat in my shower flashed before my eyes and fed my rising panic.

'Stop, Les. *Stop*! Don't do anything you'll be sorry for.'

He pried my fingers from the door. I felt myself sliding across the bench seat as he yanked me toward him. Then I saw a shadow loom over the car. Then another. And another.

They were faces. Missing and broken teeth, matted hair, dirty faces, ragged clothes. Wild-eyed homeless people. They'd surrounded us.

I stopped struggling and stared through the windshield back at them. Then Les realized they were out there, too.

He dropped his grip and stared at them like they were from outer space.

The first face shouted, 'Are you okay, lady?'

Nobody had ever looked more beautiful.

'No!' I shouted back.

Suddenly fists started pounding on the glass.

'Who are they?' Les demanded.

I didn't know and I didn't care. Whoever they were, they looked better to me than he did. I scrambled over his paralyzed body and threw open the car door before he realized what I'd done.

They were the homeless and they smelled bad, like they hadn't seen a bar of soap in years, but that was fine with me. They helped me out with kind hands, then one of them, a stooped, toothless woman, asked, 'You okay?'

I nodded. 'I am now, yes. Thank you. Thank you.'

I kept moving, moving away from Les and his car and the group.

'I'm okay,' I kept saying. 'Thank you.'

'We saw what he was doing,' one of the guys said. 'We'll take care of him.'

Right then, Les's engine started up. The group – I counted about fifteen men and three women – all surged toward the car.

With their attention diverted, I took a couple of deep breaths, then started down the street. As I fell into an easy jog, behind me I could hear Les's shouts and protestations. Somehow, whatever they did with him, I was certain it'd be just.

50

There are some situations you like to handle on your own and some you have to. Then there are those you shouldn't. Confronting a possible murderer, in my book, ranked in the last category.

So I tracked Blackie down at his favorite after-hours place, hoping he'd be sober enough to be my muscle so I could roust Hank Nesbitt. But when I found him, it was too late – he'd been working on his Saturday night too long. The bartender had already cut off serving him. So instead of rousting Nesbitt, I ended up driving a wobbly, singing Blackie to his house and putting him to bed.

Then I picked up the phone and called Glen Faddis.

'Do you know what time it is?' he demanded when he answered the call.

He sounded groggy but he obviously wasn't groggy enough not to be annoyed at being awakened.

'Can you act tough?'

'What? It's three thirty in the morning. What are you talking about?'

'You said you wanted an exclusive. Can you play a heavy?'

'What's this about?'

'I'll tell you when I see you.'

'This is crazy.'

He grumbled some more, then agreed to meet me on a corner in the Excelsior.

'Wear leather,' I said.

I didn't tell him I'd picked the meeting spot because it was just down the block from Hank Nesbitt's house.

My first thought once I'd reached the safety of my Toyota an hour earlier had been to track down Hank Nesbitt. As brutish and violent as Les Barton had behaved, I knew he hadn't killed Match. He'd shown me he didn't have the intelligence or the skill to pull it off and get away with it. He was a simple, lumbering thug, clumsy, no aptitude.

But Hank Nesbitt could have. And Hank could have put Les up to tonight. The only problem was, no matter how hard I tried, I couldn't come up with a motive.

Hank had everything to benefit from Match's success. In fact, the whole band's fortunes were riding with Match. And Sharon had said Match was as loyal to them as they were to him, that he wouldn't fire any of them, even after she'd asked him to. The bottom line was: none of them had a motive.

My intention was to find one.

Glen Faddis was fifteen minutes late when he drove up in his silver BMW Roadster. I jumped out of the Toyota and waved him over. He got into the passenger side and rubbed his hands together for warmth. His eyes were alert behind his wire-rimmed glasses.

'Do you have to wear those?' I asked.

'What? My glasses? Yes. I usually wear contacts but I was rushed.'

He looked more like a professor than the heavy hitter I'd hoped would scare Nesbitt into talking. I reached under my car seat and handed him a crowbar.

'What's this?'

'Don't say anything. Just make sure he sees that and try to look tough.'

I opened my car door and jumped out. He popped out on the other side and said, 'Wait!'

'Sshhhh. Keep it down. Let's go,' I whispered, and set off down the block.

Faddis came around the car and fell in beside me. 'Where are we going?'

'You know Match's drummer?'

'Nesbitt?'

'Right. We're going to ask him why he killed Match.'

'Did he?'

'I don't know.'

'This is crazy.' But he was smiling.

I stopped him in front of the house and reached down for the crowbar.

'Hold it up like this. Looks tougher that way.' I showed him.

He said, 'I don't want to hit anybody.'

'Don't say that. You will if you have to. Just follow me. And don't talk. Ready?'

I didn't wait for his answer. I charged up to Nesbitt's door and jammed my thumb on the buzzer. I gave it two short rings, then held it down. I would have pounded on the door but the neighbors might have heard and called us in.

Finally, I heard some movement inside. A light went on. Half a second later, Hank Nesbitt, drowsy, hair tousled, bare-foot in pink boxer shorts and no shirt, opened the door.

He wasn't much taller than I was, and thin, so I didn't feel as outclassed by him as I had by Les Barton. I put my hand on his chest and pushed him inside and prayed Glen Faddis had seen enough forties gangster films to know he was supposed to follow.

'It didn't work,' I said.

He saw Faddis and the crowbar behind me and kept backing up into the living room, arms raised defensively.

'Hey, Hey!' he kept saying.

I pointed to a chair. 'Sit down.'

He dropped into it, too terrified to speak.

'Your plan didn't work.'

'What plan?'

'Don't pretend you don't know. You told Les Barton to attack me.'

'What?'

'At the Riff. Before you left us.'

'That's crazy. Why would I do that?'

His voice was gaining strength and, with it, conviction.

'To keep me from investigating Match's murder.'

I heard movement behind me.

'Uh, Ronnie?' Faddis sounded frightened. He was supposed to just stand there and look mean. Why couldn't he follow instructions?

'*Ronnie!*'

I wheeled to face him, annoyed and showing it. Then I understood.

Beside Faddis, wearing matching pink boxers but twice Nesbitt's size, was a shaved-headed man with a diamond stud in one ear and a rose tattoo above his right nipple. He was enormous, and he was frowning. And he was holding the crowbar I'd given Faddis.

'Who are you?' I said with more force and authority than I felt.

'Herbert,' he answered. 'I'm Hank's lover. Hank, what's going on?'

We ended up sitting around the living room while Herbert served us all herbal tea and I asked Hank if he'd set me up for Les. Glen sat next to me, amused but interested.

Hank seemed bewildered. 'Where did you get that idea?'

'I saw you two talking before I left.'

'Oh, God. He didn't take you to the after-hours place, did he?'

'He drove me straight to an abandoned warehouse and tried to assault me.'

'Oh, God. Please don't get mad, okay?'

It'd be pointless for me to say I already was. Herbert reached over and patted Hank's hand.

'Tell her,' he said.

Hank's face flushed. 'Les has a record, you see. He likes it rough with women. All's I told him was that you were a private detective and he shouldn't try to get rough with you. That's why I was trying to get you away from him. I was . . . Listen, he's been to jail twice for rape, okay? I just didn't want anybody to get hurt.'

He looked scared enough to be telling the truth. And Herbert,

186

who was as calm as a Buddha, vouched for Hank's story, telling us that Hank had mentioned his concern when Herbert came home from work.

'I'm a paramedic,' he explained. 'I work strange hours.'

Hank set his mug of tea on the floor by his feet and leaned forward. 'You don't think Les killed Match, do you? I mean, he's got problems but he'd never do anything like that. None of us would. We were on the way up with Match. He was our ticket, man.'

I grilled him some more about the dynamics of the band, how they related to Match and to each other, but none of his answers changed a thing. Match's band might have had the means and the opportunity, but without the reason I'd hoped Hank would provide, I had to look someplace else.

Walking back to our cars, Glen Faddis had the good grace not to laugh. In fact, he was downright understanding.

'Some you win, some you lose,' he said. 'It doesn't look like it's anybody in the band, does it?'

He handed me back my crowbar when we got to my car.

'What about Sharon?' he asked.

'What about her?'

'She's gotten a lot out of Match's demise, wouldn't you say?'

I had to agree. And the only time Sharon had seemed upset was the night Match died. Ever since, she'd been wheeling and dealing like a carnival barker.

Faddis said, 'The autopsy report proves she could have killed him. It took him a while to die. He could have been stabbed up there.'

The yellow light from the street lamp down the street made him look sallow and tired. But his eyes danced with intelligence and curiosity.

'We should take another look at her,' he said.

'*We*?'

He laughed. 'Don't you think I earned my street cred tonight?'

'I'll call you,' I said, and started to get into my car.

'Wait. I've got something.'

'What?'

'I've been sniffing around,' he began.

I waited, tired and impatient.

'It'll be better if I show you. I've got the stuff at my place.'

'Good,' I told him. 'Bring it to the Baghdad Cafe. I'll see you there in half an hour.'

51

When Glen Faddis walked into the Bagdad Cafe, it was clear he hadn't stopped to wash his face or comb his sparse, sandy hair. He had a thick accordion file under one arm and offered me a jaunty wave from the door with the other.

'Hey,' he said, slapping the heavy file down in front of me.

I'd taken a table by the window where I could watch Market Street's damp surface glisten in the butter-colored light from the street lamps above. I'd chugged down my first cup of coffee and the refill sat in front of me, going cold.

I waited while Glen went up to the counter and brought back some coffee and a slice of cake.

'Things have changed,' he said, sounding excited.

'What's in here?' I asked, indicating the folder between us.

'My notes. But I've got something better. On the drive from my house to here, I started thinking. It's better if you hear it from the horse's mouth. Ah, speak of the horse!'

He rose up out of his chair and I turned to see who he was beckoning over to the table. I didn't recognize her at first with her face scrubbed clean and wearing jeans and a plain black hoodie over a Green Day tee shirt.

'You remember Yvette Fields, don't you?'

Match's illegitimate daughter. Glen pulled out a chair for her and she dropped into it with the sensuous grace of a dancer.

'Thanks for coming, Yvette. I really appreciate it.'

She mumbled something that made me think she hadn't been given much of a choice. But after she sat, she offered me a small smile.

No false bravado. Just a simple, pretty girl with something to say. I wondered what private demons had driven her to the Tenderloin to feed the inexorable appetites of men who saw nothing wrong with paying to use another person's body.

Glen Faddis pushed the coffee and cake in her direction. He showed her the same solicitude he had me, gracious and gentlemanly.

'I remembered you like carrot cake,' he said.

She smiled at him then, and I saw courtesy in action. His calm respect for people brought out the best in them.

Faddis waited until she'd taken a couple of bites, then said, 'Tell Ronnie what you told me.'

Her blue eyes seemed enormous without all the makeup and her skin shone with the glow you only see with youth.

'It's something my mom told me. About Match,' she began. 'Mom said Match was a fake.'

I looked at Glen, then back at Yvette.

'That's the word she used? "Fake?"'

Yvette nodded and took another bite.

'What's that supposed to mean?'

'She hated him. She didn't want to marry him or anything, at least I don't think she did. But she wanted him to support us. She told him I was his responsibility as much as hers. I remember hearing that a lot when I was little. She didn't want him around us or anything like that – I mean, I had "uncles" coming and going all the time. But my mom wanted money from him. She wanted him to pay for food and clothes and schoolbooks and things. And he did. We did pretty well, actually. And my mom told me he did it because she knew he wasn't who he said he was. That's why he gave us money. Then she died and the money stopped.'

'She was blackmailing him?'

Yvette said, 'It didn't seem like it then, but looking back, I see that's what was going on.'

'Do you know what she had on him?'

She took a couple more bites of carrot cake, then smiled up at me with all the guilelessness of an ingenue.

'If I did,' she said matter-of-factly, 'the money never would have stopped.'

52

Clark Margolis might have been happier to see me at seven o'clock in the morning if he'd known I'd waited a half-hour dozing in my car in front of his house before knocking on his door. I'd been running on caffeine and adrenaline since my 'date' with Les Barton, and it finally caught up with me when I got to his house.

But thirty minutes was all I'd needed. I felt fresh as a rose, even if I didn't smell or look like one.

'This isn't a good time,' Clark said when he opened the door and found me on his front porch. 'I've got to get ready for school.'

'This is important,' I said.

He caught the urgency in my voice and opened the door wider for me to pass inside. The smell of coffee filled the house and I prayed he'd offer me a cup.

'Coffee?' he said, as I followed him back to the kitchen. 'Toast?'

I said yes to both, so he set the breakfast he'd been about to serve himself in front of me and busied himself with a second serving.

'This is about Dad, I guess,' he said over his shoulder. He pulled a mug out of a cabinet and filled it with coffee, then drank it black.

'I met with your half-sister,' I began.

He cursed. 'What does she have to do with Dad?'

'This may not sound very good, but here's what she said.'

I told him as gently as I could about the blackmail and the false identity.

'She's lying,' he said. 'She didn't know my dad.'

'She has receipts,' I said. The contents of Glen Faddis's accordion file. 'Bank statements that show the money coming in every month. Clark, she has copies of the checks your father wrote.'

The toast popped up in the toaster and we both started. Clark pulled the bread out, threw it onto a plate and began to butter it with savage little strokes.

'It's a lie,' he said. 'It's a lie.'

I pulled a stack of pages from the folder I'd brought in with me and set it on the table.

'Is this his handwriting?'

He whirled around from the counter and his eyes found the copies. As soon as he saw them, he crossed over to the table and picked them up, staring hard at the signature, crisp and legible in the same bold, back-slanted hand I'd seen on the photograph on his mantel.

Clark flipped through page after page after page. As he did, the pain in his eyes grew and deepened. They became the eyes of a little boy, filled with disappointment and hurt, born from broken promises, from neglect and deceit.

'Is that his signature?' I asked again softly.

He laid the pages down on the table and nodded.

I pointed to the copies. 'Do you have any idea what this is about?'

He shook his head, then trudged like a robot back to the counter and brought the plate of toast and his cup of coffee to the table. The papers and open folder lay between us, the ghost of a father he'd never really known.

'What can I do to help?' he said.

191

53

Clark Margolis and I spent the rest of the morning rummaging through old trunks and boxes in his attic. We found his parents' marriage license from their elopement to Reno. The name on the certificate was Matthew L. Margolis, Match's proper name, the same name he'd used on Clark's birth certificate, and on the copy of the certificate for Yvette, which we found tucked in the back of an ancient photo album.

It was close to noon when we found Match's birth certificate. Clark's fingers were trembling as he pulled it from its decorative envelope. His face fell as he read the entries in each little block. Then he handed it to me. I read the name of the newborn: Matthew Lawrence Margolis.

It seemed authentic enough, but forty years ago, before Match married his first wife, before Clark and before Yvette were born, it had been a lot easier to assume a new identity.

Sitting between the last box we'd emptied and all the trunks we'd already examined, Clark said, 'Do you think this is a fake? Can you find out?'

'Depends,' I said, looking down at the certificate in my hand and reading the names listed for Match's parents.

'What can you tell me about your paternal grandparents?'

Clark looked baffled. 'Like what?'

'Did you ever meet them?'

'Of course. They both died in an accident the year before Mom died. I was ten. That's why I ended up in a foster home, because they were gone.'

'But you knew them?'

He nodded. 'Quite well. Mom and Dad let me stay with them a lot. Mostly every weekend. Dad had the gigs, and Mom liked to go with him. She was his number one cheerleader.'

While Clark kept on reminiscing, I glanced down at the names on the certificate.

Mother: Elizabeth Jean Savros. Age: 24.

Father: Joseph Lawrence Margolis. Age: 29.

'What did you call them?' I asked.

'My grandparents? Grandma Betty and Grandpa Joe.' He smiled. 'They were the sweetest, dearest people.'

I handed Match's birth certificate back to him.

'It's not a fake,' I told him.

Match was Matthew Lawrence Margolis. Son of Grandma Betty and Grandpa Joe. You can fake your own identity, but the likelihood of convincing your parents to do so too was so remote, I'd bet the ranch that's not what had happened.

So what had Yvette's mother meant?

54

I was on my way back to the city, crossing the Bay Bridge and drinking in the view that fills my heart to the brim every time I see it, when my cell phone rang. It was probably Glen Faddis but I didn't feel like talking to anybody just yet.

I let my voicemail take it, then glanced at the clock on the dash. Four thirty. I'd been up for longer than I thought was humanly possible. The last cup of coffee I drank hadn't delivered on the usual jolt, so I was dragging. Suddenly everything ached and my brain was starting to feel like mush. My lumpy sofa bed beckoned like a siren. I shut the cell phone off and stepped on the gas.

By the time I reached the intersection of Columbus and Grant Avenue, I was thinking fondly of the soft texture of my pajamas. I was about to turn onto Grant, but what I saw drew me up short. Three black and whites stationed outside the Quarter Moon.

They could have been there to clear up an altercation between rowdy patrons. I'd seen that happen before. Or somebody could have reported another break-in at my apartment upstairs. A crowbarred door wasn't exactly easy to overlook. Then again, they could have been there for something else.

As much as I loathed the prospect of another break-in and another dead rat in my shower, it was the 'something else' that worried me.

I gunned the old Toyota and prayed nobody recognized me or my car as I sped down Columbus towards Bay. Nine blocks away, I pulled over in somebody's driveway and pulled out my cell phone.

'Yo, Quarter Moon Saloon.'

'Harry. Do you know who this is?'

'Yo.'

'What's going on down there?'

His voice dropped. 'Somebody wants to burn your ass, sister. They're searching your place.'

I had to strain to hear his voice above the noise of traffic zooming by.

'For what?'

'You know a chick name of Margo something?'

'Margolis? Sharon Margolis?'

'That's it!'

What did she tell them I stole? Harry kept talking.

'The pigs say you did her.'

'She's dead?'

'They say your hands were all over the gun.'

55

Blackie wasn't home so I picked his lock, pulled down the shades and found myself a beer. Then I phoned Rocky Piedras.

'Ah, Ms Ven-tah-na,' he said, giving my name its proper Spanish pronunciation. 'I'm so happy you called. Rosario . . .' He swore softly in Spanish under his breath. 'Rosario made me call the police and would not allow me to phone you. I regret it, but my choices, Ms Ven-tah-na, were not the best. Rosario thought it would be illegal to contact you. She put our marriage on the line, as they say. Ah well, women.' He sighed. 'It is a shame about the little widow, is it not?'

'Yes, Mr Piedras—'

'Please call me Rocky. *Qué lástima*,' he said. 'What a shame. I am so sorry to hear of this death. Rosario should have let me go over there. But she wouldn't allow it. And now, this.'

'Did you or your wife see anything? Did you hear anything?'

'Yes! Oh, yes. How stupid of me. I should have said so immediately. I saw the man this time,' he said, his voice suddenly jittery with excitement. 'Rosario did, too.'

'Did you tell the police?'

'Yes, of course, Ms Ventana. It was our duty as citizens. But because we did not see him come from inside the house, the police did not visit. They said this is San Francisco and it is not unusual for people to behave oddly. And then we went to visit my Rosario's mother in Santa Cruz. We did not return until this morning. That's when Rosario noticed the smell. We called again, and told them we saw the man and that the house was quiet and smelled bad. Then they came.'

'What did the guy look like, Rocky?'

'That is the part that is so strange, Ms Ventana. I wouldn't believe it unless Rosario saw him, too. And she did. It is all very strange. The man, he was *el Presidente Nixon*.'

'In a leather jacket?'

'Yes! How remarkable that you should know! You have met him?'

'In a manner of speaking. Did you get a better look at his car this time?'

'No. I am so sorry, Ms Ventana. His car, I do not know where it was.'

'Did you hear shots?'

'We were asleep but now that I know what happened, I believe that is the sound that woke us up.'

After I hung up the phone, I sat down on Blackie's cluttered couch and tried to figure out what to do next.

Sharon was dead and my fingerprints were all over the gun. Since I was innocent, in theory, I could turn myself in and let them test my hands for residue. But I could have picked up traces of residue just by handling the gun. It wasn't worth the risk.

If I turned myself in, chances were good to great that they'd hold me until they found the right person – and I wasn't about to bank my freedom on Philly Post's investigatory skills.

What I needed was an angle, some way to work the case, solve both murders and not get picked up by Philly Post while I was doing it. I guess the problem wasn't challenging enough, or maybe it just overwhelmed me. In either case, I didn't resolve it. Instead, I fell asleep.

56

One eye opened. It was dark. I hated to leave dreamland. It was cool and soft and vaguely pleasant. For a split second, I didn't know where I was, then I smelled the scent of stale cigarette smoke and remembered I'd come to Blackie's to hide out.

Something bumped out on the front porch and I realized that's what had awakened me. The door flew open before I managed to sit up, much less sprint out the back door.

Blackie snapped on the overhead light and sauntered in.

'Blackie!'

I was so happy to see him, I grinned like an idiot. If he was surprised to see me, he didn't show it.

'Hey, doll.'

He tossed a copy of *The Explorer* on the couch next to me, then fumbled for a cigarette.

'You want a beer?' he asked.

I was too busy checking the paper to answer. The story – with Abby Stark's byline – made the bottom half of the front page:

> WIFE OF JAZZ GREAT SLAIN
>
> Sharon Margolis, 45, was found shot to death this morning in her Miraloma Park home, apparently the victim of an armed intruder. Her death comes only six days after the slaying of her husband, legendary saxophonist and jazz composer Match Margolis, who was stabbed last Saturday night minutes after ending his first performance in fifteen years.

Investigators refused to speculate as to motive, but sources close to the department say burglary has been ruled out and there was no sign of forced entry. Police are following several leads but no arrest has been . . .

Good old Sharon. She, with Abby Stark's kind assistance, was now screwing me even from beyond the grave. It didn't matter. I still felt sorry for her. I wasn't going to miss her brassy lies, or her pushy ways. But I felt saddened by her death all the same.

Blackie set a beer on the floor next to my feet while I finished the article. It didn't say much else worth reading.

'So?' Blackie said when I looked up.

'I left her snoring like a sawmill on her living-room couch.'

Blackie grunted. 'Harry says you're hot.'

'You went to the Quarter Moon?'

He nodded and took a deep drag of his cigarette.

'Was Post there?'

'Do dolphins swim? He wants a wrap on this Margolis shit and you're it, doll.'

'Christ, Blackie. You'd think he'd know me better than that.'

Blackie snorted and managed to look disgusted and amused at the same time.

'He's a cop, doll. How many times have I got to say it?'

'I need a shower,' I said. 'Have you got a clean towel some-place?'

'Depends.'

'On?'

'What do you consider clean?'

'I'll take anything.'

Blackie nodded toward the bathroom. 'They're on the rack. Smell 'em and see,' he said, then dropped into my vacated spot on the couch and switched on the news.

The hot water worked miracles. I felt human again, and refreshed. When I walked back into the living room Blackie was still in the same spot, sitting in the same mess he calls home. It made me think of what my own apartment must look like by now. I hoped that at least the police search team wouldn't string up a dead rat in my shower.

I remembered my cell phone and sat down to check for messages. There were four.

Philly Post had called first. 'We need to talk, Ventana. Come down to the station when you get this message.'

The next call was Glen Faddis: 'Have you seen the news? Call me.'

The next one was Abby Stark, telling me that if I gave her an exclusive interview before turning myself in, she could probably convince her attorney cousin to represent me and even give me half price on his fees. I knew her cousin. I'd taken political science with him in high school and he'd flunked.

The last call was Mitch, announcing he'd found the perfect boat and did I want to go see it?

I erased all the messages and phoned Glen.

'What happened?' he said.

'I didn't kill Sharon.'

'Of course not. I'm talking about you and Clark. You went to his house and I didn't hear from you. What did you find out?'

'It was a dead end. Match is Match Margolis. He's not an impostor as far as I could make out. I don't know what Yvette's mother meant. Do you?'

'Maybe the son's in on it,' Faddis said.

'No. He's too earnest.'

I thought for a minute. 'What if she didn't mean it so literally? What if she meant he's a fraud? As a musician.'

'A fraud? What? That he couldn't play the saxophone? Come on, you heard him Saturday night. That was Match up there wringing hearts out note by note. Nobody can fake that. You can't lip-sync a saxophone.'

'All right, but what about the songs? What if he didn't write the songs?'

I was thinking of the scores stolen with the saxophone

from Match's house. Glen was listening now so I continued.

'Maybe she meant he wasn't a composer.'

We decided to split the band among us. Glen would talk to Cheese Herman and Hank Nesbitt. I'd see Rochelle Posner and Dickie Almaviva. And Blackie volunteered to track down Les Barton.

'We've got to get cracking,' I said as soon as I hung up the phone.

Blackie turned a skeptical eye on me. 'You're wanted, doll.'

I ignored him and scanned the room. Every surface was covered with some stray item that Blackie had set down, probably years ago. A navy-blue knitted cap tossed in the corner caught my attention.

'Can I borrow that watch cap?' I asked.

'Help yourself.'

I pulled it onto my head and stuffed all my hair up under it.

'Got any shades?'

'Over there.' Blackie nodded toward a pile of junk on the table by the door. I rooted through it until I found an antique pair of yellow-tinted aviator sunglasses. I slipped them on and turned to Blackie, smiling.

'How's that?'

He smiled back. 'Your own police lieutenant wouldn't recognize you.'

Most of the time I was jaded about Blackie. As a rule, I never thought about his good looks much, but every once in a while the light would catch his eyes just so, and he'd grin at me like he had just then, and in that split second I'd see him with a stranger's new eyes. He'd look so handsome it'd take my breath away.

'Ready?' I said.

He sprang out of his seat. 'Wherever we're goin', doll, I'm your man.'

57

Our first stop was Blackie's poker pal, Elwin. I'd stashed my faithful Toyota in the bowels of Blackie's garage, so Elwin loaned me his son's car – a souped-up Dodge that smelled of seaweed. The kid was a surfer.

We split up then. I drove to the Sunset district, found an isolated pay phone and dialed Philly Post. The phone booth smelled like a urinal but that was okay. I wasn't going to be long.

Post picked up on the first ring.

'I didn't kill Sharon Margolis,' I said.

'Ventana? Where are you?'

'I'm not coming in.'

'I've got questions, Ventana. You need to come in and answer them. We'll sit and talk, that's all.'

'Will you arrest me?'

'Of course not,' he said amiably. 'We just need to—'

I hung up then. Post was *never* this nice. He was lying.

Before I left the phone booth, I looked up Dickie's address in the book. Then I drove over. Even though his lights were on, nobody answered the door. I considered breaking in, but decided to try Rochelle instead. She wasn't home, either.

Logic told me they had to be working so I started trolling the clubs. Fifteen spots later, I was about to head for the East Bay clubs when I finally found Dickie Almaviva jamming at a low-rent dive down in the Mission.

From all appearances, it looked like Dickie had pulled the little band together himself. Not a single one of Match's group was there, but Dickie was handing out scores and calling the shots, and, by the expression on his face, loving every minute of it.

I scanned the audience for anybody else from Match's band. But the room was full of strangers.

As I watched Dickie play, I sat at the bar and thought of Match. Some men are great musicians. Some are great composers. Match was at least one, maybe both. Poor Dickie Almaviva was neither – at least tonight he wasn't. It seemed all the talent I'd seen the other night had been pure synergy. Dickie was trying, sure, and he was trying hard, but watching him play tonight, the only thought that kept humming through my mind was, nobody's ever going to replace Match Margolis.

When the band finally wrapped up the set, I found Dickie and offered to buy him a drink. He didn't recognize me at first, but he seemed too wrapped up in his gig to ponder my hat and weird shades once I told him who I was.

'Whew!'

He wiped his brow and laughed out loud. 'I've got time for a drink, sure. That'd be great.'

We picked up our drinks and sat down at a table nearby where Dickie cradled his glass like it held liquid gold.

A lot of jazz musicians – it seemed Match had been one – couldn't handle coming down after the all-night high of a righteous jam. Their substitute was an artificial high, like coke or heroin or even just plain booze when the real high wore off. It looked like alcohol was Dickie's ticket.

Somehow, it didn't seem right to just dive in and start asking about Match without at least saying something about Dickie's performance.

'Nice song, that last one,' I said.

'Aah, the music.'

Dickie set his glass down slowly on the table and looked at me. He seemed slightly unfocused, mildly drunk.

'You know where that song came from? I'll tell you. A little boy in Cuba whose grandfather gave him a trumpet. On his ninth birthday. The boy loved that trumpet. He learned all the local traditional songs and played for his family and friends.

'Then one day he heard a saxophone on the radio station from the United States. A sax and a trumpet, the instrument he had learned to play. From that instant, his life changed. He vowed that he'd meet the man who made that music. One day he'd shake that man's hand. And maybe, if God was willing, one day they might play together, and that man would teach the little boy the things he needed to learn. That boy, the soul of that young boy, that's who I played that bit for. Those songs belong to him.'

He shot me a lopsided smile, then downed half the contents of his glass.

'Drink up, Ronnie. So *I* can buy *you* a drink.'

'Listen, Dickie. Did you hear about Sharon?'

'Yes. It's very tragic, isn't it? It's a pity.' There was no feeling behind his words.

'Did she call you last Friday?'

'No. Why?'

'She didn't phone you?'

'Why would she?' When I didn't respond, he said, 'What about Match? Have you found who killed Match?'

'They might have some ideas,' I lied.

The ideas were all mine, though, and they were getting clearer by the minute. Something had finally clicked into place. The song Dickie's little band had played – the one I'd complimented him on, the one whose tune had seemed so familiar – was Match's. I remembered where I'd heard it: Saturday. It had been his last number, the one he'd played just before he died.

Suddenly, it was all starting to make sense. If murder ever does make sense.

58

I waited until Dickie was deep into his next set, then quietly slipped out and headed into the Bayview, a wounded part of the city ripped apart by gangs and violence and poverty, a reality of San Francisco the tourists will never see.

Dickie's place was on Armstrong, off Third, above a dry-cleaning shop. Not exactly high rent, and Dickie didn't strike me as the kind of guy to worry a whole lot about security, which was a good thing since the only tools I had with me were my trusty picks.

The bulk of the street traffic ran down Third, which was mostly shabby shop fronts and boarded-up buildings. It was one o'clock in the morning, but you couldn't tell by the number of cars rolling down Third. Armstrong was quiet, though, and even though it was mostly residential dotted with some commercial buildings, it was dark. That's how I wanted it.

I parked down the block, then headed toward Dickie's place, toward the darkest end of the street. Instead of the usual excitement I always feel before a break-in, I felt bothered and rushed. Dickie's performance wouldn't go past two, which meant I had less than an hour. Mostly, I was worried because I wasn't sure what I was looking for. I was just hoping I'd know it when I saw it.

I passed a string of trashed parked cars and dodged the empty cans and bottles scattered along the sidewalk. As I neared his apartment, my unease grew. Any other time, I'd abort the mission if I felt this uneasy. But Dickie's tunes kept playing through my head, urging me on. I kept thinking about the music and the murder and Match. And Sharon.

When a set of headlights pulled around the corner, I barely had time to duck behind a van that reeked of gasoline. For a couple of seconds, the street was flooded with light. I glanced around and right away, I wished I hadn't.

The night – the dark – had been kinder to the neighborhood. Faded, chipped paint on the houses, mountains of trash in the yards, mangled toys abandoned by the sad children who lived inside these homes. A white cat skittered across somebody's drive, then ducked behind a fence and vanished like a fleeing angel. It all jumped out at me under the glare of headlights as the car raced by, then turned the corner onto Third.

I took a step out from behind the van, then heard voices and crouched back down again, trying not to breathe the gassy fumes. The voices got louder.

'Darla, you are a *bitch*!'

'Eat dirt, Tyrone! And don't you *ever* lay a hand on me again, you hear?'

They kept trading insults and demands until Tyrone shouted his parting words: 'I ain't comin' back, you whore. Believe it!'

A door slammed, an engine started up half a block away. Headlights, the engine revved, then the car, tires squealing, raced down to Third, then squealed again as it turned and disappeared.

In the sudden silence, a woman sobbed. Already, I knew how their story was going to end: Frank and Johnny, Bayview style.

I stood across the street from Dickie's place. Light edged the drawn curtains upstairs as they had earlier. Dickie must have left a lamp on. The lights shone from the house next door, too. I could hear a radio or television droning from an open window somewhere.

Dickie's other neighbor was a big, solid brick commercial building. The sign over its door said JOHN AND SONS and, whatever kind of business it was, it looked pretty well locked up for the night.

As long as the radio neighbor stayed entertained listening to all the crackpots calling in their opinions to the host, I wouldn't need to worry about making too much noise once I got inside.

I crossed the street and walked quickly past the front door of the dry-cleaning shop to a smaller door at the corner of the building.

From a short glance at the dry-cleaners, it looked wired for security – a cheap, homemade-type job with sensor tape around the windows and exposed wires everywhere, visible from the exterior. There was probably a pressure-sensitive mat inside the front and back doors that anybody with an IQ over two would

205

step over. And the alarm box over the front door probably went off about once a week with false alarms. If I had the time, I'd play around with it just for kicks, maybe even jazz it up for them just for the challenge, but Dickie's place upstairs beckoned.

I rang the bell again and waited, like I had earlier. The lock was a Harvard. They always turn counterclockwise. I rang again, just to make sure.

After a moment, I whipped out my picks, made the lock click in three seconds flat, and congratulated myself for being my parents' daughter. Anybody watching from the street would have thought I'd used a key.

Since I didn't have any gloves, I pulled down the sleeve of my jacket to cover my hand, gripped the knob and turned it.

Inside, I found myself at the foot of a dank and narrow stairway. The only way to go was up, toward the streaming light. So that's what I did, cautiously, in silence, praying like I always do that nobody had slept through the doorbell.

At the top, I suddenly found myself in the apartment, its lights blazing. I paused and listened. Above my own breathing, I heard the faint sound of the radio next door.

'Anybody home?'

If there was an answer, I would just say the downstairs door had been ajar.

Nobody responded so I stepped into the room. It was one giant open area with vast hardwood floors, brick walls, and a disheveled mattress thrown on the floor in one corner. A doorway against the far wall led to what looked like the kitchen – I could glimpse a table and a stove.

There was no doubt where Dickie liked to put his dollars. Besides a few basic pieces of second-hand furniture, he had a reel-to-reel, a few CD players and tape decks, speakers, and a lot of complicated-looking components I'd never seen before.

In the midst of all the electronic gadgetry stood the simple upright piano, stacked two feet high with records and papers, two trumpets on the very top of it all. And beside the piano, leaning up against it with its base resting on a soft blanket, was a gleaming tenor sax.

My heart leapt to my throat. I crossed the room for a closer look. I didn't touch it but the first thing that popped out at me was the intricate filigree etched around its bell: *M.M.* amid flowers and notes.

So Sharon *hadn't* lied when she said the smashed sax in Philly's office wasn't Match's.

It might be enough. But it wasn't proof of anything beyond the burglary. Maybe Post could sweat a confession out of Dickie.

But I wanted more. I wanted a motive.

I went to the kitchen to check for a second way out. I'd been sloppy at Sharon's when she'd caught me without a quick escape. I tried the back door. It wouldn't budge. At first I thought it was jammed, but it turned out to be nailed shut. Great.

And the only window in the kitchen was too small to crawl through quickly, if at all. The whole set-up probably added up to about sixty violations of the fire code but my guess was that right this minute, I was far more alarmed about the situation than the fire marshall would be if he knew.

My only exit was the way I'd come in: down the stairs and through the front door. I considered just calling Philly Post in and taking a powder, but I wanted answers and I wanted them now.

Back in the front room, I didn't know where to start. The place was a mess, which makes things harder when you're trying to leave things exactly as you've found them.

I scanned the room, then went for the table by the piano. The papers were a jumble, but I got the impression Dickie knew exactly where everything was. I scooped up a pile of sheet music and paged through it.

I couldn't read a note to save my life but the song titles penciled in at the top of each page were in a sprawling, almost feminine hand. I didn't recognize any of them.

If I could read music, maybe I'd know if they were original compositions or just arrangements he'd done for somebody else. Whatever they were, there were reams and reams of the stuff on the table and stacked on the floor underneath it.

I looked around, then reached out and pressed the switch on the reel-to-reel. It started the tape while I headed for a chest of drawers at the opposite end of the room.

A low, sensuous stream of notes filled the room. Saxophone. It was Match playing. I'd recognize his style anywhere. He was playing the song he'd closed his gig with last Saturday night.

I stopped what I was doing and just listened. He played the number out to the end, then closed it with a slow, lingering moan that pulled at me from the inside out. *How did Match do it?* I asked myself, then in the ensuing silence remembered where I was.

The top dresser drawer slid open easily. My hand was buried in tee shirts when I heard a voice say, 'Yeah!'

I wheeled around, heart stopped, holding my breath, tense and ready to bolt as soon as I figured out which way to run. Then a second voice spoke, a man's, familiar and young, with a hint of an accent. Finally I realized the sound came from the tape.

Dickie said, 'That was great, Match. Do you like that one?'

'Beautiful, man. Bee-u-tee-ful.'

Match sounded like he was still blissed out over the music he'd just played.

'I'm glad you like it. Do you want to play it?'

'Opening night, man. We'll do it opening night.'

'All riiight!' Now it was Dickie who sounded ecstatic. 'What else have you got for me?'

The sound of shuffling papers on the tape, then, 'Here, Match. Try this one. I wrote it last night.'

Slowly I shut the drawer I'd been rifling through and crossed over to stand in front of the machine and listen.

'All right,' Dickie's voice said, 'for this one we need to scale things down. It's a little simpler in the melody. Listen.'

Piano notes sprinkled into the room, little crystals of sound that seemed trite after what Match had done with his sax.

While I listened, my eyes drifted around the room, to the piano, with its notebook of half pencilled-in sheet music on the rack; to the saxophone, gleaming simple and gold and upright against the piano; to the two trumpets, recumbent in open, velvet-lined cases atop the stacks of sheet music on the piano; and finally to a corner of a stained spiral-edged notebook jutting out from under the mass of single sheets on the table.

I pulled it out, opened it, and read what was written inside the cover: Match Margolis. The name wasn't written in the same bold, back-slanted hand he'd used to sign his marriage certificate, but in the flowery letters his wife had used.

The piano stopped.

'Try it,' Dickie's voice said, and the sax took over, playing the same tune that had sounded mediocre at best and turning it into a masterpiece of feeling and soul with perfect phrasing and timing.

I paged through the spiral-bound notebook and read the titles to Match's earlier compositions. All of it was written in the flowery script of his first wife's hand.

Then at the end of the notebook, in the back, a new style of handwriting had taken over. I read the titles. *Single Love. Home at Last. Turn it Off.*

They were all songs Match introduced Saturday night. He'd introduced them as his own.

Match finished playing the song. They went through the same fevered congratulatory exercise as before, then Match said, 'Here.'

'What's that?'

'For the songs, kid. Ten songs, twenty grand. Pretty good, huh? What do you say? You keep 'em comin' and there'll be plenty more.'

'No, Match.' Dickie sounded truly injured. 'You don't understand. For you to play Dickie Almaviva's songs, to announce that to the world, is a miracle. It's honor enough. More than I can ask for.'

'Take the money, kid.'

'And make my debt to you even greater? No, Match. I can't. Here, listen. Here's another song I wrote.'

The lilting piano filled the room, then Match interrupted.

'Kid. Dickie. I've gotta have my name on those songs, you know what I mean? Twenty grand isn't anything to sneeze at. And there'll be plenty more.'

'My compositions are not for sale,' Dickie said. 'Use them, use them as much and as often as you want. But they are mine, they came from me, from my heart.'

The sound of paper crackling, probably Match stashing the package back into his pocket or valise.

After a moment, Match asked, 'What's it gonna take?'

'You can tell the band whatever you want. All I ask is that you announce, at the end of the show, that I, Dickie Almaviva, wrote this music. That will be worth more to me than any amount of money in the world.'

Match's voice became tense. 'Fine. That's what I'll do, then.'

I switched off the tape and searched frantically for the rewind button, but just when I found it, the room went dark. The hissing on the tape droned to a dead silence and I froze.

I held my breath, cocked my head to one side, and listened. Heart pounding, blood roaring in my ears, I couldn't hear a thing.

I blinked, tried to see into the sudden blackness, but it was like I'd fallen into a bottle of ink. It would take my eyes too long to adjust. Time was something I didn't have. Without thinking, I reached out to the reel-to-reel unit and traced its surface until my hand found the spools. I fumbled and twisted and tugged until I managed to get the reels off. As soon as they were free, I tucked them inside my shirt.

Now all I needed to do was get out of there. I listened, trying to hear something that might tell me if the path down the stairs was clear. Absolute silence. Then came a quiet rustle, cloth against skin.

If I could hear that, then surely he must have heard me struggling with the tape. The soft squeak of a leather shoe came next and finally the creak of a step under a footfall. In the disorienting muddle of darkness, I couldn't tell where he was. The noise could have come from the stairwell or from across the room by the kitchen.

I listened hard, holding my breath, willing my heart to silence, and the rustle came again, this time more distinctly. I knew he was near.

Whoever had come in off the street needed to adjust his eyes to the dark also. But if it was Dickie out there, he had a distinct advantage over me. I'd only taken one quick circle around the place and couldn't really remember where everything was.

I tried to picture the layout in my head but my mind wasn't holding anything beyond the cold, black fear that kept me anchored, frozen, waiting to hit back at whatever came at me from the dark.

59

'R onneee.'
The voice was soft and melodious, almost enticing. Anything but threatening. But I got goosebumps all the same.

I blinked and stared into nothing. He knew that sooner or later I'd make a break for the stairs. Would I fool him if I went in the opposite direction?

I reached out for the table I knew was beside me and crouched down so my head was level with its top. If he was expecting me to be tall, I'd surprise him. But I didn't know if he had a weapon. Or even if he'd come alone.

Then he spoke and I knew where he was.

'You should have stayed out of it, Ronnie.'

I stared into the black and thought I could make out his

figure at the top of the stairs. It seemed to be inching toward me. I cursed the fact that my clothes weren't black, that my shoes weren't my running shoes, that I probably wouldn't get out of here in one piece, that I very probably could die tonight.

I crept along, using the edge of the table as a guide, and scrambled behind the piano, then peeked out the other end, holding my breath and listening for any movement from him. The dark lump I'd seen earlier wasn't where it had been before. I scanned the darkness but couldn't find him.

'Ronneeeee.'

I nearly jumped out of my skin. He was close now, almost on top of me. I panicked and darted into the kitchen. The instant I did, I realized my mistake. I shuffled quickly under the cheap little dinette table in the corner and waited.

I was trapped now and he was laughing softly as he strode in after me. It was lighter in the kitchen; the yellow glow from a street lamp outside streamed through the small curtainless window above the sink. He paused at the doorway and I saw the ghoulish, smiling Nixon mask over his face.

'I have a knife, Ronneeee.'

The limp form of the dead rat in my shower popped into my head. I winced, then forced myself to think while I scrunched under the table. Adrenaline coursed through my veins. The next move had to be his. I crouched and waited.

His hand was raised now. I could see the outline of the knife clutched in his fist. He edged into the small room and from the way he moved I could tell he thought I was behind the door.

The room was too cramped for me to sneak out while he had his back to me. And once he saw I wasn't behind the door, it would only take him half a second to figure out the only other place I could hide was under the table.

I set my hands, palms up, under the table, and cocked my legs. His shadow shifted and when he turned my way I froze. I could hear him breathing, panting quietly in the dark like some jungle beast of prey. Then it stopped and I held my breath, too. With a sudden intake of breath, he came at me.

I tilted the table, shoving it up and forward with all my might, yelling and growling for momentum. When I hit something solid, I heard an *ummph*! I gave the table another shove, then, clutching the tapes inside my shirt to my chest, I charged for the stairs.

Somehow I made it without stumbling. I grabbed the bannister and flew down, three steps at a time. I fumbled with the doorknob at the bottom while footsteps clattered overhead. He was coming for me.

I glanced back over my shoulder just as the front door finally gave and sprang open. He was up there, a determined black shadow at the top of the stairs.

'Ronnie, wait! Let me explain.'

I knew exactly how he'd explain – with a knife. I ran.

I was halfway down the block before I realized Elwin's car was in the other direction. I charged out into the middle of the street, then headed west toward Third, toward the traffic.

I chugged along and tried to think. Where was everybody? Minutes ago it had seemed the whole place was hopping. Didn't anybody live in these locked up little houses?

'Help!' I gasped. It came out a strangled croak.

I veered toward the sidewalk, scrambled over the trash at the curb and pounded on a door.

'Ronnie. Come back. I want to talk.'

I looked over my shoulder. He was bearing down on me. I knew there were people in these houses, but there was no sign of life behind the door I'd just knocked on. I took off again.

Third Street. Third Street. If only I could make it to Third. I glanced back again. He was gaining on me.

I dodged a row of overflowing garbage cans, grabbed a lid to use as a shield in case he caught up with me, then flung the cans into his path.

Traffic on Third flowed along so steadily when I reached the intersection that I pulled up short. Twin lights sped by in a quick sequence. There wasn't much margin for error if I crossed. I considered which might be worse – to be hit by a car or slashed by a madman who'd killed two people already.

I raised my arms and threw myself off the curb, waving from the gutter at the oncoming cars. The first car braked, then veered into the next lane and sped away, its horn blaring a fading protest in the dark.

The car behind it did the same thing. A third car flashed its brights at me, then slowed. Its passenger window came down as I scampered towards it. A stout bald head appeared in the window as the driver leaned over.

'Get out of the fucking street, you bitch!' he shouted, then accelerated in a gust of warm exhaust and shrinking red tail lights.

I raised my arms and waved at the next car.

'Stop!' I yelled. 'Please, help! Somebody stop!'

But nobody did.

Behind me, Dickie was rushing toward me, getting closer by the second. He'd circled the garbage and was shouting things at me in Spanish I couldn't even understand.

As he thundered toward me, I turned, raised my garbage can lid as a shield, and faced him squarely. He was a furious ball of venom and hate and he didn't look like he was going to stop. Shield or no shield, I was no match for him. I dropped the lid and ran.

I ran with the traffic, hugging the parked cars to my right, and choking on the upwash of exhaust, praying he wouldn't catch up. I shot a look over my shoulder and gasped. He was gaining on me.

The cars just kept bearing down on us. I saw a brief gap in the traffic, then zigzagged through the parked cars and swung back to the road again. Dickie followed. Good. I knew what I had to do.

I sped up, running with the traffic now, shooting quick glances over my shoulder to gauge the stream of cars. If my timing was off, I'd be dead. But if Dickie caught me I'd be dead, too.

Dickie was tiring, I could tell. He wasn't waving the knife at me anymore. He was pumping his arms for steam. I eased my pace. He was close now, almost so close I could have reached out and touched him. The time was now.

I saw my opening, focused on the center divider, then sprinted into the traffic and prayed Dickie would follow.

Two cars swerved around me, horns blaring and tires screeching. Headlights and red lights were everywhere. I got as far as the double yellow line. That's when I heard it: the dull, sickening *thunk*!

Then silence. Everything suddenly slowed down. I looked back. None of the cars were moving now. A truck in the next lane over had shuddered to a stop. It backed up and its headlights broke through the darkness like a spotlight revealing a stark, crumpled heap on the pavement.

I couldn't be sure. The misshapen mound on the street didn't even look human. I looked around me. Maybe Dickie was hiding, waiting for me to cross the street back to him so he could sink his knife into my back. I didn't know. But I started toward the thing in the street.

As soon as I did, the truck door sprang open. I reached the crumpled form before the driver did. The Nixon mask stared up at me, ghoulish under the harsh halogen glow of the truck's headlamps. Dickie's knife glistened from the concrete about three feet from his outstretched hand.

I leaned down and pulled off the mask. Dickie's face was contorted in pain. Somewhere down the street, somebody leaned on his horn. People were getting out of their cars now, walking toward us, but not hurrying. The truck driver came up beside me.

'Jesus, Mary, Joseph,' he said. He kept repeating the same three words over and over.

I looked down at Dickie. He was all twisted up on the ground, face up, bleeding out of his mouth and nose. He looked frail, like a child, shiny black hair splayed out on the pavement beneath his head like an ebony halo.

Behind me, the truck driver said, 'I didn't see him. I swear to God I didn't see him. He came out of nowhere.'

Funny, I thought, how people always say the same thing in situations like this.

Dickie's lips moved but the trucker's jabbering drowned him out.

'Quiet!' I said, then bent in close to hear.

The metallic smell of blood wafted up into my nose. His chest gurgled. He turned his head and coughed a fine spray of blood into the dark. My stomach lurched.

'It's all right, Dickie,' I said, then shouted to no one in particular: 'Call 911! Call an ambulance!'

60

It was daylight but I didn't care. The shades were drawn and Match's sultry saxophone dirge filled the room.

I popped the top on another warm beer from the two six packs I'd propped up by the sofa and drank a long, hot swig.

Listening to the music, I realized it didn't sound good to me anymore. It seemed false and tainted. The sax, the melody, the very soul of his sound was hollow.

I finished the beer and started another when somebody knocked on the door.

'Go away!'

The knock turned into banging.

'Open up!'

'Go away!'

I couldn't remember if I'd locked the door or not, then remembered I hadn't. The knob rattled and the door burst open.

Blackie stomped in like he owned the place.

'What the fuck are you doing in the dark, Ventana?'

He snapped up the window shade. Late-afternoon sunlight washed in, momentarily blinding me. Blackie looked around like he was seeing the place for the first time. Then his eyes found the beer on the floor beside me.

'What the hell is this? You drinking hot beer? What's the matter with you, doll?'

He stuck his hand into his pocket, then tossed a wad of bills in my lap.

'What's this?'

'The fucking reward, doll.'

He reached over and pulled a beer out of the six, then popped it open.

'The fat man sent it over – Teagues. Now you can pay your rent and get Toby off your back.'

Blackie took a deep drink, made a sour face, then choked and started coughing.

'Fuck, this tastes bad hot. You got any cold ones, doll?'

Blackie set the bottle on the floor and started for the fridge.

'I don't—'

'Hey!'

We both looked up. Philly Post was standing at the open door.

'You having a party or what?' he asked.

I didn't answer. Blackie sure as hell wasn't going to talk, but Post couldn't take a hint. He came inside anyway and sat down on the couch beside me.

'You want this?'

Post pulled a check out of his breast pocket and held it under my nose. I ignored it and drank more beer.

'Well?' he demanded.

'What is it?'

'The musician's union put up a reward, remember?'

Post flashed big white teeth at me and worked hard to ignore Blackie over in the kitchenette.

Post said, 'You're rich.'

'I don't want it.'

I pushed the check away. Then I picked up the wad of bills from Teagues and held it out to Blackie. 'Take it, Blackie. I don't want this, either.'

Blackie didn't move. He just narrowed his eyes and studied my face with concern.

'You drunk, doll?'

'It's blood money,' I said. 'I don't feel good about any of this.'

'What's that got to do with *that*?' Blackie said, pointing at the cash in my hand.

'Christ, Ventana, it's not your fault the guy got screwed and couldn't handle it,' Post said.

'I know. But it's not right. Don't you see? I should have just left it alone.'

'He popped two people,' Post said incredulously. 'And he would have popped you if you'd let him.'

I'd been reminding myself of that all morning but I just couldn't muster any antagonism towards Dickie, dead rat and all.

'I don't want to make money off people's misery,' I said. I finished my beer and flicked open another one.

'Say, doll—' Blackie began.

'No. Listen to me. Let me explain. Dickie worshipped Match and look what Match did to him. He raped the kid, artistically speaking. He stole his songs, then laughed in his face when Dickie asked for the credit. You saw him at the end of his last set Saturday. Dickie said he kept waiting for Match to say his name, to call him up front to take a bow. His own idol did that to him. In a way, I think I can understand how he felt.'

'I'm with you, doll,' Blackie said. 'Margolis was a fuck. But he's dead. Dick's in jail. Why go broke over it? Take the money.'

Post scowled.

'Almaviva should have taken him to court. He had the evidence on tape. You don't knife somebody just because they steal your songs.'

I'd asked Dickie about that in the ambulance on the way to the hospital. Although he was barely conscious, I could tell the question had angered him.

'Court!' His snarl had been a bare whisper. 'Who . . . do you think they'd . . . believe? The Marielito Cuban . . . or the great Match Margolis?'

I understood, but I didn't think Post would.

'Probably woulda got thrown out anyway,' Blackie said, and shot Post a withering look. 'Fuckin' law and order.'

Post smiled back coldly. 'Law and order. You've got that part right, Coogan.'

Post still hadn't gotten over the fact that Match's gangster friends weren't guilty. He'd spent tons of man hours on surveillance and had come up with nothing.

I remembered the call I'd had this morning.

'Clark Margolis said he's going to credit Dickie with all the new songs on the new CD,' I told them. 'And the old ones, the ones Clark's mother wrote for Match, he said she's finally going to be credited for them. Glen Faddis is going to do a biography of Match and Clark's cooperating.'

'Yeah,' Post said. 'It's all in the papers. Hell, Margolis was a fraud.'

'It's never all black and white, Post. Match happened to be a great musician. He just couldn't write music.'

'So he *stole* it?'

'He did some bad things, okay. I agree. But he's dead now. What's the point of maligning a dead man?'

The legend had clay feet. Lots of them do.

'Yah, yah, doll,' Blackie said sympathetically. He'd given up on the fridge and came back to eye the money in my hand again.

'Sounds good on paper, but what about the cash? That Margolis witch stiffed you. How the fuck you going to pay Toby and his boys? How are you going to pay for this place?'

There was always Mitch's house in Marin. Myra had canceled on him so he'd phoned this morning to renew his plea. But I'd told him no and I'd meant it.

I turned to Blackie, then to Post. Post had been looking around the room, taking in the table, the chair, the hot plate, the yellowed shades above the windows and the general tininess of my space. I glanced around, too, trying to imagine what the place would look like to somebody else. It wasn't anything fancy, but most of the time I could afford it, and it was mine.

The tape of Match's music ended with one of the last grand songs Match had played, the one that had become his theme twenty years ago. The machine clicked off and we sat in silence.

Then from somewhere down below on the street, I heard the clear and pure and sweet sound of children laughing. It seemed like sunshine in my heart.

I glanced down at the money in my hand, then slowly separated the bills and started counting them while the others watched. Twenty thousand dollars. Teagues had doubled his reward.

'The check's for ten thousand,' Philly said, extending it toward me.

I hesitated. Blackie winked at me and grinned.

'Take it, doll. You earned it fair and square.'

I thought about jazz and Match and Dickie. I thought about talents that come to life not when they're born, but only when they're nurtured. Nurtured and rewarded.

'All right,' I said. 'But half of this is going to the musician's union scholarship fund.'

Blackie's grin widened. 'Now you're talking.'

I pushed myself off the couch and pocketed the check.

'Let's go find the landlord,' I said. 'And Toby. After that, the first round's on me.'

I paused at the door.

'You coming, Post?'

27.93